JILL

by Philip Larkin

poetry
The North Ship
XX Poems
The Fantasy Poets No. 21
The Less Deceived
(*The Marvell Press*)
The Whitsun Weddings
High Windows
Collected Poems 1938–1983
(*edited by Anthony Thwaite*)

The Oxford Book of Twentieth-Century English Verse (Ed.)

fiction
Jill
A Girl in Winter

non-fiction
All What Jazz: A Record Diary 1961–71
Required Writing: Miscellaneous Pieces 1955–82

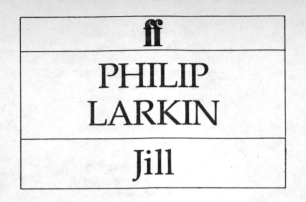

ff

PHILIP
LARKIN

Jill

faber and faber
LONDON · BOSTON

First published in 1946
by The Fortune Press
First published in this edition 1975
by Faber and Faber Limited
3 Queen Square London WCIN 3AU
Reprinted 1977 and 1981
Reissued 1985
Reprinted 1986, 1987 and 1990

Printed in Great Britain by
Richard Clay Ltd, Bungay, Suffolk
All rights reserved

British Library Cataloguing in Publication Data

Larkin, Philip
Jill
I. Title
823'.914[F]   PR6023.A66

ISBN 0-571-10691-9

To
JAMES BALLARD SUTTON

INTRODUCTION

I

An American critic recently suggested[1] that *Jill* contained the first example of that characteristic landmark of the British post-war novel, the displaced working-class hero. If this is true (and it sounds fair trend-spotter's comment), the book may hold sufficient historical interest to justify republication. But again, if it is true, I feel bound to say that it was unintentional. In 1940 our impulse was still to minimize social differences rather than exaggerate them. My hero's background, though an integral part of the story, was not what the story was about.

As a matter of fact, the Oxford of that autumn was singularly free from such traditional distinctions. The war (American readers may need reminding) was then in its second year. Conscription had begun with the twenties and upwards, but everyone knew that before long the nineteens and the eighteens would take their turn. In the meantime, undergraduates liable for service could expect three or four terms at the most: if they wished then to become officers, they drilled with the un-uniformed Officers' Training Corps half a day a week (later they got uniforms and drilled a day and a half a week).

Life in college was austere. Its pre-war pattern had been dispersed, in some instances permanently. Everyone paid the same fees (in our case, 12s. a day) and ate the same meals. Because of Ministry of Food regulations, the town could offer little in the way of luxurious eating and drinking, and college festivities, such as commemoration balls, had been suspended for the duration. Because of petrol rationing, nobody ran a car. Because of clothes rationing, it was difficult to dress stylishly. There was still coal in the bunkers outside our rooms, but fuel

[1] James Gindin, *Postwar British Fiction* (Cambridge University Press, 1962).

rationing was soon to remove it. It became a routine after ordering one's books in Bodley after breakfast to go and look for a cake or cigarette queue.

With new men coming up every term, too, there was hardly any such thing as a freshman, and distinctions of seniority blurred. Traditional types such as aesthete and hearty were pruned relentlessly back. The younger dons were mostly on war service, and their elders were too busy or too remote to establish contact with us—often, in fact, the men of one college would share a tutor with another, whom they would never see socially at all. Perhaps the most difficult thing to convey was the almost-complete suspension of concern for the future. There were none of the pressing dilemmas of teaching or Civil Service, industry or America, publishing or journalism: in consequence, there was next to no careerism. National affairs were going so badly, and a victorious peace was clearly so far off, that effort expended on one's post-war prospects could hardly seem anything but a ludicrous waste of time.

This was not the Oxford of Michael Fane and his fine bindings, or Charles Ryder and his plovers' eggs. Nevertheless, it had a distinctive quality. A lack of *douceur* was balanced by a lack of *bêtises*, whether of college ceremonial or undergraduate extravagance (I still remember the shock during a visit to Oxford after the war of seeing an undergraduate in a sky-blue cloak and with hair down to his shoulders, and of realizing that all that was starting again), and I think our perspectives were truer as a result. At an age when self-importance would have been normal, events cut us ruthlessly down to size.

II

I shared rooms with Noel Hughes, with whom I had just spent two disrespectful years in the Modern Sixth, but my tutorial-mate was a large pallid-faced stranger with a rich Bristolian accent, whose preposterous skirling laugh was always ready to salute his own outrages. Norman had little use for self- or any other kind of discipline, and it was not uncommon, on returning from a nine o'clock lecture, to find him still in his dressing-gown, having missed breakfast by some ninety minutes, plucking disconsolately at a dry loaf and drinking milkless tea. To learn where I had been (Blunden, perhaps, on Biography) did nothing to raise his spirits: "That bugger's a waste of time . . . I'm better than that bugger." His eye falling on his empty cup, he would pitch its dregs messily into the grate, further discouraging the fire, before reaching again for the teapot. "A gentleman," he would aphorize with dignity, "never drinks the lees of his wine."

Norman at once set about roughing-up my general character and assumptions. Any action or even word implying respect for qualities such as punctuality, prudence, thrift or respectability called forth a snarling roar like that of the Metro-Goldwyn-Mayer lion and the accusation of *bourgeoisisme*; ostentatious courtesy produced a falsetto celestial-choir effect, ostentatious sensibility the recommendation to "write a poem about it". For a few weeks I uneasily counter-attacked along predictable lines: all right, suppose it *was* hypocrisy, hypocrisy was *necessary*, what would happen if *everybody* . . . After that I gave it up. Norman treated everyone like this: it made no difference to their liking for him. Indeed, his most hilarious mockeries were reserved for himself. Like the rest of us (excepting perhaps Noel), he was clearer about his dislikes than his likes, but while we were undergoing a process of adjustment Norman's rejection of his new environment was total. At first this strengthened his influence over us: as time went on, it tended to cut him off. Not in fact until he was with a Friends' Unit in Poland after the war did he seem to be doing what he wanted.

We quickly invented "the Yorkshire scholar", a character embodying many of our prejudices, and conversed in his flat rapacious tones in going to and from our tutor, Gavin Bone. "You're gettin' the best education in the land, lad." "Ay, but you must cut your coat according to your cloth." "Had tea wi' t' Dean on Sunday—I showed him I'd been reading his book." "Never lose a chance to make a good impression." "What play have you written about?" "*King Lear*. You see, I've DONE *King Lear*." "Ay." "Ay." This comedy probably gave Norman more emotional release than myself, for he had been through

13

the hands of the late R. W. Moore at Bristol Grammar School, but I was sufficiently acquainted with the climate of the scholarship year to enjoy keeping the game going. I cannot imagine what Gavin Bone thought of us. Already in failing health (he died in 1942), he treated us like a pair of village idiots who might if tried too hard turn nasty. The highest academic compliment I received as an undergraduate was "Mr. Larkin can see a point, if it is explained to him".

During these first two terms our friends were mostly outside College; Norman had a group in Queen's, while I kept up with other Old Coventrians or enjoyed jazz evenings with Frank Dixon of Magdalen and Dick Kidner of Christ Church. At the beginning of the Trinity Term, however, Norman, who had been idly looking over the notice-board in the lodge, hailed the mention of a newcomer, name of Amis.

"I met him at Cambridge on a schol. . . . He's the hell of a good man."

"How is he?"

"He shoots guns."

I did not understand this until later in the afternoon when we were crossing the dusty first quadrangle a fair-haired young man came down staircase three and paused on the bottom step. Norman instantly pointed his right hand at him in the semblance of a pistol and uttered a short coughing bark to signify a shot —a shot not as in reality, but as it would sound from a worn sound-track on Saturday afternoon in the ninepennies.

The young man's reaction was immediate. Clutching his chest in a rictus of agony, he threw one arm up against the archway and began slowly crumpling downwards, fingers scoring the stonework. Just as he was about to collapse on the piled-up laundry, however (Oxford laundries were at that time operating a system described by James Agate as collecting every two weeks and delivering every three, so that the place was generally littered with bundles in transit one way or the other), he righted himself and trotted over to us. "I've been working on this," he said, as soon as introductions were completed. "Listen. This is when you're firing in a ravine."

We listened.

14

"And this when you're firing in a ravine and the bullet ricochets off a rock."

We listened again. Norman's appreciative laughter skirled freely: I stood silent. For the first time I felt myself in the presence of a talent greater than my own.

No one who knew Kingsley at that time would deny that what chiefly distinguished him was this genius for imaginative mimicry. It was not a BBC Variety Hour knack of "imitations" (though in fact he had a very funny imitation of the man who used to imitate a car driving through a flock of sheep doing his imitation); rather, he used it as the quickest way of convincing you that something was horrible or boring or absurd —the local comrade ("Eesa poincher see . . . assa poincher see"), the Irish tenor ("the sarn wass dee-cli-neeng"), the University CSM ("Goo on, seh"), a Russian radio announcer reading in English a bulletin from the eastern front ("twelf field mortars"), his voice suffering slow distortion to unintelligibility followed by a sudden reversion to clarity ("a-berbera mumf mumf General von Paulus"). As time went on, his scope widened: "remind me", a post-war letter ended, "to do *Caesar and Cleopatra* for you." Films were always excellent material: the gangster film (with plenty of shooting), especially a version entirely peopled with figures from the University Faculty of English; the no-work film (this was largely silent); the U-boat film ("Wir haben sie!"); and one that involved Humphrey Bogart flashing a torch round a cellar. One day after the war Kingsley, Graham Parkes and Nick Russel were strolling along to The Lamb and Flag when a motor-cyclist clearly with the same destination propped his machine against the kerb near by. When he had got some distance across the pavement towards the arch, Kingsley (I gather for want of something better to do) made his motor-bike-failing-to-start noise. The man stopped dead in his tracks and stared at his machine narrowly. Then he walked back and knelt down beside it. Some minutes later he entered the pub with a subdued expression on his face. Kingsley's masterpiece, which was so demanding I heard him do it only twice, involved three subal-

15

terns, a Glaswegian driver and a jeep breaking down and refusing to restart somewhere in Germany. Both times I became incapable with laughter.

From this time on my friends all seemed to be in College, and a photograph taken on the sunny lawn the following summer reminds me how much our daily exchanges were informed by Kingsley's pantomimes. In the foreground crouches Kingsley himself, his face contorted to a hideous mask and holding an invisible dagger: "Japanese soldier," my note says, but I have forgotten why. Edward du Cann is withdrawing the safety pin from an invisible hand-grenade with his teeth (*In the Rear of the Enemy*, one of Kingsley's Russian documentaries); Norman and David Williams are doing the "first today" routine,[1] Wally Widdowson has a curiously stiff thumbs-in-belt stance ("Russian officer"—was this part of *In the Rear of the Enemy*?), and David West ("Roumanian officer") is attempting to represent a contemporary saying that every Roumanian private had a Roumanian officer's lipstick in his knapsack. The rest are engaged in the eternal gang warfare.

This is not to say that Kingsley dominated us. Indeed, to some extent he suffered the familiar humorist's fate of being unable to get anyone to take him seriously at all. Kingsley's "serious side" was political. In those days of Help For Russia Week, when the Hammer and Sickle flew with the Union Jack in Carfax, he became editor of the University Labour Club Bulletin and in this capacity printed one of my poems. (A second, much less ambiguously ambiguous, was denounced by the Committee as "morbid and unhealthy".) In his contentious mood he could be (intentionally) very irritating, especially to those who thought party politics should be suspended until the war was over. Sometimes he was the target of delighted laughter and violent abuse in the same evening and from the same people. I shared his convictions to the extent of visiting the club's social room in the High once or twice for coffee after closing time.

About jazz we had no disagreement. Jim Sutton and I had built up a small record collection at home and had brought it

---

[1] Not Kingsley's invention, but see his story "The 2003 Claret", in *The Complete Imbiber* (Putnam, 1958).

to Oxford (he was at the Slade, then exiled to the Ashmolean), so that we need not be without our favourite sound. There was not much live jazz to be heard at Oxford in those days until the Oxford University Rhythm Club was set up in 1941 and provided public jam sessions, but on the advice of Frank Dixon I had found a number of scarce deletions in Acott's and Russell's (then separate shops) and in one or other of our rooms there was usually a gramophone going. Kingsley's enthusiasm flared up immediately. I suppose we devoted to some hundred records that early anatomizing passion normally reserved for the more established arts. "It's the *abject entreaty* of that second phrase. . . ." "What she's actually singing is *ick-sart-mean*. . . ." "Russell goes right on up to the first bar of Waller. You can hear it on Nick's pick-up." "Isn't it marvellous the way Bechet . . ." "Isn't it marvellous the way the trumpet . . ." "Isn't it marvellous the way Russell . . ." Russell, Charles Ellsworth "Pee Wee" (b. 1906), clarinet and saxophone player extraordinary, was, *mutatis mutandis*, our Swinburne and our Byron. We bought every record he played on that we could find, and—literally—dreamed about similar items on the American Commodore label. Someone recently conscripted into the Merchant Navy had reputedly found his way to the Commodore Music Shop in New York, where the "proprietor" had introduced him to "one of the guys who helped make these records"; yes, leaning against the counter had actually been . . . Long afterwards, Kingsley admitted he had once sent Russell a fan letter. I said that funnily enough I had also written to Eddie Condon. We looked at each other guardedly. "Did you get an answer?" "No—did you?" "No."

At the end of every term somebody left. Sometimes it was a false alarm: Edward du Cann disappeared in December 1942, waving cheerfully from the back of a taxi, but he was back next term, when he promptly swallowed a pin and was rushed to hospital. But more often it was permanent. Norman was commissioned in the Artillery and ironically found himself in the kind of regiment where revolvers were fired in the mess after dinner. Kingsley was commissioned in the Signals, where within an hour a major reprimanded him for having his hands in his pockets. Friends remained plentiful, but contemporaries were becoming scarce. I lost touch with the freshmen, among whom it was reported there was "a man called Wain". Years afterwards John told me that our acquaintance at this time was limited to a brief bitter exchange at lunch about Albert Ammons's *Boogie Woogie Stomp* and the poetry of George Crabbe. If so, it was a great opportunity lost.

None the less, it was almost my last term before I met Bruce Montgomery. In a way this was surprising: among the handful of undergraduates reading full Schools in the humanities friendship was generally automatic. In another it wasn't: Bruce's modern languages-Playhouse-classical music-Randolph Hotel ambience conflicted sharply with my own. Of course, I had seen him about, but it hardly occurred to me that he was an undergraduate, not in the same sense that I was. Wearing an air raid warden's badge and carrying a walking-stick, he stalked aloofly to and fro in a severe triangle formed by the College lodge (for letters), the Randolph bar and his lodgings in Wellington Square. In his first year he had been partnered at tutorials with Alan Ross; having observed that their tutor's first action was to wind up a small clock on his desk, they took advantage of his lateness one morning to wind it up for him. The tutor was an energetic man and I always understood that the result was disastrous. But now Alan had long since gone into the Navy and Bruce, like myself, was something of a survivor. This did not make me less shy of him. Like "Mr. Austen", he had a grand piano; he had written a book called *Romanticism and the World Crisis*, painted a picture that was hanging on the wall of his sitting-room, and was a skilled pianist, organist and even composer. During the vacation that Easter he had spent ten days writing, with his J nib and silver pen-holder, a detective story called *The Case of the Gilded Fly*. This was published the following year under the name of Edmund Crispin, launching him on one of his several successful careers.

Beneath this formidable exterior, however, Bruce had unsuspected depths of frivolity, and we were soon spending most of our time together swaying about with laughter on bar-stools. True, I could make little of Wyndham Lewis, at that time Bruce's favourite writer, and my admiration for *Belshazzar's Feast* was always qualified, but I was more than ready for John Dickson Carr, Mencken and *Pitié Pour les Femmes*. In return I played him Billie Holiday records and persuaded him to widen his circle of drinking-places. One night the Proctor entered one of these and I was caught by the bullers at a side door: Bruce, on the other hand, simply stepped into a kind of kitchen, apologized to someone he found ironing there, and waited until the coast was clear. "When will you learn," he reproved me afterwards, "not to act on your own initiative?"

I sometimes wonder if Bruce did not constitute for me a curious creative stimulus. For the next three years we were in fairly constant contact, and I wrote continuously as never before or since. Even in that last term, with Finals a matter of weeks away, I began an unclassifiable story called *Trouble at Willow Gables*, which Bruce and Diana Gollancz would come back to read after an evening at The Lord Napier. Possibly his brisk intellectual epicureanism was just the catalyst I needed.

III

Jill was in fact begun that autumn, when I was twenty-one, and took about a year to write. When it was published in 1946 it aroused no public comment. Kingsley, who by that time was back at Oxford, wrote to say he had enjoyed it very much, adding that its binding reminded him of *Signal Training: Telegraphy and Telephony*, or possibly *Ciceronis Orationes*. Later he reported that he had seen a copy in a shop in Coventry Street between *Naked and Unashamed* and *High-Heeled Yvonne*.

On looking through it again in 1963 I have made a number of minor deletions but have added nothing and rewritten nothing, with the exception of a word here and there, and the reinstatement of a few mild obscenities to which the original printer objected. It will, I hope, still qualify for the indulgence traditionally extended to juvenilia.

1963   P.L.

19

The main location of this story in time and place—the Michaelmas Term at Oxford University in 1940—is more or less real, but the characters are imaginary.

As, despite its length, it remains in essence an unambitious short story, chapter-divisions have been dropped, leaving it merely as a narrative with breathing-spaces.

John Kemp sat in the corner of an empty compartment in a train travelling over the last stretch of line before Oxford. It was nearly four o'clock on a Thursday in the middle of October, and the air had begun to thicken as it always does before a dusk in autumn. The sky had become stiff with opaque clouds. When they were clear of the gasometers, the wagons and blackened bridges of Banbury, he looked out over the fields, noticing the clumps of trees that sped by, whose dying leaves each had an individual colour, from palest ochre to nearly purple, so that each tree stood out distinctly as in spring. The hedges were still green, but the leaves of the convolvuli threaded through them had turned sickly yellow, and from a distance looked like late flowers. Little arms of rivers twisted through the meadows, lined with willows that littered the surface with leaves. The waters were spanned by empty footbridges.

It looked cold and deserted. The windows of the carriages were bluish with the swirls of the cleaner's leather still showing on the glass, and he confined his eyes to the compartment. It was a third-class carriage, and the crimson seats smelt of dust and engines and tobacco, but the air was warm. Pictures of Dartmouth Castle and Portmadoc looked at him from the opposite wall. He was an undersized boy, eighteen years old, with a pale face and soft pale hair brushed childishly from left to right. Lying back against the seat, he stretched his legs out and pushed his hands to the bottom of the pockets of his cheap blue overcoat. The lapels of it curled outwards and creases dragged from the buttons. His face was thin, and perhaps strained; the expression round his mouth was ready to become taut, and a small frown lingered on his forehead. His whole appearance lacked luxuriance. Only his silky hair, as soft as seeding thistle, gave him an air of beauty.

He had been travelling all day and was hungry because he

21

had had no proper lunch. When he started out that morning from his home in Lancashire, he had had two packets of sandwiches in his pockets, made the night before by his mother. The egg sandwiches were wrapped in white paper and the ham in brown; they were each tied firmly, but not tightly, with string. But at a quarter to one he was sitting in a full compartment, with no prospect of changing for fifty minutes, and as he was shy of eating in front of strangers he looked anxiously at the other passengers to see if they were going to produce food themselves. They did not look as if they were. One man pushed out to take lunch in the dining-car, but the others—two elderly ladies, a beautiful girl and an old clergyman who was reading and annotating a book—all sat on placidly. John had not travelled much before and for all he knew it was considered bad manners to eat in a public carriage. He tried to read. But at one o'clock he had grown desperate and had slunk along to the lavatory, where he locked himself in and bolted a few of his sandwiches before a furious rattling at the door made him cram the rest out of the ventilator, noisily flush the unused water-closet and go back to his seat. His return might have been a prearranged signal: the shorter and fatter of the two old ladies said: "Well!" in a pleased way, and produced a leather shopping-bag, from which she took napkins, packets of sandwiches, small fruit pies, a thermos flask, and they both began to eat a small picnic. Meanwhile the beautiful girl took out some coarse-looking rolls and cheese in silver paper, and even the old clergyman was crumbling biscuits into his mouth, with a handkerchief stuffed into his collar. John hardly dared to breathe. He could sense the old ladies exchanging glances, and sat miserably turning the pages of *A Midsummer Night's Dream*, waiting for what he knew must come—the charitable offer of food. And sure enough, in five minutes he felt a nudge, and saw the shorter and fatter of the two leaning across, holding out a packet in a napkin. She had a rosy face and her false teeth were bared in a smile.

"Would you care for a sandwich, my boy?"

The beat of the train obliterated some of her words, but her gesture was eloquent.

"Er—no, thank you—it's very kind of you—*no*, thank you—I——"

He could not explain that he had thrown his own lunch out of the lavatory window, and she continued to hold the bag out, shaking it determinedly:

"Go on, my boy . . . plenty . . . you'll be hungry . . ."

She wore a cream blouse under her beige travelling-coat and a steel brooch set in the collar. As John continued to show by signs and words that it was very kind of her, but he really wouldn't, she withdrew the sandwiches and unsnapped her handbag.

"You're not feeling ill, are you?" One chubby hand fumbled inside the bag, among letters, keys, a lavender-scented handkerchief and a bottle of tablets. "I have some smelling-salts, if you've a headache . . . lie down. . . ."

But by this time he had taken a sandwich, for anything would be better than being dabbed with eau-de-Cologne, or made to sit by an open window. The beautiful girl was staring at him amusedly as she licked the tips of her fingers, and even the clergyman, paring a russet apple with a silver penknife, paused to gaze at him cheerfully. In the end he was forced to accept not only three sandwiches from the ladies, but a piece of cake from the girl and a quarter of the clergyman's apple. He kept his eyes fixed on the dirty floor as he chewed, utterly humiliated.

So now, four hours later, he was hungry, but so near the end of the journey his restlessness prevented him from wanting to eat. And as if the train knew his destination was near it seemed to quicken speed, plunging on with a regular pattern of beats. He looked from the window and saw a man with a gun entering a field, two horses by a gate, and presently the railway line was joined by a canal, and rows of houses appeared. He got to his feet and stared at the approaching city across allotments, back-gardens and piles of coal covered with fallen leaves. Red brick walls glowed with a dull warmth that he would have admired at another time. Now he was too nervous. The train clattered by iron bridges, cabbages and a factory painted with huge white letters he did not bother to read; smoke dirtied the sky; the train swung violently over set after set of points. A

23

signal-box. Their speed seemed to increase, as they swept towards the station round a long curve of line through much rolling-stock, among which John noticed a wagon from near his home. Then the eaves of the platform, hollow shouting, the faces slowing down as he dragged down his heavy suitcase from the rack, the shuddering halt and escape of steam.

"Oxford," cried a porter, "Oxford," walking the length of the platform because all the nameplates had been removed in time of war. John got out.

He did not hurry through the ticket barrier, and when he walked out of the station all the taxis had been taken. He stood on the pavement, not sorry to be delayed a little, for he was coming to reside at the University for the first time and was so afraid that even now, if he had had the chance, he would have turned and fled back into his previous life. The fact that he had worked for years for this moment made no difference: if he could not run back home, he at least would prefer to loiter about, getting nearer by degrees only to the college on whose books he was enrolled as a scholar.

During this last hesitation he stared down towards the town, aware that behind him a young man was arguing with a porter about a lost bag of golf-clubs. What he could see did not look very remarkable; there were hoardings advertising beans and the ATS, people pushing towards a red bus, a glazed-brick public-house. A pony and cart creaked down the road, the man holding the slack reins, a bowed figure in the faint dusk. John looked about for colleges and old buildings, but could only see distantly a spire or two, and watched a woman buying some sprouts at a greengrocer's fifty yards away. His bag stood beside him on the kerb.

It was because he had crammed everything he had into that bag that it was so heavy and forced him to take a taxi, a thing he had never done before. Only his china had gone before him in a little crate: everything else had been packed in his case, which was like a small trunk with a handle. He could hardly carry it twenty yards, it was so heavy.

Anxiously he waited. The driver of the first taxicab back

grinned and switched off his engine as John gave him the address of his college.

"Sorry, sir, I'm goin' to 'ave my tea."

"Oh."

He went back to the kerb again. The second driver was willing, and after a short, blurred ride, set John down at his gates for two shillings. John gave him half a crown, and, afraid that the man would try to give him sixpence change, stepped quickly through the gate into the college porch. He heard the taxi drive away.

Already the sound of traffic receded a little. He recognized the quadrangle (for he had been there once before) and looked about him.

I must ask the porter where my room is, he told himself to quell his rising bewilderment, that is the first thing to do.

So he left his bag stand and turned into the doorway of the set of rooms at the gates that was given over to the porter as a lodge. Here the post was laid out and a few tattered railway time-tables and telephone-directories hung for the use of the students along one wall. John remembered the porter, a fierce little man with ginger whiskers and a regimental tie, and saw him leaning against the inner door talking to two young men. He was better dressed than John himself.

"Don't tell *me* that. Don't tell *me*. That's what I was saying all last term."

"Anyway, no one'll bother to do it," said one young man languidly. "No one in their senses, that is."

"I'll tell you what it is," the porter began in an even crosser voice, but broke off when he saw John. "Yes, sir?"

John swallowed, and the two young men turned to look at him.

"Er—I've just arrived—er—can you—er—my rooms——"

"What, sir?" snapped the little man, bending an ear nearer. "What d'you say?" John was speechless. "A fresher, are you?"

"Yes——"

"What name?"

"Er—Kemp—er——"

"Kent?"

25

The porter picked up a list and ran his thumbnail down it: the two young men continued to look at John as if he held no particular significance for them. It seemed hours before the porter exclaimed:

"*Kemp!* Kemp, are you? Yes, room two, staircase fourteen. With Mr. Warner. That's you, sir," he repeated as John did not move. "Fourteen, two."

"Er—where?——"

"Founder's Quad—second arch on the left. Staircase fourteen's on the righthand side. You can't miss it."

John backed out, murmuring thanks.

Who was Mr. Warner?

This was something he had dreaded, though not very intensely because there were other more immediate things to shrink from.

He had thought that once he had found his rooms, he would always have a refuge, a place to retreat to and hide in. This was apparently not so.

Who was Mr. Warner? Perhaps he would be quiet and studious.

The news upset him so much that he forgot to ask the porter if his crate of china had arrived, and instead, picked up his case and set off in the direction indicated. The quadrangle was gravelled and surrounded by sets of rooms on three sides, with the Chapel and Hall on the fourth side. The windows were dark and hollow: archways, with arms and scrolled stone, led off into other parts of the college, and one or two pigeons flew down from high ledges from among the rich crimson ivy. John, panting under the weight of the bag, passed through one of the arches where a tablet commemorated the previous war, and found himself in a set of cloisters with the statue of the Founder in the middle, surrounded by iron railings. His footsteps echoed on the stone, and he walked on tip-toe, unaware that the sound would become casually familiar to him in a very few days. In this inner quadrangle silence was almost complete, only broken by the sound of a gramophone playing distantly. He wondered who the Founder was and who Mr. Warner was —perhaps he was a poor scholar, like himself.

26

There were three staircases on the right-hand side of the quadrangle, and the last one was number 14: the numbers had been newly painted. New also were the names of the occupants painted in a list at the bottom of each stair: he read them apprehensively, Stephenson, Hackett and Cromwell, the Hon. S. A. A. Ransom.

The next was 14. Kemp and Warner.

What alarmed him was not so much the sight of the door (room number 2 was on the ground floor), but the fact that he could hear laughter and the sound of teacups coming from it. There were people there! He listened, first at one door, then at another, but it was undoubtedly coming from his own room: cautiously he put his suitcase down, and was just preparing to creep away—for he would as soon have intruded as rung the doorbell of a strange house—when the door suddenly opened and a young man came out holding a kettle.

John retreated. "Er—I——"

"Hallo, did you want me?"

The young man was taller and stronger than John, with dark dry hair brushed back from his forehead, and a square, stubbly jaw. His nose was thick and his shoulders broad; John felt a twinge of distrust. He wore a dark grey lounge suit and dark blue shirt and on his right hand was a square-faced gold ring. There was a swagger in his bearing, he held himself well upright.

"Er . . ." John made a taut, inexpressive gesture. "That is, I think this is—my name's Kemp."

"Oh, you're Kemp? How d'you do? I'm Warner—Chris Warner."

They shook hands.

"We're just having tea: there's rather a crowd inside, I'm afraid I've sort of taken possession." He began filling the kettle from the tap. "Come from Town?"

"From Huddlesford," said John, not knowing that Town meant London.

"Oh, yes. Good journey?"

"Yes——"

He was acutely aware that the conversation in the room had

27

stopped and that the unseen tea-party was listening to the colloquy outside.

"Well, come in and have some tea, if there's anything left." John followed him in. "Friends, my better half has arrived, Mr. Kemp. These are Elizabeth Dowling, Eddy Makepeace, Patrick Dowling and Hugh Stanning-Smith."

He smiled blindly from face to face. They looked at him, and smiled too.

The room was large and airy, and in a terrible mess. Tea was laid on the hearthrug and dirty cups and plates were littered about, while the table was covered with wrapping paper, crumbs from a half-loaf, a pot of jam, a pile of books, and other things recently unpacked from the trunk that stood open under the window. A fire burned brightly in the grate. The room was bigger than any in his own house.

He looked at Elizabeth Dowling first, because she was a girl and because hers was the only name he had caught. She was broad-shouldered, with a regular face, and sat in one corner of the sofa. She was powdered carefully, had a reddened mouth, and her golden hair was brushed fiercely up from the sides of her head, so that it formed a stiff ornament, like a curious helmet. Her right hand lay quiescently holding a burning cigarette, and she wore a check tweed costume.

Then he looked at Eddy Makepeace, who wore a yellow silk tie with horseshoes on it. He had a youthful, spotty face, that expressed great confidence and stupidity, and his eyes bulged.

Patrick Dowling lounged foxily, with a faint resemblance to Elizabeth that showed they were related, and stared back at John with unpleasant candour: Hugh Stanning-Smith was quiet-voiced and white-fingered.

"Chris, you are impossible," said Elizabeth fretfully. "Filling it so full. . . . It'll take *hours* to boil. Simply *hours*. And I'm *dying* for another cup."

John stared at her, never having heard before this self-parodying southern coo, and a sense of his alien surroundings came over him. "I think . . ." he muttered, casting about for an excuse to go. "I think. . . ."

"Here, have some cake." Christopher roughly whacked a

large slab on to a plate and held it out. "Come on, take your things off and sit down," he added kindly. "Pat, get up and give the gentleman a seat."

"It doesn't matter," said John hurriedly, who would have liked to sit down. "I've been sitting all day."

"*So* has Pat," cooed Elizabeth. "But he's *lazy*."

"And he's going to sit all night, too." Patrick gave a sudden disconcerting roar of laughter, then stuffed cake into his mouth. As no one showed any signs of rising, John took off his coat and leant against the wall.

"Have you come a long way?" Elizabeth pronounced each word very clearly, as if speaking to a foreigner, and looked up at him. Staring down at her lips, he perceived that they were actually much thinner than they were painted.

"From Huddlesford."

"M'm. Quite a distance."

As John did not say anything else, the conversation turned away from him again and became general. "What were you saying about Julian, Chris?" inquired Eddy, moving irritably in his chair. "Did you say he'd volunteered?"

"That's right. In the Signals."

"Oh, I see. I thought there was something in it."

"You bet."

"Aren't the Signals dangerous, then?" Elizabeth asked, with an air of intelligence, tapping ash into the saucer of her cup. "Is that what you mean?"

"Can't be if Julian——"

"Is that the person we met in Town, Chris?" Elizabeth turned to Christopher Warner, who was carelessly shuffling plates together, the meal being more or less done. He nodded. "At the Cinderella, after the theatre? I didn't think he was very clever."

"What Lizzie means", said Patrick sarcastically, "is that he——"

"*Shut* up!" Elizabeth made as if to throw a cushion at him, and pouted instead. "You're just a swine." For a second her eye caught John's, and she looked down at her lap. Otherwise the atmosphere of the room was almost the same as before he had entered it.

29

He had finished his cake, and dare not ask for more, so he gave his attention to the room. It was large, impressively conceived, though the details were shabby: windows on one side of the room looked out on to the Founder's Quad (he could see the statue), and on the other on to what he later discovered was the Master's Garden. Long curtains hung by them to the floor. The walls were panelled and painted cream: on each side of the fireplace was a set of shelves in the wall, and the furniture consisted of a table, a desk, two armchairs and a sofa.

Christopher's things were tumbled everywhere. Besides books and clothes, he had taken things at random out of his trunk and put them down anywhere—a bottle of hair lotion, a squash racquet, a few illustrated magazines. Several pictures were propped against the wall. Another suitcase, unstrapped and partly empty, was pushed behind Eddy's chair.

Even with the big fire and comfortable furniture, though, it was not a cosy room. John thought of himself reading a volume of essays in front of the hearth with snow falling outside, but in reality the windows were large and draughty and the room never became properly heated.

The five of them were sprawled round the fire, while John stood behind them by the wall. When he brought his attention back to them, he found that they were not, as he had thought, forgetful of him. As his eyes moved, startled, from face to face, they each hurriedly looked away from him: the one called Eddy had actually been grinning vacuously at him. He flushed, for while it seemed only natural that they should ignore him, he could not believe they were actually pointing at him amongst themselves and laughing together. Yet this was what it looked like.

"Hurry up, kettle!" fretted Elizabeth. He looked at her suspiciously, but with lowered eyelashes she merely recrossed her legs and straightened her skirt. Could he be imagining things? All their faces bore expressions of unconcern: Christopher Warner—John had begun to study him the most, as he knew that Christopher and he were already linked together—Christopher sat on the edge of the fender seat, staring lightly at the carpet, occasionally glancing sideways at Eddy. The gap in the conversation widened second by second. What was wrong?

Cautiously, beginning to feel a twisting apprehension like the beginnings of seasickness, he inspected himself, noting that his fly-buttons were fastened, finding nothing unusual about his appearance, so that his blush intensified, and he tried to stand very erect and militarily. Then he thought this was silly, and tried to adopt a nonchalant pose, crossing his feet and staring out of the window. Eddy Makepeace cleared his throat with a sharp, artificial sound. And Elizabeth took a handkerchief from her handbag and wiped her nose carefully, so as not to disturb the powder. Christopher, extending his silver cigarette-case, said with an uneasy smile:

"Tube for anyone?"

But his words were drowned by the frothing of water on the hot fire as the kettle boiled over, and he quickly took it off, using a handkerchief to hold it. Everyone reached for their cups, stretching and shifting. "Oh, what an *age*," cried Elizabeth, trying to obscure the pause that had been broken by holding out her cup childishly. "Me, Chris, *me*. Oo, do buck *up*."

"Visitors first," said Christopher Warner, filling a cup for John. "Do you take sugar?" He paused, changing his grip on the teapot. "Christ, the damn thing's hot."

"Oh—er—thanks," John, still fiery red, struggled for something to say: "Do you know—er—rather a funny thing, I think we've both brought the same kind of china——"

He was interrupted by a howl of laughter so sudden and boisterous that he jumped and looked round him in alarm. Everyone was wildly amused. Elizabeth snatched her tiny handkerchief again, and, holding it to her eyes, shook with merriment. Eddy Makepeace gave short barks of laughter, that were irritating because they sounded forced: Hugh Stanning-Smith was chuckling in a well-bred way, and Patrick Dowling looked sideways up at him with a foxy jeer.

"What—what's wrong?" he exclaimed, startled for once into natural behaviour.

More laughter. His bewilderment caused a second, cruder

31

burst, as if a comedian, having told a funny story, had proceeded to sit on his hat.

"Oh, God," gasped Christopher Warner at last, taking his handkerchief from around the teapot handle and mopping his eyes with it. "Oh, dear! My dear fellow, these *are* your crocks. . . . Oh, Lord!" His face creased in another spasm of laughter, and gusts of it coughed from his chest. "Oh, God, I shall spill the——" He put the teapot down and a little tea slopped out of the spout on to the cloth. "I say, you must excuse us. I haven't any crocks: I'm afraid we broke your crate open and gave your things a christening—I say, I do hope you don't mind——"

John understood at once. Like every freshman, he had received a list from the Bursary giving a list of domestic articles that he should be provided with on coming into residence, such as two pairs of sheets, a set of china, a kettle, a cruet and so on. Three weeks ago his mother had insisted that they spent an afternoon among the shops buying these things: it had been a touching little expedition, meaning, he realized, far more to her than to him. They had had tea afterwards in a cinema café, with teacakes.

Most of the things they had bought lay dirty and scattered around the room; in fact, John wondered they had lain unrecognized for so long. The crate (he saw it now) was behind Christopher's trunk, broken open carelessly, so that it would be impossible to use it again, as he had intended to do. These, then, were his cups and plates: his coffee strainer (choked with tea leaves); his shining kettle blackened by the fire. His breadknife, his sugar basin.

"God, I thought he'd never notice," gurgled Eddy Makepeace, drying his bulging eyes. "How *damned* funny."

Elizabeth Dowling burst into another peal of laughter. "And the *exquisite* way. . . ." She gulped, to strangle her laughter. "He brought the subject up *so* politely. . . . Oh dear, oh dear!"

John sipped his tea, which was hot and burnt his mouth. He was acutely conscious of being referred to in the third person, but it expressed his mood. While being trapped in their laughter, he only wanted to drag himself stiffly away and hide.

32

"I say, you don't mind, old man, do you?" asked Christopher Warner, with an anxious tone that seemed flattering.

"Oh, no—no——"

"Hell, there's nothing to *mind* about," said Patrick Dowling sneeringly. "It's only that it was so damned funny. He must have thought he was seeing things."

"Haven't you really got *anything*, Chris? You are awful. I spent *days* in Harrod's making up my mind about patterns and colours and shapes and things. If anyone *dares* to break them, oo, I'll—I'll——"

Christopher, laughing loudly, kicked the fire into a blaze and straddled the hearthrug.

"Well, I only brought glasses, so we can share and share alike."

"Trust you, Chris," said Eddy Makepeace knowingly.

"Well, I mean to say. That list they send you's enough to make a cat laugh. Breakfast china and tea china—do they think you're made of money? Anyway, it'll only get pinched or broken. No, I just picked up some beer mugs and sherry glasses from home—and God help the bastard that breaks any of them, too. Well well, I expect Kemp'll be using my glasses soon enough."

John muttered something, too embarrassed at being the centre of the situation and at hearing the word "bastard" used in front of a girl to consult the feelings that raged inside him. When he did, he found them a turmoil of anger and bitter humiliation and self-pity. While the light conversation moved around the subject and eventually away from it, he found himself staring at the coffee-strainer that had been used to strain tea, and feeling sorry for it, as if they had suffered in the same way. His impulse to run away was neutralized by the fact there was nowhere to run to. This was home for him, now.

"What's on at the flicks?" demanded Eddy Makepeace loudly, dropping ash into his cup. John stared with growing dismay at the bulging eyes and spotty face, feeling he had wandered into a place where he had absolutely no counterpart. Putting down his cup, he continued to remain silent.

It seemed too much to hope that they should ever go, but just before six they all got up and at last departed. Christopher saw them to the gate. Evening had more than begun to fall, and John heard them go laughing round the cloisters. Left alone, he sat dejectedly down on the sofa, among the litter of dirty china, feeling that if he were left alone for long he would begin crying. But this feeling changed to alarm as he heard Christopher Warner coming back, for the idea of living with a stranger made him shrink. Would they have to share the same bedroom? He had never done that before, and was intensely shy. Further, he felt nothing but dislike for Christopher Warner so far.

"Now," said Christopher briskly, slamming the door. "Most of this mess is mine, I think. . . . I say, bung a bit of coal on the fire, would you?"

John obeyed. Christopher Warner began carrying armfuls of clothes into the bedroom, not paying much attention to John, who knelt down awkwardly beside his ridiculous semi-trunk and undid it.

"I've taken the farther bed—I suppose that's all right?" said Christopher, as they passed in the doorway. The farther bed was away from the door, and was nearest the small lamp.

"Oh, yes."

John put his three shirts into the corner of one drawer, hearing the sound of Christopher screwing up wrapping-paper, and looked about the bedroom. It was small, and held two beds, a washstand and a large clothes-cupboard. On the marble top of the washstand Christopher had grouped his shaving things, which John studied cautiously. What was 'shaving lotion', and 'talcum powder'?

"I'm glad you met some of my friends," said Christopher as he cleared up. Taking the first of the framed photographs, he began scanning the walls for nails. "I know them pretty well in Town. . . . Elizabeth is Patrick's sister, you know. That Hugh fellow's a pal of Patrick's. I was at school with Eddy—at Lamprey, you know."

"Oh, yes."

"A fine place. A bloody fine place." Christopher hung his

34

first picture, and stepped back, wiping his hands on his trousers. "That's it. Etching, you know."

John had not heard of Lamprey School, but looked deferentially at the etching while Christopher hung up three other pictures, two of which were Lamprey teams with Christopher represented.

"That makes the place look more like home. I say, I'm sorry, you haven't anything, have you?"

"No, no, that's quite all right."

"I was afraid you might be the sort of guy that would want to hang lousy modern daubs about. It's a bore, having to share, isn't it?"

John would have thought this exceptionally rude had he said it himself. From Christopher Warner, who was burrowing for his lighter with a fresh cigarette in his mouth, it did not seem so.

"Lord, you don't catch the dons sharing. You'll know there's a war on when they do." A cloud of smoke hid his face, then parted. "Not that I blame them."

"What are you going to read?"

"I'm supposed to be doing English."

"Yes—so am I."

"Oh, then that's why we're together." He took another look round the room. "I think most of the mess is cleared up now."

It was becoming dark, and the sitting-room was filling with shadows. Christopher pushed a pile of magazines carelessly on to one of the shelves of the bookcase; far away and near bells were beating the half-hour, the sound spreading mellowly through all the arches and stone traceries to John's ears. He bent his head, thinking of words like "angelus" and "refectory".

There came a knock on the door.

"Come in."

A thin, delicate-looking man in an apron entered and stood by the door.

"Good evening, gentlemen. I'm your scout."

"Oh, yes—put the light on, will you? That's right. I'm Warner. This is Kemp."

35

John ducked his head shyly.

"I'll put the black-out up, sir, if you wouldn't mind watching. . . . You'll be wanting to do it yourselves when the days get shorter."

They watched him fit the sheets of plywood across the windows in the bedroom and close the shutters in the sitting-room. Then he began collecting the used tea-things on a tray, working swiftly and methodically while they watched. "You know I'm entitled to take your dusters?" he said, glancing up. "For the cleaning——"

"Oh, yes, of course. They wouldn't be much good to us!"

"No, they wouldn't, would they, sir?" The scout began to put the bread and sugar away. "I don't suppose you'd want my job as well as your own, would you? No, I don't suppose you would." He laughed quietly the while, as though his chest hurt him. "Hall's at seven, gentlemen, you know that? Have you your gowns?"

"Yes——"

"No, I haven't——" John looked startled at them both, having in the strain of the last hour forgotten the rule (which had been worrying him) that everyone who ate in Hall must wear the gown of their degree.

"You haven't, sir? A scholar, are you, sir? I'll get you one— just a few moments, if you'll hang on." And, taking the tray, he went out, closing the door quietly. John was relieved, both at this promise and at the fact that Christopher had been there to deal with the man. He had not been looking forward to the unfamiliar experience of speaking to a servant.

"I got mine from the porter for half a dollar," explained Christopher, picking up a scrap of black cloth. He yawned. "I'm going to the Junior Common Room. A man was telling me you can get sherry there."

Then there was dinner in the big Hall, with rows of black-gowned students standing down the white tables while a Latin grace was read. During the meal John hardly lifted his head, but was aware of the casual chatter, the servants carrying plates and trayfuls of tankards, and the tall, gilt-framed oil paintings high up on the panelling. He finished the three courses very quickly, waited till someone else left, then walked out himself.

Christopher Warner had eaten at the Commoners' table with Patrick Dowling, and they were sitting over their beer when John went, so that he went back to an empty room, to be alone at last. In the electric light the cream-painted walls seemed unfriendly. After taking off his gown, he sat on the sofa again, but at once got up, as restless as a cat in a new home, and looked around him. A dismal melancholy was beginning to expand inside him, a great loneliness. It was the knowledge that he had nowhere to go more friendly, more intimate than this room that depressed him so, and particularly because the room was not his alone. He could not fortify himself inside it against the rest of the strangeness, for at any moment Christopher Warner and Patrick might come in and make coffee in his coffee-pot or break one of his plates through trying some balancing trick. He had hoped that at least there would always be his own room, with a fire and the curtains drawn, where he could arrange his few books neatly, fill a drawer with his notes and essays (in black ink with red corrections, held together by brass pins), and live undisturbed through the autumn into the winter. This was apparently not to be.

No one would think that two people lived here, he thought, looking round the room. Christopher had laid a leather writing-wallet on the desk, a fancy stone ashtray on the mantelpiece and a pair of silk cushions on the sofa. His wool-lined slippers were by the coal-scuttle: John had left his own under the bed because they were badly worn. It was strange how other people's clothes grew seasoned, bettered, by use: his only became tattered and worn out. He looked around the room for evidence of his own presence, but found very little. It was hardly better in the bedroom. At least he had a bed to himself, with his pyjamas folded neatly on top of it, but Christopher's scarlet bathrobe was the first thing to catch the eye, and his towels, and in the cupboard his bright scarfs and shirts.

Out of curiosity he began to inspect Christopher Warner's things, to try to deduce his character from them. Who was he? He was rich and from London. There were a few hairs on his

37

comb, and his hair-brushes were in a leather case. John snapped and unsnapped the catch. The pockets of his jackets hanging behind a curtain were empty, but the clothes bore the tab of a tailor in London and John felt the cloth and the leather buttons with interest. His two drawers were not enlightening: as well as the shirts and light underwear, there was a jumble of socks and silk ties, collars, a set of studs and cuff links, a pile of white linen handkerchiefs. There were also a few unopened packets of razor blades and four contraceptives. He felt as alarmed as if he had found a loaded revolver.

Drifting into the sitting-room, he glanced along the bookshelf, where Christopher had roughly stacked a number of things, including a few books. They were a complete Shakespeare, *The Shropshire Lad*, an *Omnibus of Humour*, a book by Siegfried Sassoon, and one or two detective novels. Inside the covers was written "Christopher R. W. Warner" in a huddled, sloping hand, not without character. On the top of the books lay a squash racquet in a press, and there were also five or six notebooks, stamped "Lamprey College" in thick Gothic letters, one of which John opened, his eye catching the words:

Thus we see that in creating the character of Shylock, Shakespeare's original intention was deflected, and instead of a comic moneylender, he produced a figure of tragic significance.

The awareness that he himself had written something very like that gave John a strange thrill, part rivalry and part kinship, with a dash of disappointment that something he had in the past prided himself on knowing should be the common property of any stranger.

Behind the books he found a pack of cards, a newspaper and a pair of rubber shoes.

The letter-case would probably tell him more, he decided, and, crossing to the desk, he switched on the reading lamp. But it contained, besides sheets of notepaper, envelopes and blank postcards, only one letter and a photograph of a girl in a white dress, with "To Christopher with love" written across the white part. He looked at it wonderingly. The letter ended "With love to you, my darling" and was unsigned, but after reading it through he concluded it was from Mrs. Warner, Christopher's mother. It was dated the 9th October from a house in Derbyshire, where she was apparently staying with friends, playing golf and watching it rain. Elspeth had finally gone into the WRNS. John noted the extravagant, well-formed writing, and, putting the letter back and closing the wallet, crossed to a little triangular shelf in one corner of the room where Christopher had put a double photograph of his parents. The picture there showed her as dark and boldly attractive, not at all as old as she must be. She had the same broad jaw as Christopher, and a friendly look that coincided with the style of her letter, which was as casual as if Christopher were her equal, merely a friend or a friend of the family, quite unlike the kind of letter John associated with parents. Although, of course, he had hardly ever received one, as he had never been away from home for any space of time before.

He then gave up the search for he did not know quite what, knowing only it had not been successful. Christopher Warner seemed as distant and as hostile as ever; John had been looking for a sign of kinship, and had not found it, and also for a sign of weakness—a diary or some sentimental letters—that would compensate him for the business of his china. In fact, the weakness would have been kinship. But he paused, at a loss in the big room, seeing his face in the large mirror over the fireplace, and behind it the photograph of Mr. and Mrs. Warner in the double frame. This reminded him that he had not written to his own parents since arriving, and he sat down at the desk to do it, glad of the job.

Dear Mum and Dad,

I arrived here safely after four o'clock. I am at present sitting in my room, which I am sharing with a man called Warner: it is quite big, and in the Founder's Quadrangle. My china has also arrived safely, and has already been used. Nothing has started yet, as term doesn't officially start till Sunday.

Hope you are both well.

Your loving son,
John.

As an afterthought he added:

The sandwiches were very nice.

Then he addressed the envelope:

Mr. and Mrs. J. Kemp,
48, King Edward Street,
Huddlesford,
Lancashire.

He stamped it with a blue stamp. The room was quite silent
apart from the flapping of the flame among the coals, and as he
tried to sit reading the quietness rang in his ears, making him
grow tense for the least sound. He fancied he could even hear
the electric light burning. Time crawled by at an intolerably
slow speed, every minute seeming four times as long as usual:
he did not know if he wanted Christopher Warner to come back
or not; it was not so much that he wanted to see him again, but
that if he did it might show he had some comradely feeling,
even that he wanted to compensate for the wounds they had
inflicted during the afternoon. At length he threw *A Midsummer Night's Dream* aside, and opened the door to listen to
the night outside, advancing cautiously down the steps into the
cloistered quadrangle. Looking up from the stone enclosure, he
could see the sky full of innumerable trembling stars, and all he
could hear was extravagant sounds at a distance—drunken
howling from a far street, something that might have been a
revolver shot, and, from somewhere in the College itself, the
hysterical crying of a jazz record. Close to all was quiet: the
slightest of winds breathed over the grass and around the stone
pillars, while from the Master's garden came the restless sound
of trees. He wondered if a time would ever come when these
things would assure him and seem pleasant.

He went to bed at half-past nine, quite unable to endure it
any longer. Because the day had tired him, he went to sleep
sooner than he had imagined, despite the unfamiliar smell of
the sheets; but towards midnight he was startled out of sleep
by a tremendous crash in the next room. His terrified thought
was that a gang had come to rag and bully him, and he started

up shaking in bed, but almost immediately the bedroom door burst open and Christopher lurched in, switching on the light. His dark hair was disordered and he wore a savage expression on his face, and he took no notice of John at all. The first thing he did was to use the chamber-pot noisily, breathing hard as if he had just run a race; then he pulled off his tie and jacket and the rest of his clothes. When he was in his pyjamas, he leant over the slop-pail and vomited copiously three times, and at last climbed into bed, where, after turning and mumbling a good deal and giving a loud belch like the ripping of canvas, he subsided into sleep.

Whatever John had expected, he had not expected this, and he lay shuddering with fear and horror for several minutes in the dim light, until he realized he must switch it off. With infinite caution, refusing to look at the pail or even at Christopher Warner, he slid out of bed and pushed the switch gently down, plunging the room into blackness which made Christopher's heavy breathing and occasional snorts sound terrifying to him.

Whatever wretchedness he felt, crouching there in the dark and trying to recapture sleep, was quite overlaid by fear. His heart kept beating fast lest Christopher should rouse up again, and come lurching over to him, and when at last he did sleep, his dreams were full of pursuits and brutal attacks. At every steady chiming of the hour from the College clock he stirred uneasily.

When the servant called them at half-past seven the next morning, John had already been awake for nearly two hours, lying listening to the squealing of castors and the to-and-fro sound of the carpet-sweeper as the man cleaned the sitting-room, and earlier than that hearing nothing but the faraway crowing of a cock and watching the light grow round the edges of the shutters. He had examined in his mind all the events of

41

the day before, for they were startlingly vivid compared with the rest of his memories: the rest of his life seemed only a passing thought, that counted for nothing.

The shape of his clothes on a chair depressed him: the sound of snoring and heavy breaths from Christopher's bed scared him. He did not want to go any further with this new life. Already he was fearing what would come next: he feared being formally called, he feared breakfast, he feared all that still lay before him, measuring it against the trifle he had already experienced. How much pleasanter it would be to go back, though the past was even by this time unemphatic and twilit. Yet the only remembrance that came to his mind was one afternoon, months ago, when his mother had gone out to the doctor, leaving him an egg to boil for his tea: he had placed the egg on the kitchen table, looking round for a saucepan, and, before he could stop it, the egg rolled over the edge and smashed on the brick floor.

However, when the man had taken down the shutters and John had got up, washed in cold water and dressed, his fear had diminished a little, and he looked doubtfully at the bed where Christopher Warner slept. He had not awoken and still lay in deep sleep, his mouth ajar, his black hair tousled and the stubble thick on his jaw. As John stood by him, the stale smell of beer was noticeable, and he looked so different that John could not but feel that their acquaintanceship of the day before was a mirage, and here was a complete stranger. Should he wake him? He hesitated uncomfortably, hearing in his mind Christopher Warner's sharp voice inquiring: "Why the hell didn't you wake me for breakfast?"

"Warner," he said nervously.

No answer.

"Er—Warner," he repeated, touching his shoulder tentatively. "Wake up."

There was slow movement in the bed: Christopher grunted. His mouth shut. His eyes opened, and he began struggling to get his hand up to rub them.

"Eh? . . . urrh . . . ah. What's the time?"

"I—I don't know. It must be nearly breakfast time."

42

Christopher stared at the wristwatch he still wore, and after a second's thought he began to wind it, as if mentally composing an answer.

"Thanks. I won't get up for breakfast."

"Oh—er—sorry——"

"All right!" said Christopher reassuringly, turning over with his face to the wall, while John withdrew, flushing at his own stupidity.

John ate his breakfast among a crowd of self-conscious freshman scholars, speaking to no one. For some reason he could not take his eyes off Patrick Dowling, who was also a scholar, but who sat at the commoners' table, wearing a smart and townified lounge suit, and when Patrick happened to catch his eye he did not return John's half smile.

After breakfast he handed in his ration book at the Bursary, looked at the notice-board till he found a mention to himself, and then drifted back to his room. Christopher was now lying awake, and called:

"That you, Kemp? What time is it now?"

"Er—it's about nine."

"My watch has stopped. Do you think you could give me a glass of water?"

"Yes, of course——"

John filled a tooth-glass and handed it to him. "Thanks," said Christopher, his forehead wrinkling as he drank. "Ah, that's better. Did I cat last night?"

"Er—I beg your——"

"Did I cat? Was I sick?"

"Yes, you—er—were——"

"I thought I should be." Christopher handed back the empty glass and lay silent a moment. "We got into a pub about half-past nine, you know, and I got some pints. And as soon as I'd had one mouthful, 'Eddy,' I said, 'this beer's piss.' And he agreed. And I said: 'If there's one thing that makes me cat, it's pissy beer.' I wonder how he got on." He pursed his lips in resignation, then yawned. "What did you say the time was?"

"About nine——"

"Oh, God!"

43

The bed creaked as he sat up on the edge of it, feet searching independently for slippers, one hand scratching his dark head. John was comforted by his mildness and went back into the other room, where a strong fire glowed in the grate and a few bars of sunlight fell on to the worn carpet.

"We—er—we've got to see our Tutor this morning."

"What?"

"I—there's a notice—we've got to see our Tutor——"

"Oh hell and damnation! When?"

John thought he said "Where?" and replied:

"In his rooms, at eleven."

"I'm meeting some people at eleven."

When Christopher came out of the bedroom, he was wearing his scarlet bathrobe and smoking a cigarette. He crossed to the fire and crouched before it.

"What a blasted nuisance. Where does he live, d'you know?"

"No—in College somewhere——"

"Oh, God, I should hope so. I don't want to have to be chasing all over the town for him."

"We're the only two freshmen reading English," said John, vaguely passing a hand over his hair and looking down at the fender. Christopher paid no attention, and eventually sat back on the sofa until he had finished his cigarette. Then he lit another one, and went out of the room, taking his shaving things and a bath-towel. As he slammed the door, he burst into roaring, theatrical song:

> See 'im in . . . the 'Ouse of Commons . . .
> Passin' laws . . . ter put down crime . . .

and this echoed away round the cloisters, till other noises overlaid it.

John was relieved by Christopher's friendly attitude, and, noticing the letter he had written the night before, went out to post it, wondering where the nearest pillar-box was. He did not know that there was one in the College Lodge, but in any case he was glad of the walk, and he looked curiously around him at the shops, the broad white pavements and the brightly-polished knockers on private doors. Even the new red brick

44

air-raid shelters looked attractive in the sun, and he found them as pleasant as the old buildings with their tall windows and turrets. Suddenly he felt that he was going to enjoy Oxford: his early depression lifted clean away, and he threaded his way through the town whistling a few notes to himself. Here and there he noticed bookshops, and paused uncertainly before their windows.

Towards eleven o'clock his apprehension returned, and when they entered the Tutor's carpeted room he hardly dared to raise his eyes. Christopher made a few casual remarks about the weather and rooms as they sat down, and John looked nervously about him, noticing a large illustrated book on heraldry the Tutor had just laid aside as they came in. He was a tall cadaverous man, very slow in his movements and shy to make a definite suggestion; it was by a series of these suggestions that he brought the conversation round to literature, and before John had time to be alarmed, they were speaking of the term's work. Christopher sat frowning seriously, his brief answers revealing to John's surprise that he knew hardly anything, but his self-confidence seemed to increase with every admission of ignorance, and his manner suggested that the Tutor was a personal friend who insisted upon talking tediously about literature. John carefully concealed the pride he felt when he was able to say, yes, he had read this or that.

The Tutor opened a tiny notebook, but just then a telephone buzzed on his desk, and with a weary movement he went to answer it, so John looked round the room. It was decorated in pink and grey, and with its light oak bookcase was almost like a drawing-room. A bronze head of a boy stood where the sun would catch it; and really John had never seen so many books in his life outside a public library. The idea of one man possessing them all made him stare at the Tutor with renewed interest, feeling the hint of another different way of life. How differently he must see things!

"Yes," said the Tutor into the telephone. "Yes, yes." He replaced the receiver and came back to them. "I'm afraid it is impossible for me to take you separately at the moment. A colleague of mine in another college has taken up"—he gave

45

a faint conventional smile—"work of a very different nature since last term, and a number of his pupils have fallen to me ... yes. Well, shall we say. . . . Would Friday, at eleven, suit you both?"

He gave them a list of books to read and the subject for an essay, and they left, Christopher hurrying away immediately to have coffee, pausing only to toss his gown into the lodge on the way.

Left alone, John subsided into vacancy. After lunch he walked round the gardens—a remnant of their summer beauty, which was still faintly perceptible—and then sat in his room considering the essay subject for a while. At last he put on his overcoat and strolled into the town: was there nothing else, then, till next Friday, a week hence? What was he going to do? It seemed wrong to waste so many hours of the day. What should he do next—start working immediately? What was the rest of the University doing? Looking round, he saw dozens of students, pushing into teashops or bookshops, wearing new college scarves and talking at the top of their voices, and to get away from them he walked down the High Street as far as the river and stood on the broad bridge. From there he could see trees on the river banks and the water running quickly under stone walls. Farther up, a swan plunged its neck deep into the weeds, and, lingering by the balustrade of the bridge, he lost himself for a moment in the tranquillity of the scene, watching the dead leaves drifting away with the current.

But he was tired of his own company by the end of the afternoon, and on returning to College he was distinctly pleased to find Christopher Warner at home. He had already begun to admire Christopher so much that the shock of the previous day was being rapidly dissipated, and even now he was pleased rather than not to see him. By this time he was half-drunk again. An opened bottle of beer stood on the mantelpiece, and Christopher, in his shirt-sleeves, was tinkering with a radiogram that had arrived since John left. Patrick Dowling lay watching him from an armchair, another bottle held to his mouth, his eyes moving idly round as John came in.

"There, now let's see if the sod will—— Oh, hell, where's

the——" Christopher savagely turned the volume-control on full, and the room was filled with a deafening, gigantic piece of piano playing. He lowered it. "That's better. Yes, that's fine. Now, will it get past that? No! Pat, the sod's stuck again." Not bothering to lift the lid, he gave the cabinet a violent kick, and the needle jumped clear, but this time the mechanism itself rebelled, and the record came to a halt. Christopher swore viciously and put the bottle to his lips.

"You are a fool, Chris," said Patrick thickly. "What d'you want to cock it up for, you haven't had it two hours." He rolled his eyes round to John. "Hallo, Kemp or Hemp or whatever your name is."

"Hallo," said John timidly.

Christopher Warner turned round to him.

"Now look at that bloody radiogram, Kemp, it's only been here since three and it will not bloody well play. . . . I've done all I can. I don't know what's wrong. What the hell do they think I paid thirty bob for?"

"Er—that's cheap, isn't it?"

"He hasn't bought it, you fool," put in Patrick offensively. "You can hire them for that a term. Aren't you going to stand your whack?"

John was saved from answering by the entrance of another young man, a second-year student, who wore spectacles and carried a sheaf of papers. "Pardon my intrusion, gentlemen," he said, coughing and speaking in an impressive voice. "I have the honour of representing the Oxford Union. Is anyone here interested in this body? If so, I have a leaflet——"

"Oh——" Christopher paused in the action of pulling off his necktie. "You're one of those people who come in and leave bumf lying around, are you?"

"As you so crudely put it, sir. The subscription is thirty shillings a term, entitling you to free use of the Union premises, including the reading and writing rooms, billiard tables, library, bar—that, I feel, sir, would recommend itself particularly to you——"

"See here, old boy." Christopher had dropped the ends of his tie, and came over to the visitor. "I may look a bit simple,

47

but when I want to pay thirty bob for the privilege of having a drink, you'll know the end is near. Good-bye."

"However," said the young man, stepping back, "I will leave what you are pleased to call some bumf for you to peruse at your no doubt extensive leisure." He looked hard at John as he spoke, as if hoping for support, but John was watching Christopher with a grin, trying to stop himself bursting into laughter. "Good afternoon, gentlemen. I leave you to your Bacchic revelry."

Christopher retorted by belching grossly as the door closed. "Who was that sucker?" he demanded loudly. "I'm getting definitely fed, yes, quite definitely fed, with them all." He rolled up his shirt sleeves, and let his tie dangle loose. "Where's the beer, Pat? Surely we've not drunk the lot?"

"There's one left," said Patrick, holding up a full bottle he had been keeping under his chair. Christopher unscrewed the stopper and drank. His cheerful insolence was infectious: John could have laughed delightedly at the way the person from the Union had been dealt with, knowing that had he been alone, he would probably have parted with thirty shillings very quickly. He was thrilled, too, by the fact that he himself had nothing to fear from Christopher—or so he thought—being within his circle of friends; the idea of Christopher as a protector crossed his mind, Christopher as a large dog that was savage to strangers. It was queer that already the affair of the tea-things was beginning to fade in his memory, falling into perspective as one of the harmless things Christopher did without thinking. He had never seen a person so free from care.

The attention he paid to Christopher saved him from committing several actions that he immediately recognized as unnecessary when once Christopher had objected. On the first Sunday of term, for instance, he had actually taken down his gown from behind the door, when Christopher looked round from where he was lying on the sofa.

"What's cooking?"

"Freshman's sermon—aren't you——?"

"I didn't know there was one."

"The Master says he hopes every Freshman will attend."

"Hopeful type," commented Christopher, returning to his magazine.

"Don't you think people will go?"

"*I* shan't go."

So John put his gown back, and wrote some letters, one home to his parents, and one to his sister, who was an elementary school teacher in Manchester; and afterwards, having obtained one of the books the Tutor had mentioned from the college library, sat reading and making notes. Christopher yawned and read and smoked cigarettes until twelve o'clock, when he got up to go out. As he was putting on his big heather-coloured overcoat, he remarked:

"Cute file that. I suppose I shall have to be getting something in that line soon."

"Do you like it?" said John, surprised, looking up from the file.

"Very cute."

"I think they've got one left, at the shop. Shall I——?"

"Oh, lord, no; don't bother. Are you getting a line on that stuff? Can I look at it when you've finished?"

"Yes, of course."

Nevertheless, when John returned home the next day with an identical file from the same stationer, Christopher had forgotten all about it, to judge from the wrinkling of his forehead as he stared at it.

"Me? I said so?"

"Why, yes." John felt himself going very red. "I thought you said——"

"I really don't remember." Christopher looked at John almost suspiciously, as if John were trying to deceive him in some way. "Still . . . I haven't any change now. I'll pay you tonight."

John felt a sudden chill, as if a door had swung open and revealed his loneliness still awaiting him: for one moment he felt the waste desert that would receive him if Christopher were not there as a friend: for a moment it seemed almost that Christopher Warner did not give two pins for him. But on the scholars' table that night he heard Christopher referred to as "that rowdy man Warner", which seemed in some way to compensate him. As he ate he could hear Christopher shouting and talking loudly down on one of the commoners' tables.

He was, indeed, by the end of the first week established as the most turbulent of the freshmen, and people had formed their attitudes towards him accordingly. John could not but admire the easy way he got on with the servants: with the porter he would talk about racing and drinking, while with Jack, the scout, he would hold long conversations on the subject of early rising, all on a plane of facetiousness that John found richly amusing.

"Good morning, Jack."

"Good afternoon, sir. Up at last, sir."

"What's that, Jack?"

"I says, up at last, sir. An' about time."

"Well, there's gratitude for you." Christopher, standing before the fire in his pyjamas, would smoke at his cigarette in a satisfied way for a bit, while Jack clattered about in the bedroom, emptying slops and making the beds. Then he would call:

"Here, Jack, make mine first. It's been a hard day: I'm ready for bed."

"Ah, I should say you are. Fair nippy today's been. Too cold for you, sir."

"Too cold, eh?"

"Oh, far too cold, sir. It'd wither you up soon as look at yer."

"Why, Jack, you terrify me."

"Ah——" Jack would reappear with his mop and disgusting pail of slop water, pausing to breathe delicately across the room:

"You should try getting up when I do, once in a while, sir. Five o'clock. Then you can talk about cold. Take 'em off a brass monkey, it would."

At this Christopher would wheeze with laughter, and offer Jack a cigarette, which he always accepted and put behind his ear where his hair was beginning to turn grey. John had heard people say that his lungs were bad.

50

"Sound type, Jack," Christopher would comment after the door had closed.

Although he thought of Christopher as his only friend, John's days were all similarly vacuous as he lived the unfamiliar hotel life of the undergraduate, and in particular he had no one to talk with at meal-times, as Christopher and Patrick both sat on the commoners' table. This gap was eventually filled by another scholar named Whitbread, who remarked one evening at dinner:

"Noisy crowd down there."

"Er—I beg your pardon?"

"Noisy crowd down there—regular bad set, I fancy."

"Oh, I share rooms with Warner," said John, with a little laugh.

"Do you? That's a bit of bad luck. Can't you ask the Dean to move you?"

"Oh, he's all right when you get to know him," said John casually, fingering a piece of bread. "Not at all bad."

"A fellow like that does no good to himself or anyone else," Whitbread enunciated. He had a pale stubbly head, queerly like a dormouse, and thick steel-rimmed spectacles: he spoke with a flat Yorkshire accent that made John suppose wrongly that he had a sense of humour. John could tell by his clothes that he was not well-off, and he remembered a phrase from one of his mother's letters (it was still in his pocket) that said that she hoped he had made some friends "of his own standing". With a gust of indignation he realized that she meant people like Whitbread. "Of course, the College takes a number of fellows like him to keep up the tone," the latter continued, scraping up custard with his spoon, "but they look to us to bring home t'bacon."

Whitbread seemed to take a fancy to John, and after the meal was over asked him back to his room for coffee. They crossed the pitch-dark quadrangle together, Whitbread holding a bicycle flashlamp to show the way, and climbed to a tiny set of rooms in the attics, where a dull fire smouldered. One side of the room sloped with the roof, the mirror was spotted with tarnish, and through the bedroom door, which stood ajar,

51

John could see the other's blue and white pyjamas neatly folded on the bed. Whitbread went into the bedroom to fill the kettle from his water-jug, and while the kettle boiled on the gas ring outside they sat over the fire and talked.

"Not very matey, the other students, are they?" said Whitbread, his knees apart. "Take some getting to know. Of course, you have to choose your friends carefully. No good going about with millionaires."

"Well, I hardly chose Warner," said John, flushing slightly.

"No, no, I didn't mean it personal," Whitbread protested, looking honestly at him through his metal-rimmed spectacles. "Of course you didn't. An' you can't help but see a good bit of him. But if you take my advice, you'll let him know where he stands, pretty sharp. Can't have him mucking up your work."

"Do you find it easy to work here?"

"Why, yes." Whitbread was puzzled. They heard the kettle boil over, and as he went out to make the coffee John noticed the surprising stockiness of his shoulders and arms. "I didn't do anything for the first day till I'd settled a bit. But now I've settled into a routine more—why, it's easy." He made the coffee by pouring boiling water into two cups, into which he had first added a little coffee essence, and stirring quickly. "My word, you don't want to be one of these fellows that slacks off as soon as he gets his scholarship. Why, that's only half t'battle." He produced a bag of biscuits, and offered them. "I got these from home. Go on, take two."

They sat sipping and munching, and discussed the scholarships they had won: John found that Whitbread had slightly more a year than he had himself, through his grammar school's being more richly endowed. "I could make something if I liked," said Whitbread, with a gnomish grin. "Nothing easier."

"Why don't you?"

"Eh, there's no call to be stingy. Besides, it don't do to get the reputation of being close. T'dons respect you if you have additional hardships to face, but they don't like you to be miserly. You've got to cut your coat according to your cloth."

"Yes, of course."

John lay, a slight figure, in the armchair, holding his coffee-

cup and looking round the room once more. There were no
pictures, but a calendar hung over the desk, on which lay an
open classical text, a dictionary and some notes. The books in
the bookcase were all classical texts, with a few sixpenny edi-
tions of popular works and five large scholarly books bearing
the arms of the college, borrowed from the library. A card
giving the programme for the term of preachers of the University sermons stood on the mantelpiece. Whitbread finished
his coffee quickly and made some more. As he was doing so
there was a tap on the door and another scholar looked in by
the name of Jackson.

"Oh, sorry, I didn't know you had a visitor. . . . Have you
done with those Tacitus notes?"

"Come in, have some coffee," said Whitbread, taking another
cup from the cupboard and smiling broadly. "Yes, I've nearly
done."

"No, if you don't mind—I'm working—I really mustn't
stop——"

"Ee, come in, just for five minutes. Kemp's not staying long.
I'll be starting myself at half-past eight."

So Jackson, who wore a curious stiff collar, came in and
sat down, and the three of them sipped the thin coffee and
talked about the College. John was surprised by the amount
Whitbread knew, not only about the College's past history, but
about the other undergraduates, the dons and the present con-
ditions in the University itself. He knew, for instance, that
Christopher came from Lamprey College, and Lamprey's exact
social status as a public school (which was less high than John
had imagined), he knew that the Senior Common Room
cellars were better stocked than those of the Junior Common
Room; he knew the offences for which men had been debagged
in the past; he knew where the ancient silver sconces had been
sent in case Oxford was attacked from the air. John was impressed, but also slightly embarrassed: Whitbread's eagerness
was embarrassing: it was like watching a man scouring his
plate with a piece of bread.

They broke up when half-past eight struck, Jackson going
back to his own room with the Tacitus notes and Whitbread

switching off the main light, so that the room was dark except for a pool of light from the reading lamp on the desk. John watched him unscrew his fountain pen and settle himself in his chair, like a man preparing to answer an examination paper.

"Thanks for the coffee," he said adding curiously, "How late will you work?"

"Oh, not late—eleven, perhaps."

John felt his way down the dark stairs, seeing the light under other doors and hearing music from wireless sets, which were allowed to be played till nine o'clock. As he walked round the cloisters to his own room, he felt exceedingly depressed by the glimpse he had been given of this hard, tenacious life, and he was filled with grudging admiration of Whitbread. He remembered his own disciplined study, and raged at his powerlessness to carry it on: he was reminded, too, of his home, and the pride his parents had taken in seeing him work and be rewarded. For the first time since arriving at the College his home life and boyhood seemed vivid to him: he could almost hear the clinking of railway wagons from the sidings below the back garden and the sound of electric bells ringing simultaneously in all the classrooms of his grammar school.

As he went up the steps of staircase fourteen, he decided to work steadily all night till bedtime.

But he found Christopher and Patrick in his room, and Eddy had come round, bringing with him another Old Lampreian by the name of Tony, and although Eddy and Tony had kept their raincoats on, it was clear that they would not leave that evening. It was Christopher's fault: he sat askew in an armchair, lazily refusing to go out and drink; he had no money, he said. And there was nothing on at the flicks. In the best of humours, he waved a burning cigarette at them all. "You men are restless, nervy types," he admonished. "Calm yourself, Eddy. Suppress this itch to be on the move. Let's have a quiet evening at home for once—Patrick, go to the Buttery and get some beer. We're the hosts."

"I shall get it all in your name," said Patrick, leaving the room.

"Patrick's a mean swine, if there ever was one," said Eddy, unbuckling the belt of his raincoat. "Have you got enough cigarettes?"

Christopher stretched backwards to pull open one of the desk drawers, and took out a brand-new box that held two hundred. "Yes, he is cussed mean. He's all right, though. Do you want one?" he added, breaking the seals of the packet and extending it, open.

"Where's he from?" asked Tony, taking one.

"Nowhere in particular. D'you know, I only found out the other day that he was a Catholic? He goes to Mass on Sunday morning and has to cut breakfast."

"Damned if I would."

"No. Still, they get something to eat there."

As the joke spread in ripples of appreciative chuckling, Eddy and Tony pulled chairs nearer the fire, stretching out their legs and expelling cigarette smoke in long contented breaths. Patrick came back with a large wicker basket full of bottles, which he placed on the hearthrug: John, feeling he should justify his presence in the room, took out some tankards from the cupboard, including one for himself, and handed them round.

"Oh, thanks. old man," said Christopher. "I say, Pat, did you really put all this down to me?"

"Why not go and have a look?" suggested Patrick, grinning. "Are you overdrawn again?"

"Well, this stuff is blasted dear," said Christopher complainingly, pulling out dark little bottles of stout. "We shall want an opener. Is there one in the drawer, John?"

There are numerous passages in music where the whole orchestra, which has previously been muttering and trifling along some distracting theme, suddenly collects itself and soars upwards to explode in a clear major key, in a clear march of triumph. Any of these moments would have described John's feelings exactly as he bent over the drawer, repeating again and again to himself that Christopher had called him by his first name. When he turned round he could hardly keep from smiling. Almost the best part of the joke was his irrelevant remembrance of Whitbread's words: "If you take my advice, you'll let him know where he stands, pretty sharp."

"Thanks." Christopher took it carelessly. "Now then, glasses forward."

"Pale ale for me," said Eddy.

"Those four there are College Old," said Patrick, pointing with the stem of his pipe. "I asked Bill for some specially. I'll have that."

"Right," said Christopher, pouring.

Tony—his second name was Braithwaite—was one of the people who become boisterously excited as soon as they take a sip of anything alcoholic. Holding out his glass tankard in both hands, he laughed till his fair wavy hair flopped uncontrolledly, his broad shoulders heaving. "And do you remember when Potty Hurst brought that white rabbit in, and the thing just sat in the middle of the floor, too scared to budge?"

"Lord, yes; I'd forgotten Potty Hurst."

"And Baxter thought it was a bit of white paper, and bent down to pick it up. The thing jumped ten yards, and old Baxter had such a fright he banged his head on a desk."

The conversation continued to circle around Lamprey College, and Patrick (the only person, bar John, who was not a Lampreian) sat filling his pipe with a sardonic smile, cramming the hanging ends into the bowl expertly, and rolling up his pouch with care. "I remember we had rather a good rag at our place. The trouble is, I really can't remember how or why it started. I know a rotten little rat of a prae fell foul of our dorm —something about a House game, I think it was."

The others listened contentedly, their eyes not on him.

"At any rate, a gang of us—four or five—called round on him one night after lights-out in his room—praes had separate rooms at our place—and shaved his bush off."

Eddy gave a cackle. "I'm damned," he said. Patrick grinned at them.

"We kept it up that we were going to castrate him, you know. Lord, I've never seen a man so white. Absolutely as white as paper, white as this bloody wall. And there was damn-

56

all he could do about it, either. It's not exactly the kind of thing——"

"Ha, ha, ha!" roared Tony. "My God, no."

"Of course, old Chris was a man for night work," Eddy said, rubbing one eye with his finger. "Every night after lights out, you'd hear Christopher's bed creak. 'Where are you off to, Chris?' 'Oh, just a stroll round.' Couple of hours later: 'That you, Chris?' 'Sure thing.' 'Where was it tonight?' 'Oh, round and about.' 'Have a good time?' 'Fair to middling, thanks.' Fair to middling. Ha, ha, ha! He was a close devil, was Chris."

Christopher sat smiling softly, like one who is being praised. "Ah, those were the days," he murmured. "Sound stuff."

The glowing structure of embers in the grate collapsed, and Patrick added coal and two small logs, knocking out his pipe and relighting it. Sprawled in attitudes of enjoyment, the four of them lazily kept the conversation going, giving the impression of speaking on this subject for want of a better. Their stories were lustful and playfully savage, and John found they had extreme physical effect on him. He sat crouched on a hard chair, his fists clenched on his knees, gripped by an unreasoning terror that seized him whenever he heard of experiences that would have left him dumb. The life they described was intensely primitive to him. He tried to imagine himself set down amongst it, but blackness fortunately descended on his imagination before he could savour the whole impossibility of it. The astonishing thing was that he could catch here and there a note of regret in their voices, a nostalgia even. In the intervals of comparing notes and customs, they would sigh and gaze sadly at the fire, as if they were exiles gathered together far from their homes. And little by little John himself came to understand their sorrow, as what they had lost became clearer in his mind. To him it was wild and extravagant, a life that was panoplied and trampling compared with his own: it seemed to him that in their schooldays they had won more than he would ever win during the whole of his life. At first ill-treated, they had lived to be oppressors whose savagest desire could be gratified at once, which was surely the height of ambition. As the picture grew in his mind, he ornamented it with little marginal additions, until in the end the thing was an unreal as a highly-coloured picture of an ancient battle, but he had no inkling of its untruth, and he looked on them with curious respect. The pimply Eddy; Christopher, dark and unshaven as a boxer; the selfish and smiling Patrick, and even Tony Braithwaite—all took on a picturesqueness in his eyes, as if they were veterans of an old war.

Later in the evening, when nearly all the beer had been drunk, a quarrel broke out between Eddy and Christopher about money. Christopher insisted that Eddy owed him fifteen shillings, and he only contradicted Eddy's denials with a perverse smile, lying back in his armchair and kicking Eddy repeatedly on the shin with each contradiction.

"Chuck that," said Eddy.

"Give me that fifteen bob."

"I said chuck that, you——"

Eddy leant forward suddenly and gripped Christopher's ankle, jumping up and dragging him off his chair with a bump on to the floor. The others started up in alarm. Eddy, exerting all his force, managed to keep Christopher's foot high in the air, grinning down at him the while.

"There, you fool——"

But with a sudden wrench and twist, Christopher got Eddy's legs, and the two of them rolled furiously about the carpet, knocking over a half-full bottle. The air was full of their panting and oaths as they struck at one another with intent to hurt, for they were both rather drunk. John stood behind his chair nervously, while Patrick leant against the chimneypiece, hands in his pockets.

Christopher was much the stronger and in a moment had a wrestler's hold on Eddy, pushing his head down so that he was powerless, his neck and ears growing a deep crimson. With a sudden exultance Christopher threw his whole weight on the grip, and Eddy screamed, and Tony took a step forward, raising his hand, but in a few seconds the whole incredible scene had dissipated. Eddy squatted on the hearthrug, sticking his horseshoe tiepin into his tie again, saying, "God, Chris, you are a swine," while Christopher stood before the mirror combing his hair, and John picked up three pennies and a propelling pencil that had fallen during the struggle. As he put them on the table, he noticed his own unused glass tankard: Christopher had not noticed he had taken one and had not offered him any beer.

John always regretted they did not spend more time together. After their first tutorial he suggested timidly that they should walk round the gardens, but Christopher said rather abruptly that he was meeting some people, and left him. But it was nevertheless this regret that came first to his mind when their Tutor, the day after, sent him a note asking him to be good enough to call on him.

"Come in, Mr. Kemp." The Tutor smiled kindly, keeping one finger in the book he was reading. "Sit down. I wanted to ask you if perhaps you'd prefer me to take you alone in future."

"Alone?"

"Alone, instead of with Mr. Warner."

"Why—er—no, I don't think so, sir." He was flabbergasted and spoke without thinking.

"Are you sure? You don't feel the present arrangement hinders you in any way?"

"Oh, no, sir."

The Tutor covered his eyes for a moment with his hand and rubbed his forehead. His long body was clothed in a rough green tweed suit.

"Well, as you please. It wouldn't be any trouble." He waited a few seconds, but John said nothing, keeping his eyes fixed on the brightly-polished fire-irons in the hearth. "All right, that's all I wanted to say."

John left the room, and walked back round the cloisters, the shadows of the pillars falling across his path and his long black gown billowing out behind him. He met Christopher just lounging down the steps of staircase fourteen and told him eagerly what the Tutor had said.

"I hope you put a stopper on it."

"Oh, I did, yes."

"Good show. I suppose he thinks if he gets us alone he can screw more work out of us."

"I'm glad you think I did right."

Christopher nodded briefly, and strolled off, keeping his hands in his pockets and his head erect. John watched him go, and then went into the rooms. He was trembling slightly as he hung up his gown behind the door, partly from the nervousness that any contact with authority produced, and partly with pleasure that he had done Christopher a service. If the empty days that meandered past had any object at all, it was to please Christopher and win his favour. Whenever Christopher entered the room, John could not help brightening up and getting ready to laugh: he did not expect to be included in the talk, but it seemed a great privilege simply to be allowed to listen to them as they stood talking casually, the collars of their coats turned up, discussing where they should go of an evening. He had a keen sensation of their presence, like the smell of a fine cloth or leather. The night before their second tutorial, when they had known each other for exactly a fortnight, Christopher took John's notes and hashed up a careless rigmarole to present in the morning, sitting in the lamplight with a cigarette in his mouth. His pen moved quickly over the paper. When he had done, he pushed the papers aside with a sigh of relief.

"Thank God that's finished. White of you to lend me all this." He studied his wrist-watch, yawning unconcernedly. "What about a drink?"

John laid his pen very carefully down across his notebook.

"A—er—where, d'you mean?"

"Oh, somewhere out." Christopher stood up and picked up his scarf from the top of the cupboard; he blinked at John in a way that suggested that he had only just realized who he was talking to. "Oh, it doesn't matter, if you're working."

"But of course—yes, of course!" John shoved his chair back, jumping to his feet. He bundled on his overcoat, keeping an eye on Christopher, as if he might suddenly disappear or the invitation be rescinded. Christopher crossed to the looking-glass and passed a hand over his hair from back to front: then, catching sight of the small clock that stood on the mantelpiece, picked it up and wound it a few times.

"Ready!" said John, by the door. There was a look on his face that fleetingly recalled the expression of a child who is being taken to a circus. As they walked round the cloisters and across the first quadrangle together, he regretted it was too dark for them to be seen. A light came on in the Master's lodgings, but almost instantly a maid drew a heavy plush curtain across it, and there was no light anywhere. Christopher paused at the Lodge, where he found a postcard inviting him to play in a trial football match. He put it in his pocket.

"We'll go to the Bull, shall we?" he said. "Eddy might be there."

John did not want to see Eddy, but he was content to let Christopher go where he wanted, so they turned left on leaving the great gates. The bells were chiming for half-past six, and from the centre of the town came a mournful hooting of traffic, while from a taxi-rank near by a telephone rang persistently. The night air was cold. An aeroplane, bearing red and green pilot lights, flew diagonally across the sky.

As they turned up a little alleyway, John wondered what the Bull would be like: it had figured prominently in the anecdotes he had heard, and he had always pictured it as a tiny den. He was surprised, therefore, to enter a dazzlingly bright bar, where the light glanced off the chromium fittings and the mirror behind the counter, and a powerful coke fire slumbered in the grate. The room was empty except for the landlord, who read the newspaper, and a tremulous old man sitting in a corner with an untouched pint of beer before him.

"Evening, Christopher," said the landlord, folding the paper up.

"Good evening, Charley. Two bitters, if you please."

John took his with a gesture so casual that he nearly spilt it. It would never do to let Christopher think he had never drunk before, as was the case; that was something to be hoarded up till it had ripened into an anecdote. He imagined himself saying in the future: "D'you remember that time we went to the Bull, old boy. In our first term? D'you know, that was really and

61

truly the first time I'd ever seen the inside of a bar. . . ." ("Oh, come off it, old boy!") "S'fact! My dear fellow, it's absolutely bloody gospel! Here, after you with the—whoops! Don't drown it. . . ." His voice would be rich and husked with tobacco.

Aloud he said: "Thank you."

"Not busy yet, Charley."

"Not yet, sir." Charley laid his hands palm downwards on the counter and watched Christopher light a fresh cigarette from the stub of an old one. "It's the black-out. That's what it is."

Christopher nodded seriously.

"It is, I tell you. I've just been reading a bit in this paper"— he made a gesture as if to unfold it, but contented himself with tapping it several times—"all about the British pub Jerry can't kill. Garrh! 'E's killing it. 'E is! Why, at this time we'd have an 'ole barful of fellers—commercial, office chaps. . . ."

John listened impatiently, but as Christopher looked interested and amused, he tried to look interested and amused also.

"You won't be sorry to see the lights go up again, then."

Charley gave a short burst of laughter and drank: John drank too. Ugh, what a vile taste. The old man in the corner parted his mouth in a grin, and, speaking as if with difficulty, said:

"I reckon you'll shut down—an'—an' drink the place dry yerself!"

It was hard to hear what he said.

"Now that," said Christopher, with a laugh, "is what I call taking a really unfair advantage.

Charley grinned too, and wiped the bar down with a foul wet rag. But before he could think of an answer more men came in, and the conversation dropped. John and Christopher took further swallows of beer, John trying to decide whether he really disliked it or whether he just found it unpleasant. Then he beat desperately about his mind for something to say: he felt that unless he flung nets of words over Christopher he might escape, borne off by another unaccountable whim, perhaps to seek Eddy or Patrick. "Do—er—do the Proctors ever come in here?" he inquired with a nervous laugh. "Have you ever seen them here?"

"I've never seen them anywhere," replied Christopher, stirring. "They don't bother about the little places much."

"Is this a little place?"

"Fairly, but you see it's early yet. They don't come out till after Hall."

When Christopher blew out smoke, it was like cloudy breath —why was that?

Suddenly realizing Christopher had finished his beer, he drank his own and ordered two more, noticing that a group of men in the corner had switched on the light over the dartboard and begun to play. His pale face, with a hanging lock of yellow hair, looked back at him excitedly from the mirror, and he wondered how soon he would begin to feel drunk.

"I expect you managed to drink a good deal at school," he ventured.

As expected, Christopher looked interested at once. "I don't know about a good deal," he began, lifting his full glass. "It wasn't so easy. But there were ways, you know . . . I remember once——"

But before he could say more, the door swung open and Eddy Makepeace with another young man appeared, both dressed in raincoats, and after a second's squinting in the light, made straight for Christopher.

"There you are, you elusive bastard," greeted Eddy, coughing noisily. "It's foggy outside. Here, come down to the King's. Know who's there?"

"Who?"

"Brian Kenderdine."

"No."

"Fact. Here for a night. He's been to Narvik. He asked after you—we called at your rooms, but you weren't there. I said I'd look for you here, while Brian and the boys went along to the King's."

Eddy stopped, licking his lips, and took a swig of Christopher's beer. John, vainly trying to compose his disappointed heart, noticed that Christopher was already tightening his muffler and looking more animated than he had yet done that evening.

"It'll be good to see Brian again. Is he tight? I know he always liked to get off a train tight, to make an impression."

"He hitched," said the young man in a disagreeable mincing London voice.

"No, soon will be though. Actually he's been in a naval hospital—looks much thinner."

"What was the matter with his navel?" grinned Christopher, buttoning his scarf inside his jacket. "Here, finish that beer, Eddy, you bloody pig."

"I only wanted to see if the bitter was still the same old Bull's piss. I can't think why you don't have mild."

"Jesus!" said Christopher disgustedly. "Leave it then. Here, oh damn, I've got no real money. Can you see me through, Eddy?" His hand searched his pockets sketchily. "A quid will do."

"No can do," said the other young man. Eddy opened his pocket-book, a cutting about a horse his father owned fluttering to the ground. John silently picked it up. "Sorry, Chris, I've only fifteen bob till I go to the bank. Get it off Pat."

"I owe Pat two quid," grumbled Christopher. "You haven't a quid handy, have you, John, old man?"

"Why, of course."

John felt in his pockets. Rather belatedly, Christopher said: "John Kemp—Dick Dowdall."

John smiled uneasily, trying as he handed the note over to catch Christopher's eye to seal the loan with a friendly glance, but Christopher was looking at the money.

"That's white of you, old man. You'll get it back tomorrow without fail. Right, let's go."

They pushed out of the bar, calling good night to the land-lord and leaving the half-empty glass standing on the bar. A soldier grunted and said something sarcastic to his comrade. John heard Eddy's high laugh in the alleyway outside—why did he laugh?

Frowning, tasting his beer reluctantly, he went over the con-

64

versation as with a small hammer, tapping and assessing every word. Perhaps it had not been too bad, for a start. He thought about it until he noticed the time shown by the bar clock, which alarmed him and made him leave hurriedly to get back in time for dinner. He did not know it would be fast.

During dinner he thought constantly of the pound: it was the second of the five pounds pocket-money he had to last him through the term and should have covered the coming fortnight. Now he could not help feeling as uneasy about it as if he had used it to back a racehorse. He told himself that Christopher would pay it back out of sheer courtesy, but even so his mind was not at rest. He avoided sitting by Whitbread.

To comfort himself, he ordered another half of bitter, and when he had returned to his rooms he found himself too drowsy to concentrate on the work he had intended doing. Even though he took out his sheaf of notes and unscrewed his fountain pen, his mind wandered. In the grate the servant had constructed an enormous fire that was just reaching its best: the heat thrilled and stupefied him; he turned over a few pages, wondering where Christopher was at that moment. Some of the notes he had made yesterday, others dated from several years ago. He tried to remember when he had written them, and failed.

He had not noticed the precise date when Mr. Joseph Crouch had been appointed to the staff of the Huddlesford Grammar School as English master, and at the time knew nothing about him. Joseph Crouch was a young man with an excellent London University degree. Indeed, his ability was such that he was put in charge of all senior English work within a few months, and the other English master could only shrug his shoulders more or less philosophically. Mr. Crouch was very pleased about this. He found some comfortable rooms on the edge of the park, and transported at some expense all his books and book-shelves thence from his home in Watford. There were hundreds of volumes: not expensive, but there was some sort of a copy of every important work in the language, and many works of criticism, all with "Joseph Crouch" scribbled carelessly in soft pencil on the fly-leaf. Passages he approved of had a straight pencil-stroke by them: those he disliked were marked with a wavy line: without exception the books bore traces of having been exhaustively and intelligently studied.

He also brought a suitcase full of his University notes, which in themselves explained his academic success. They covered every book he had read in one way or another, giving synopsis of the plot, the argument, the style and the book's history; they were written in black ink on single sides of thin sheets of paper, and the headings were underlined in red. Scraps of supplementary information had in some cases been pasted in; all were frequently studded with cross-references and these were in green; the sheets were held together with brass pins. They were numbered carefully, each figure with a little circle round it, and the handwriting on the first sheet was not in the slightest way different from the handwriting on the last one. They filled one of the drawers of his writing desk.

Mr. Crouch was not a good-looking man. He was rather short, with a sallow, yellowish skin, untidy hair and features of a slightly Mongolian cast. When he smiled, his face split into a malevolent crease, and though he was young, his walk recalled an old man's shuffle; he wore a pair of thick-lensed spectacles. His teaching was unusual in that he delivered complete, rather formal sentences in a measured voice; the boys, accustomed to the colloquial and even incoherent manner of the rest of the staff, found him hard to attend to, and the word went round "Joe's dull". This made him less popular than if the verdict had been that he was "a real swine".

All the same, he was pleased with himself. Huddlesford Grammar School was large and of a fairly high standing, and he regarded his post there as nothing but a stepping-stone to better things. He liked his rooms, and after tea would sit placidly in the armchair before the fire correcting work, reading intelligent books or magazines, or translating (for his own amusement) poems he liked from other languages. At intervals he would sit, dreamily watching the gas fire, thinking how, when his salary had risen, he would indulge himself in luxuries his means had so far denied him—expensive clothes, cigars, new books. Surprisingly, his nature had a sensual streak that longed for idleness and freedom. And because everything he had worked for he had so far won, he looked forward to this future with expectancy, almost with satisfaction. He felt like a man who has finished his first course of a meal, found it excellent, and has a keen appetite for what is to follow.

His only discontent in the present was that his work was not exacting enough. It was humiliating, he found, to deal with boys who had not the slightest understanding of his subject: humiliating when the discussion of an essay resolved into a discussion of its handwriting, its brevity, or even its non-existence. Too often it was borne in upon him that his work as a schoolmaster ended at a point below that at which his work as a graduate began, and that the standard of appreciation he was forced to deal with fell below any but the coarsest contempt.

"Well, it's the old story, of course," said the junior science master, a pleasant, disillusioned young man to whom Crouch had taken a fancy. "I don't see that you *can* do anything. If you wanted to do advanced teaching, why didn't you try for a university job?"

"Ah! Why didn't I?" Mr. Crouch was not to be drawn into a discussion of his private affairs.

"It wears off. For instance, I didn't exactly need a Cambridge degree to teach fourteen-year-olds the difference between an ohm and a watt."

"No," said Mr. Crouch. Bunches of boys swung past on bicycles (they were both walking home after school) trying to ride on the right side of the road and to lower their voices momentarily.

"After all, you're senior man in your subject here—you can train people for university work, if you want. I'm only allowed to tamper with the junior intelligence."

Mr. Crouch raised his eyebrows.

"Yes. That would be a good idea."

"Is anyone in the sixth specializing in English this year?"

"Jarrett is, odious creature. I'm afraid it's quite hopeless thinking about him. Still, it's a point worth keeping in mind."

Mr. Crouch nodded a thoughtful farewell, and turned down the avenue that led him home.

He was pleased to find his landlady had boiled him an egg for tea and that there was a new cherry cake. Not till he had satisfied his appetite and was smoking a cigarette did he reconsider the idea, but when he did it seemed more and more attractive. If he could catch a boy in the present fifth form, for instance, and encourage and develop his talents; if he could act the role of a tutor, lending him his dusty little texts and meticulous notes, by judicious suggestion and direction of his reading bringing the whole of literature within the range of the boy's mind. . . . How tired he was of expurgated copies of *Macbeth* and *The Golden Treasury*. How he longed to ascend once more to the remoter plains, to talk of Marlowe and Norse literature, to draw sweeping parallels and make irrefutable assertions.

Picking up the empty eggshell that his spoon had scoured clean, he gazed at it solemnly. What should he do? Should he indulge this fancy? He sat grinning, increasing the pressure of his thumb and forefinger, until with a sudden smash the shell collapsed.

It was unfortunate that his first choice fell upon a bright fifth-former whose conduct was troublesome and whose literary style was racy and impressive. "William Wordsworth", Mr. Crouch read, "drew back appalled as heads that had smiled in London drawing-rooms rolled in clotted Parisian sawdust." Undeterred, he made a few private inquiries about the boy's future intentions, and received nebulous and slightly impertinent replies. The boy finally left after taking his School Certificate to become a junior reporter on the local paper. On the last day of term, he contrived to pin one end of a roll of toilet paper to Mr. Crouch's gown, and Mr. Crouch shuffled the whole length of a corridor before finding out.

It took the whole of the summer holidays to reconcile him again to his original idea. During this time, he had returned to his home, spent much time in London with old friends from college and elsewhere, and lived for a fortnight in a cottage in the Lake District, where he had ironically read nothing but William Wordsworth. Everyone had congratulated him on his quick promotion, and one or two had specifically mentioned the opportunities it provided for training advanced students. As soon as the grammar school settled down at the beginning of the autumn term, he decided to make a second attempt.

Accordingly he collected the essays of the new School Certificate form as he was teaching and took them home one evening, and as soon as his landlady had cleared the table he put the pile of exercise books on the table, opened a packet of cigarettes and sat down. The essay had been on "The Supernatural in *Macbeth*". His intention was to read each essay through and mark it without looking at the name on the cover of the book: he would select the most attractive of the essays and investigate its author. The idea of being a judge gave him childish pleasure.

He sat there all evening, light from the shaded lamp falling on to the straggling, wispy hair and a little ashtray at his elbow collecting cigarette ends. Occasionally he scrawled a neat, acid comment on the margin; occasionally he grinned or raised his eyebrows. The task was not greatly interesting, for thirty boys with identical resources and knowledge produce thirty very similar essays. Four were of a fairly high standard of competence, and these he laid aside to return to later; the rest received marks from thirteen to three out of twenty, and a variety of calculated insults.

One sentence in one of the four essays made him pause. It ran: *Macbeth does not feel remorse, for he does not feel he has done wrong; evil is embodied in the witches, and he is not as bad as they are.*

He gave his attention to that essay and read it slowly through once more. At the end, he had to admit it was the best of the lot—not outstandingly so: it was not a brilliant essay, but that was not to be expected. It was not exactly original, but nor was that. Its great virtue was one of extreme efficiency. The boy knew the play and could quote appropriately from it; he knew the introduction and could paraphrase that. The style was not excessively immature, and the unfamiliar handwriting was neat. And the sentence that arrested his attention was like a fancied

69

streak of light in the sky before dawn: perhaps it was imagination, or the sun might be near.

With sudden decision, he snapped the book shut to read the name on the cover.

J. Kemp.

Kemp?

For a moment he frowned, quite at a loss. A pale boy in a corner? Kemp?

Momentary annoyance possessed him, but faded quickly as he realized he was glad that it was someone unknown to him. There were boys he could think of who would have been great disappointments.

He stood with his hands in his pockets, studying the hearth-rug. Kemp. A pale boy in a corner, with fair hair. Never spoke unless he was spoken to—sometimes not even then. Pulling his mark book across the table, he opened it to find that Kemp had won three reasonably high marks from him during the three weeks they had been back at school. This surprised him. He began to feel quite curious about the boy and was delighted at the result of his private examination.

"What do I know about Kemp?" repeated the language master next day. "Mousy."

"Is that all?"

"He comes fairly high up most times. Why?"

"I was wondering," said Mr. Crouch pleasantly, and moved away.

"A quiet lad—gives no trouble, no trouble at all," said the history master, who asked no more of any boy if he gave no trouble.

"Would you say he was intelligent?"

"Oh, quite—yes, quite. A very good standard of work. It's just that one doesn't notice him much," he ended with a nervous smile.

"I've noticed him," said Mr. Crouch.

"Kemp?" boomed the mathematics master, an enormous beaky-nosed caricature of a man, whose suit was eternally covered with chalk dust. He had been at the school nearly thirty years. "Why, yes. A very good all-round intelligence, there. Picks up knowledge like a magnet picks up iron filings. His father's a policeman, I think—or was. I know they aren't well off."

Mr. Crouch thank him politely and shuffled off to his classroom.

When he took that particular form, it was the last period of the day, and the lights were on. Outside cars and lorries ploughed through the rain along the road that ran some distance from the school buildings. Mr. Crouch set them some parsing to do, and then called them up in turn to give back their essays: many just received them with a word of praise or blame: others he kept while he expounded some point they had raised or settled some issue they had imperfectly handled. Deliberately he allowed half an hour to go by. But at last he locked his yellow hands before him, surveyed the rows of bent heads and said in a harsh voice:

"Kemp."

There was a movement at the back of the room, and the boy came up between the desks.

"I like this essay, Kemp," Mr. Crouch began, not bothering to open the book. "It showed care, thought and good sense." He paused. "You're a pretty hard worker, aren't you?"

"I don't know, sir."

Mr. Crouch surveyed him speculatively. He was thin and pale and poorly dressed; his eyes glanced nervously up and then fell again; his hands were held behind him. It was difficult to imagine an expression of happiness on his face. Only his silky hair, like pale thistle-seed, was agreeable to look at.

"I've heard that you are." Mr. Crouch began to play with his silver propelling pencil, slipping his thumb-nail under the clip. "What are your plans for the future?"

"When I leave school, sir?"

"Are you going to leave? This year, I mean?"

"I suppose so, yes, sir."

"What are you going to do?"

"Don't know, sir."

"No ideas at all?"

"I suppose I shall go into some sort of office, sir."

71

Mr. Crouch grinned.

"Ever thought of staying on into the sixth form and taking a university scholarship?"

Kemp stared at him for a moment with frightened blue eyes.

"No, sir."

"I see no reason why you shouldn't think about it. You're on a scholarship here, aren't you? Well, it's only the next step. You'll get a pretty good School Certificate by all accounts, and if you stay on another two years with a Sixth Form scholarship you'll get a pretty good Higher School Certificate. Then you can spend a year collecting scholarships for the university—Oxford, Cambridge, London, whatever you like."

He paused, but the boy made no comment.

"When you get to the university, you'll get a good degree— and make a lot of very useful contacts. Then you can start thinking about getting a job in some sort of office." He held the silver pencil by the tips of his forefingers. "How does the idea strike you?"

The boy's glance fell away towards the ground again and his mouth tightened. He looked bewildered.

"Well?"

"Don't know, sir."

Mr. Crouch was not displeased with the boy's unresponsiveness: it made the idea all the more fascinating. Like a sculptor, he would mould passivity.

"You see, I think you could specialize in English very satisfactorily. If we began to work together now, I could over a period of three years, say, tutor you up to university standard easily. In my opinion, you'd walk away with a university scholarship. Perhaps you think that sounds a tall order," added Mr. Crouch maliciously, noting the dismayed look. "I can assure you it isn't as tall as it looks."

The boy raised his hand to his mouth nervously. His wrists were red and his nails bitten.

"What would your father's reactions to the idea be?"

"I don't know, sir."

"Will you ask him? You see, I don't anticipate any difficulty about the financial side of it. The governors would give you a

72

grant easily enough. I don't think there's any call for you to run off into some sort of an office just yet."

The boy blushed.

"Well, think it over, and mention it to your father; I'd like to talk to him about it, if he could see me some time. Will you do that?"

"Yes, sir."

"All right, then. Here, take your book," he added.

He watched the boy return to his seat and sit down with his hand hiding his face. The faint hum of the classroom as the industrious worked and the idlers idled came suddenly to his ears, and he brought the flat of his hand down with a sharp smack on the desk.

Everybody looked up.

"There is too much chatter at the moment," he remarked evenly. "It will be very unpleasant for anyone I catch talking. Bleaney, come up here."

The discussion of essays proceeded.

Mr. Crouch enjoyed his visit to the Kemps' house a few nights later. Holding his hat in his hand, he walked with pretended humility into the front room, where a fire had been lit (he guessed) specially for the occasion. The house was small, but not poverty-stricken: there were a table of photographs, a fern and some heavily-framed sepia reproductions of execrable pictures on the walls. Mr. Crouch stood before the fire. He felt like a diplomat on a visit to some barbarous ruler, with the job of persuading him to allow a railway to run through his territory.

Presently Joe Kemp, having put on his jacket, came in, passing a huge hand over his oiled hair. He was a retired policeman, who now supplemented his pension by job-carpentering; his enormous body was topped by a small head, with ears closely set against it. He had an expression of agreeable truculence, and wore a ludicrous pair of gold-rimmed spectacles which gave him at times a puzzled look. Mr. Crouch held out a hand:

"Good evening, Mr. Kemp. My name is Crouch."

73

"How d'yer do?"

They shook hands.

"Sit down, will yer?"

"Thank you. . . . I expect your son has told you what I suggested to him. I should like to hear what you think about it, Mr. Kemp."

Joe Kemp passed his hand over his hair again and kept it there to scratch perplexedly.

"Ay, well, it's a bit of a winder. I reckon it's a bit of a tall order."

"I think John is capable of it, Mr. Kemp. Otherwise, I wouldn't suggest it."

"Ay, he's a clever enough lad. . . ."

"And the advantages of a university education are really very great, you know. It's not just a sausage machine for turning out school teachers. It's the stepping-stone to all the higher professions—the bar, the Civil Service, Parliament——"

"You missed t'road, it seems," said Joe Kemp, looking at him shrewdly.

"Ah, but I chose to be a schoolmaster. As a matter of fact, I wanted to be able to help boys like your son—help them to reach the positions their intelligence deserves."

Mr. Kemp raised a few half-hearted objections. But it was clear that his imagination had been caught by the scheme, and only a fixed determination "not to be rushed into anything" prevented him from agreeing with what Mr. Crouch said.

"I don't think there'd be any difficulty on the financial side, either, Mr. Kemp. . . . The governors——"

"Nay, well, that's not so important. I want to do what's right by John——"

"Yes, of course."

"I mean, we don't want, Mr. Crouch." Joe Kemp looked at the schoolmaster with dignity. "I know some chaps as've taken their lads away from school as soon as they could—well, I'm not blaming them, I'm just luckier than what they are. Between you an' me, it was more of a struggle ter get t'lass settled—she's a teacher, yer know, in Manchester. You ain't talkin' to a man with backward ideas, Mr. Crouch, not like some fellers I could

74

name. As I say, I want to do t'best by the lad as I can. But——"

"Yes, Mr. Kemp?"

"Don't yer think you're lookin' a bit far ahead and aimin' a bit high? What I mean is, you say 'e'll get a good Certificate. Granted. But then suppose you find 'e's not up to what you thought?"

"It's not a matter of chance, Mr. Kemp. I can tell from his work that he will win a good School Certificate. And if he does that he'll win a good Higher School Certificate. His mind will develop as time goes by."

"Well, I'll let him decide for himself," said Joe Kemp. He threw open the door and called to his son. "After all, it's his life, and if he fancies it I'm not goin' ter stand in his light. Ay, come in, John, lad. I've been 'aving a talk with yer teacher. Now, what about it? Does ta want to go to Cambridge, or Oxford?"

The boy kept glancing from one to the other of them, painfully shy. Mr. Crouch kept his eyes on his face, smiling encouragingly, shifting his hat in his hands.

"If—if you think I could," he said hesitatingly.

"Eh, well, that's up to you, lad." Joe Kemp chuckled and put an arm round his son's shoulders. "But ta would like a bang at it, eh?"

. The boy kept glancing from one to the other, painfully shy. Mr. Crouch kept his eyes on his face, smiling encouragingly, shifting his hat in his hands.

"If you think I'm—good enough?"

"No danger—eh, Mr. Crouch? No danger!"

From this night onwards, Mr. Crouch regarded himself as John Kemp's particular guardian, but of course he was far too wise to make any move in this role until the School Certificate was over and done with. John Kemp won seven credits in this examination and informed the Headmaster of his intention to stay on into the sixth form.

Just before the end of the summer holidays, Mr. Crouch invited John to have tea with him at his lodgings, and chatted amicably to him about things in general, what he had done during the holidays, what he had read and so forth. He was conscious that the boy watched him warily without relaxation, and this charmed him, as if he had the task of taming some elusive animal. By casual questions he discovered the extent and directions of the boy's reading, and made some suggestions for what he should read in the future. Soon he had put aside four of his own books for John to take home.

"And when you read anything, make notes on it." He had taken off his spectacles to polish them, and his face looked blind and simple. "Look, in this manner." Crossing to his desk, he replaced his spectacles and pulled a sheaf of notes out of a drawer: he held them out, and the boy stirred to take them. "It's an invaluable habit. You'll see the qualities and points to look for; they form the headings of your sections. . . ."

A deep sense of pride filled him as he saw the boy begin turning over the notes, his head bent; the feeling that he was delegating his knowledge caught at his heart, and made the action seem noble and queerly unselfish. He began to walk about the room. "You must remember that what you are reading from now onwards will not be useful for a week or a year even, but for all time, until your last examination is over. And naturally you can't expect to remember every single thing you read, so you must make notes. You must aim at reproducing the book you are reading in miniature. When I made those notes," he continued, halting in front of the window and looking out over the park, "I couldn't afford to buy a quarter of the books I read. And even if I had been able to own a copy of every one, I couldn't have read them all before an examination—so the obvious thing to do was to make careful notes, gutting each book so that when the time came I could turn up my notes on it and there have all the essential facts under my hand on one page."

The boy looked at the notes with admiration.

"Perhaps you'd like to borrow some, to get the idea of what to look for?"

"Oh, yes, thank you, sir."

"But don't copy them. Second-hand notes never did anyone any good."

Despite the fact that when school restarted John had other subjects to attend to, Mr. Crouch was more than satisfied with the progress he made. He had not known the full measure of ability the boy had. His brain was tireless. He could read swiftly, remember what he read and was quick to point out analogies between dissimilar things and to take suggestions that Mr. Crouch made. At first the master had made a habit of saying carelessly: "You should have a look at so-and-so" or "It's a pity we've no time to read such-and-such," but at their next meeting Kemp would invariably say, shyly, "Oh—er—I had a look at the things you mentioned, sir——" so that he quickly realized he had to be very careful what he said. It was like manipulating a powerful but delicate machine. By the end of John's first year in the sixth form, he had scampered through all the important English writers, and was beginning to explore critical theory, philosophical and social backgrounds, and elementary philology. His knowledge became remarkable: hardly ever was he at a loss for a quotation or a reference.

Some months later Mr. Joseph Crouch was sitting in his lodgings reading a newspaper. "Pilots and crews of the aircraft which took part in the successful attack on the German naval bases of Wilhemshaven and Brunsbüttel, at the entrance of the Kiel canal, returned to their bases in fine fettle," it said. "They were proud to have been chosen to strike the first blow at the German war machine."

As he turned the page to read of news elsewhere, he heard the landlady admit someone at the front door, and in a few moments John was shown in. He wore a blue overcoat and no school cap, and Mr. Crouch saw him for a moment as merely an undistinguished boy of sixteen, who might be earning his living in a shop or as a clerk in some sort of office.

"Hallo, Kemp; come in. I'm glad you've called. This is something we hadn't bargained for."

"No, sir."

"No, indeed we hadn't. I haven't quite decided what the effect will be." Mr. Crouch folded up his newspaper, lighted a long spill at the gas fire, and applied it to his cigarette. "You're sixteen, aren't you?"

"No, sir. Seventeen last month."

"And they're calling up the twenties and over." He stood looking over the park once more, where working men were digging an air raid shelter. The trees that lined the railings were still in full luxuriance of autumn decay. "Do you know," he said slowly, "I almost think it would be better if you had a shot at that scholarship *this* year—after Christmas."

"But——"

Mr. Crouch could feel without looking at him the bewilderment that his face held. It annoyed him slightly: he did not feel sufficiently secure himself to be over-considerate about the futures of others.

"Yes, why not?"

"But, sir—— Surely I couldn't, sir."

"You mustn't be so pessimistic." The master turned to him with a grin that was almost hostile; a bar of sunlight on the wall by his head dimmed slightly. "Nothing venture, nothing win."

"But surely, sir——"

"My dear boy, circumstances have changed. Nobody knows what's going to happen. In five years time it may well be that Oxford and Cambridge will be nothing but ruins." Mr. Crouch made an expressive gesture. "It seems to me that if you went up next autumn, you'd have nearly three clear years, if they allowed you deferment. . . . Of course, one just doesn't know what line they're going to take."

The boy moved to the table, his eyes lowered, and, taking up a strand of the tablecloth's fringe, began to twist it and turn it slowly. Obviously Mr. Crouch's suggestion had come as a great shock, and he was loth to adopt his mind to it. Mr. Crouch watched him impatiently. The outbreak of war had quickened the growth of a feeling he now recognized to have been growing for some time: an indifference to Kemp and his career, and a desire to get the whole business over as quickly as possible. The idea of tutoring the boy for two more years seemed intolerable, and he was prevented from being more curt than he was by the belief that in a few months, or perhaps even weeks, they would be scattered irrevocably by greater events. Further, during the summer holidays he had come as near to falling in love as his temperament allowed, and being parted from the girl made him not sorrowful, but irritable, as a child is vexed by confiscation of a box of sweets.

Finally, he felt he had been cheated. Although Kemp worked hard and intelligently, being quick to take suggestions and with a memory retentive enough to add every fresh thing to his mind, he was a burden to teach. His character was almost purely negative: if there had come one spontaneous idea from him during all the span of their acquaintanceship, Mr. Crouch would have felt repaid, but the hesitancy and heaviness that he had imagined would wear off as the boy's imagination widened and deepened persisted month after month, until Mr. Crouch was forced to admit it was native to him and would never go. He could not advance a step without guidance. The poetry and good writing he studied seemed to mean nothing personal to him: at first Mr. Crouch was pleased with this (Jarrett having been insufferably boring on the subject of the Romantics), but later on he found it a leaden weight. There was no fun in teaching so matter-of-fact a mind, however swift it was to take and develop points that ordinarily the immature mind would miss.

"The fact of the matter is," thought Mr. Crouch to himself bitterly, "he could be a really efficient engineer with as just as little trouble and with probably more benefit to the community at large."

Aloud he said:

"In any case, it would be experience."

"But an open scholarship, sir. . . . Surely at my age no one——"

"Not in ordinary circumstances, no. But these circumstances aren't ordinary, surely you realize that. I think you'd stand a fair chance."

He questioned John about the progress he had made during the holidays, and decided to see the Headmaster next day.

The Headmaster could not give him more than half his attention, for he was badgered by problems of blacking-out many windows and of conducting a ballot among the parents regarding evacuation. "No, I don't agree," he flung back over his shoulder as he strode along a corridor. "My advice to anybody now is to get all the scholarships they can in the normal way, and then to go into the Army. Oxford'll wait. It's waited long enough."

Mr. Crouch shuffled obediently after him.

"That's true, sir, but I think he's got the ability. . . . It's only a question of this year instead of next—in his own interests I think it would be advisable for him at least to try. . . . And in any case, it would be experience."

"Does he want to? What does he say?"

"Oh, he's very keen, sir."

"Well, he can if he likes. I don't advise it, but he can if he likes." The Headmaster took out a carpenter's rule and began measuring a window. "Tell me when you want the arrangements making. Twelve by five and a half."

John was irritated by the calm way Mr. and Mrs. Kemp received the news that he was to sit for a scholarship not in a year next spring, but next spring—in a little over six months.

"Next March?" said Joe Kemp at tea. "Well, that's a hustle-up."

"You'll not be eighteen—eh, we're all 'aving to change our plans." Mrs. Kemp put the teapot down. "Take yer tea, John."

"Yes, but it's not just a matter of time—I shan't know enough. No one ever sits for an open scholarship till their third year——"

"Nobbut clever 'uns," grinned Joe, folding a piece of bread-and-butter to eat with his tinned fish.

"You don't understand, dad!" John's nervousness became flecked with bad temper. "It's a silly idea. . . . I don't know what Crouch is thinking of."

"Eh, there's no harm in trying," said the father, munching.

"But there's no *point*! . . . I can't get a scholarship before I've even sat for Higher—no one ever has."

"You never know what you can do till you try." Mrs. Kemp

tilted the bowl of fish. "Here, John, have some of the liquor."

He held out his plate resentfully. "Oh, you don't understand. It's all daft. I s'll fail, so what's the use of trying? As sure as I'm sittin' here——"

"Well, no one'll think owt less of you for that," said Joe Kemp in a reasoning voice. "An' it'll be practice."

The boy fell silent. Later, when the six o'clock news had been switched off, he renewed his complaints to his father, who was sitting comfortably in the armchair. Joe Kemp said nothing but things he hoped would comfort the boy, but privately he decided to have a word with Mr. Crouch, and later that evening called round to see him. Mr. Crouch was packing a suitcase; he was returning the next day to Watford. The Headmaster had called all the masters together for an emergency staff meeting immediately following the outbreak of war.

He was not over-pleased to see Joe Kemp, but welcomed him in, and they sat by the fire with the half-full suitcase open on the table. When he listened to what Joe Kemp had to say for three minutes he began nodding his head wisely, in order to halt Joe's monologue by suggesting that he knew everything he was going to say next. "Yes," he said. "Yes . . . yes. . . . What you're afraid of, Mr. Kemp, if I see it rightly, is that John will try for this scholarship and the Higher School Certificate in one year—and miss both of them. I don't think there's any danger of that. Even if he doesn't bring the scholarship off, he'll still have four months to prepare for the Higher Certificate, and he'll meet the second examination with all the more experience and confidence through having taken the first. But apart from that, I think he has a very good chance of success in both. Next year it would be a certainty: this year it's just very likely. I'm not suggesting the impossible, Mr. Kemp. John has an exceptional brain. In fact, he is the most remarkable pupil I have ever taught. I don't deny that I would rather have waited, but circumstances have changed, and we have to change our plans too. And the authorities will recognize this, and make all due allowances. No, I understand your doubts, but they're quite groundless—you can take my word for it."

"You take my word for it," said Joe Kemp later that evening

to John, who sat miserably by the fire unable to concentrate on the book he held. "Mr. Crouch knows what he's doin'. You needn't worry; you think too little of yourself, lad. You don't know what you can do. You're shapin' fine, I reckon; don't worry thaself."

"Eh, John was always a modest one," put in Mrs. Kemp, who was putting a new heel on a sock. "Wasn't 'e?"

The boy sighed, guessing his father had been to see Mr. Crouch, and feeling too weary to struggle against the alliance. He pushed his hair back and bent his attention to the book again. Resistance was useless.

Not even Mr. Crouch had foreseen the energy with which John threw himself into his work during the autumn and winter, that haphazard period when hours were topsy-turvy and lessons were frequently interrupted by real or imaginary air-raid warnings. Indeed, it passed unnoticed for a week or two, until Mr. Crouch noticed the number of notebooks Kemp was using up and the number of books he borrowed from the school library, and the pallor of his face. He had always, of course, worked hard, but effortlessly, within his own capacity: now there seemed a danger that he would outrun even his own powers. Mr. Crouch noticed that when he was asked a question in class, a momentary flash of panic came into his face, as he sought about his brain for the answer, caused by the fear he would not know, that he would be found wanting. Indeed, Mr. Crouch forbore to ask him questions for this reason.

At home he was treated like an invalid. The front room was set aside for him to work in, and when he was working the wireless was never played and visitors were asked to keep their voices low. His mother made special dishes that she imagined were "strengthening", and gave him large helpings at mealtimes: this aggravated him and his irritable outbursts were excused on the grounds that he was "tired from workin' ". It seemed impossible to do anything naturally: if he offered to run an errand for his mother, he saw her hesitate lest she would be keeping him from his books; if on the other hand she asked him casually to fetch something from the general shop on the corner, he fancied she was trying to make him take exercise and get some fresh air. The neighbours, of course, knew all about it: they never greeted him with any other phrase but "Workin' 'ard?"

Mr. Crouch knew he was working too hard, but did nothing to stop him. It was such a delightful change to have him working independently, without need for guidance; Mr. Crouch felt strangely as if a mechanical man he had painfully constructed had suddenly come to life. And in this sudden luxury an indifferent cruelty came to him: it interested him to see to what pitch the boy could drive himself. He did not hold himself responsible in any way.

Lying in his armchair one night after tea, the heavy curtains drawn and the lamplight showing the smoke from his cigarette curling up around the ornaments on the mantelpiece, he thought about the last two years with some surprise. It did not seem likely to him now that he would ever leave Huddlesford, at least of his own free will. The war had wrought some curious change in him: he no longer bothered to read intelligent books, or subscribe to weekly reviews; the book that lay face downwards on the carpet by his chair was an indifferent novel, and he was smoking many more cigarettes a day. The chief interest of his life was a correspondence he was conducting with the girl he now wanted to marry.

"The business was queer, very queer," he said to himself, thinking of the afternoon he had first lent John Kemp some of his own notes. "What on earth can have made me. . . . No, I can't imagine. A most curious episode." He heaved himself to his feet, scattering ash, and frowned at his waistcoat. Must wear the blue suit more. Then, putting on his hat and coat and taking up a torch, he went out to a nearby public-house, where he expected to meet the junior science master.

"So your protégé's actually gone, has he?" Mr. Crouch and the junior science master were hanging about the playing fields one afternoon in March, during the running-off of some junior heats. "When was it? Thursday?"

"Yes, Thursday." Mr. Crouch pulled a flag out of the ground and stuck it back again. "He should be back today. Empty-handed, I fear."

"I thought you said he was the cat's whiskers."

"Oh, yes, he is in a way. Certainly he is a phenomenal worker. Do you know, starting on Christmas Day, he got up at seven every morning to work?"

The junior science master raised his eyebrows.

"He kept that up till Thursday, I hear. I had it all from his father. They were proud of him at first, but towards the end they became a little frightened, I feel."

"You mean, he was working too hard?"

"Frightened for him, yes, and even frightened of him in a way. It was uncanny the way he worked. ' 'S'not 'uman,' as old Kemp said to me. He'd hardly eat or speak or anything."

"Well, surely he should get a pretty good result on those lines?"

"I wonder. I can't help thinking the Oxford people will send him back to grow up for another year."

"Do you think that would be a good thing?"

"Possibly, but I don't want to teach him for another year. You remember Jarrett?"

"The youth who was always quoting *Adonais*?"

"That's the one. He's in the Army now, I hear. Kemp is almost exactly the opposite. You don't feel that reading a poem means any more to him than adding up a column of figures. All he can do is work, work, work in this mechanical, inhuman way. He'll just wear himself out."

"Strange."

"Very. He's a curious character: one of these mysteries that are not worth solving."

"That's a mighty expressive phrase," said the junior science master, fumbling in his pocket for a cigarette. "Oh, lord, they've finished the jumping. Get your end of the tape."

Mr. Crouch obeyed, wondering if the expressive phrase expressed the truth.

As he was shuffling out of the school gates at four twenty-five he was met by John, who had been standing awkwardly there in his blue overcoat, his hair blowing in the wind.

"Sir——"

"Why, hallo, Kemp. So you're back. How did it go?"

"Oh—well, average really. I did some things wrong."

"Got the papers?"

"No, they kept them."

"Oh. Well, tell me about it."

They walked along the avenue, discussing the questions. "And the viva?" Mr. Crouch settled his hat more firmly on his head as the wind tugged at it. "What did they ask about? Did you tell any lies?"

John blushed scarlet at the memory.

"I said I edited the magazine."

He gulped and looked away. "Well, that's all right, they won't bother to verify it," said Mr. Crouch, as they came to his front gate. "I shouldn't worry: you seem to have done very creditably on the whole. At any rate, you aren't over-depressed." And that in itself is a bad sign, he thought. Looking at the boy's face in the sharp afternoon light, he could see lines of strain that had not been there six months ago. He became aware John Kemp was holding out his hand nervously.

"Thank you, sir, for all you've done."

Late in the next week John was informed that he had won a scholarship worth a hundred pounds a year.

John saw little of Christopher the next morning, who did not get up till nearly twelve, when after a cold shower he went off to the Bull and Butcher for meat pies and beer and a game of darts with Patrick. John spent the morning working with a dreary persistence, while the rain fell outside. After lunch he went and read a book in the Bodleian Library and returned at five o'clock to find Christopher, Eddy and Patrick having tea. Christopher's face, pallid in the early morning, had regained its normal flush, but he was as unshaven as a soldier who has fought in a battle lasting several days. They were discussing the evening they had spent.

"You were a fool to break that glass door."

"I don't remember a thing about it." Eddy was complacent. "Not a thing."

John poured himself a cup of strong tea and, looking round, found there was no milk left. His spirits had sunk when he realized that Christopher was seeming to disregard the pound he had borrowed, and he told himself in vain that this casualness was in itself the very sign of intimate friendship. Friends did not dun each other for small loans, but he could imagine Whitbread saying in his flat voice: "I'd be glad of that pound, if you could let me have it, Warner." The fancy depressed him, and a suspicion crawled about his mind that it was a direct personal slight.

On the Saturday morning he finally gave up hope and drew out another pound from his Post Office account, the pound that should have covered the fortnight from November 10th till November 24th. He was acutely aware that it was only October 26th. The streets were busy as he walked back towards the College for lunch, but they aroused no corresponding excitement in him, for an unconquerable sense of isolation was starting to possess him as he grew aware that people who had come into residence when he did had now made their own ways and had fallen into definite ways of life. They had run up the framework on which their university careers would be woven. John had not done so. Christopher was his closest friend. And this money business was creating a gaping hole of uncertainty in his mind, so that there was nothing to build on there.

He sat silent among the chatter at lunch, hearing Whitbread joining in a discussion on coal-tar products farther down the table, and lingered over the bread and cheese that finished the meal. It had begun to rain again lightly outside and people intending to play games turned on their benches and regarded the sky indignantly. The captain of the football team came and talked to Christopher as the latter ate. Groups of students strolled off to the cinema.

After lunch John sat on the sofa, his elbows on his knees, recollecting that the libraries were closed till Monday morning. He stared a long time at the carpet beneath his feet and when he looked up suddenly to see the time there was not a trace of expression on his face. There was a sound of someone in rubber shoes running fast and calling voices echoed round the cloisters. In the distance two o'clock struck.

For a few seconds he felt unbelievably calm.

Then feet clattered up the steps and Christopher Warner banged the door open in the way he had of kicking the panelling and twisting the knob at the same time. He was dressed for sport in flannels, a sweater and a blazer, and his hair was untidy.

"Thank God you're here. Here's a go." He pulled a telegram from his pocket, roughly crumpling it open. "Are you doing anything today—this afternoon, I mean?"

If it had been anyone else, John would have tried to play for time.

"No——"

"Well, this is from my mother. It says 'Meet 3.45 train for tea.' As it happens, I can't—there's this match, and I don't want to cut that, even if I could. Silly of her to send it so late; it was only handed in at ten. Will you go for me?"

"Go—for you? . . ."

"Yes, and take her somewhere for tea, where I can meet you."

John had twisted round on the sofa, and an expression of alarm replaced one of bewilderment.

"I . . . But I don't know her——"

"Oh, hell, you know what she looks like. You know her photograph." He gestured towards the double frame that stood on the little shelf. "Tall and dark. Just explain, you know, and apologize, and take her somewhere—the Green Leaf will do."

"But——"

"I've rung up Eddy," said Christopher patiently. "And the fool isn't in College. . . . Elizabeth and Patrick have gone off to Banbury to see some cousin of theirs. You're the only person I can ask."

87

John thrilled at this, managing to say:

"Yes, but—but what shall I do with her?"

"I've told you," said Christopher impatiently. "Just take her to the Green Leaf. I'll meet you at half-past four." Glad to have settled the matter satisfactorily, he went out. The door banged with its usual double-jointed sound.

An hour later John showed his platform ticket and passed on to Oxford station, looking about him uncertainly. Of course he was too early. His hair was plastered down with water and he had rubbed his shoes with the tablecloth; into the breast pocket of his overcoat he had tucked a white handkerchief in an attempt to look smart. His alarm at the mission had been replaced in part by a determination to do Christopher justice, and he was keenly aware of the great compliment Christopher had paid him by indicating that he was a fit person to welcome and escort his mother.

What would she be like? he asked himself, forgetting that only a fortnight ago he was thinking the same about Christopher. Christopher never talked directly about her, but he would sometimes tell an anecdote deliberately in which she figured as a distant acquaintance; he used an objective tone that would separate them completely. She was very fond of bridge and golf and (John remembered) it was all Christopher could do to outdrive her. He also recalled her squabble with the Rural District Council to bring the water main up to their house, and the sports car she drove. How was he going to receive a person like that?

Secretly he hoped she would not come.

Looking round among the baskets of pigeons, the bicycles with labels tied to their handlebars, and the mailbags, he sought for some memory of the station as he had reached it a fortnight ago. How long back that time seemed. All that had since happened had left an equal, confused impression, all of similar importance: the bronze in the Tutor's room, Elizabeth's voice, Christopher's endless smoking, Eddy's clothes.

With a sudden increase in apprehension he saw the engine come hissing up the platform, and as the few people who had collected to meet the train moved forward he backed behind an empty chocolate machine. The long line of coaches drew in; doors opened and porters began handing out parcels from the guard's van. John watched the travellers stroll to the barrier, scanning each woman for any familiar features; a small feeling of delight was just rapidly expanding inside him when after all he saw her, a long way behind the rest, looking round her expectantly. He recognized her not from the photograph, but from the likeness she bore to Christopher. She had the same broad forehead and jaw and her dark hair was drawn down to her neck, with no sign of grey.

Like Christopher, she dressed in tweeds, with a felt hat, low-heeled shoes and an artificial spray of berries and leaves at her left lapel. These suggested maturity. She looked far too young to be Mrs. Warner; the light swing with which she carried a small green case expressed the mobility and youth of her being. He stared at her, and as her eye searched the platform it rested a moment on him, passing onwards incuriously. But he recollected himself, and stepped forward, knowing dejectedly that he would be too nervous to speak the words he had made up.

"Er——"

"Yes?"

"Er—I—— Excuse me, but are you Chr—— Are you Mrs. Warner?"

"Yes, I am. Can't Christopher come? Are you a friend of his?"

"No. I—yes. He—he asked me to meet you. He—he's playing in a——"

"Oh, I see. When did he get my telegram?"

"At lunch. He couldn't alter his arrangements. . . . If you—— He'll meet you for tea at the—the Green Leaf."

Scarlet, he mouthed it out.

"Where? I don't know it."

"The High Street—I'll show you. . . . He asked me to show you."

"I see." They began walking towards the exit. "What's he doing? Playing rugger?"

They passed out into the street together, Mrs. Warner

89

straightening her gloves. "So this is Oxford," she remarked, looking round her. The sky was a complete blank of clouds, giving no sign of rain or sun. "Who are you, by the way?"

John blushed again, realizing he should have introduced himself in the first place.

"I'm Kemp—er—John Kemp. I share rooms with Christopher, you know."

"Do you really, now? He never told me that. How odd of him, don't you think?"

"Oh—yes——"

And indeed, on thinking it over, he did think so, remembering his own first letter home.

"Where are we going? Is it far? Shall we take a taxi?"

"I don't think—I mean——" Her luxuriant glance put him off. "Christopher said, to meet him there at half-past four, so, if we walk——"

"We shall be in nice time, shall we?" she finished brightly. "Right, let's walk."

His heart expanded towards her, now that the most awful part of the encounter was over, and now he perceived she was one of those rare people who could construct his meaning from the few truncated phrases and gestures his nervousness permitted him to utter. As they walked towards the town, he looked admiringly at her easy stride, her breasts and youthfulness, and, holding himself erect, he hoped he did her credit. He wanted the passers-by to think that he was her son.

She asked him some questions about the life they led, revealing that Christopher had told her absolutely nothing, not even the most trivial things such as how many rooms they occupied, or what they were doing. He tried to answer her amusingly, but she only smiled faintly, and looked about the streets. This was the old, pre-industrial part of the town, where canal transport offices were, coal merchants and corn and hay dealers. Remnants of the Saturday crowd strayed about in their best clothes, pushing perambulators or pausing to stare into the showrooms of a second-hand furniture shop. Paper blew about in the gutter.

John thought of his own mother, and drove her angrily from

his mind. As he walked beside Mrs. Warner, he felt the same air of pride that he felt when with Christopher: their similarity was instantly noticeable; the same characteristics manifested themselves, and what might be called the same aroma of personality—something fierce and careless. How could he do anything but admire them? They seemed to live without a second thought.

"I don't suppose you've settled down yet," she said. "You're northcountry, aren't you?"

"Yes—from Huddlesford."

"I'm afraid our family has a terrific prejudice against north-country people. It's my husband's fault, really. I think one of them got the better of him in a business deal!"

She burst into a crow of laughter as she said this, recovering immediately. "I don't know. As a matter of fact, I've never been farther north than Crewe."

"That's funny—I'd never been farther south than Crewe," said John eagerly, looking up at her.

"And what d'you think of us, now you've crossed the border?"

"Well, I don't know." His face grew puzzled, and his voice bore the shadow of pure Lancashire dialect, as he sought about for a true comment. "The people—I don't know, they're so sure of themselves——"

"You think so?" Her voice was amused. "Perhaps they've only got smoother tongues."

He was startled by her friendly smile and overcame an impulse to take her hand.

The Green Leaf teashop was full, many people eating slowly or waiting amiably to be served, and John felt at a loss, feeling that it was incumbent upon him somehow to create an empty table. As they walked through the centre of the town he had half assumed the role of guide, pointing out the buildings he knew, and explaining that Carfax was a corruption of *carrefour*. It pleased him to imagine she was his own mother. She had listened pleasantly, occasionally asking questions.

The café was a long low room, partitioned regularly into

91

alcoves which seated four, and every one of these was full. Mrs. Warner gazed about her with a comic expression of helplessness on her face, which John had observed in Christopher and knew did not mean any such thing. He was uncomfortable as they stood conspicuously there, and suggested they took two places that were just being vacated.

"But we want a three, don't we?" Mrs. Warner turned to look at him, and then looked past him to the door. "Hallo, there's Christopher. Yes, obviously he's been playing some game. What a ragamuffin he looks."

Christopher, after a moment's hesitation, came to them. His hair was ruffled and he was untidily dressed in sweater, blazer and flannels. John felt his own significance diminish rapidly.

"Hallo, Mother."

"Well, my son. You look a mess."

"I didn't stop to dress properly. I say, can't we sit down?"

As if in answer, four undergraduates got up and left a table free, one of them nodding to Christopher as he passed him, and waving a black cigarette holder. As Mrs. Warner led the way to the table, John thought uncomfortably that perhaps he ought to go now as his part in the afternoon was finished and they might want to talk privately. "I think . . ." he muttered, as they reached their seats. "Er—I think perhaps——"

They paid no attention, so, his courage failing, he sat down by Christopher with Mrs. Warner opposite. As she put her bag and gloves on the seat beside her, he could see that she was in early middle age, though it was easy to see how she looked as a girl. Her broad, dark good looks and sturdy shoulders would have been more attractive in the long run than more brittle beauty. He looked again at her, and then at Christopher, and it seemed that their resemblance was so strong that the third party—his father and her husband—was eliminated entirely.

Christopher said:

"What time does your train go?"

"Heavens, what a question." She glanced laughingly at John, sharing the joke. "You don't come to meet me, and the first thing you ask is, when am I going? Half-past six, if you must know. What would you like to eat?" she added, as one of the

92

ladies in print overalls came and stood by them. "What is there, please?"

"Bread and butter, cakes, scones, sandwiches, teacakes——"

Her voice trembled slightly on the last word as if she were very fond of them. Mrs. Warner listened critically.

"Teacakes sound nice," she said. "Everything sounds nice. We'll have everything. What are the sandwiches?"

"Fish, lettuce, tomato——"

"Tomato, then, and lettuce. And scones, bread and butter and jam, all for three."

"Yes, madam."

"And the tea? Do you like China tea, John?"

"Oh, yes," said John, never having had any.

"China tea, then, and cakes, of course." The lady went and Mrs. Warner turned back to them. "This does remind of me when we used to motor down to Lamprey and take Christopher and his friends out to tea. Haven't you always read, John, about schoolboy appetites? I used to order most lavish banquets. But do you know, they'd hardly eat anything. I had to coax them to the fruit salad, and as for the cream buns . . . Why was it, Christopher? Weren't they hungry?"

"Oh, they were just shy. I think you frightened them."

"Frightened them? Pooh!" She gave a little snort of laughter, directed mainly at John. But the effect of the memory had made Christopher look exactly like a small boy in John's eyes; with his tousled hair and mingled jaunty-guilty expression, he looked remarkably like one. He welcomed the fancy that Christopher and himself were brothers, who were still at school, and who were being visited by their mother and taken out to tea.

She had made everything sound appetizing when she ordered them, and when it all came she lent delicacy to the scene by the way she poured out and arranged the food on the table. The silver teapot she held with a small handkerchief, and she whipped the silver cover off the teacakes as if to reveal a rare dish. They were crisp, with scorched, broken tops.

"Please help yourselves: I always drink my tea first."

She sipped it softly, without milk or sugar.

"I've quite forgotten when you went to Derby," said

93

Christopher, his mouth full. "Did the Leylands invite you specially?"

"Yes, of course. Don't you remember, we had them to stay last summer?"

"I remember trying to teach that girl golf—Elspeth, was her name?" Christopher growled theatrically, cutting his teacake a second time. "Was she there?"

"She was, as it happened—on leave. She's in the Wrens, you know. We had a round on Sunday."

"Was she any better?"

"Well, it's not fair to judge anyone who hasn't played for ages. Now for my teacake." To John's astonishment, she picked it up and bit it hugely, making as she did so a shy little gesture that further endeared her to him.

By the end of the meal John would have concluded that Christopher's schoolfriends had been too busy watching Mrs. Warner to eat much, if he had given the matter any thought.

He himself ate, but did not talk, sitting not dumb with fright, but naturally silent as if watching an actress on the stage. Her least action was a pleasure to watch, as if at some time or another she had taken lessons in deportment. Erect, her shoulders square and commanding, she conducted the meal with alert friendliness. Every now and then she would say or do something (as when she bit the teacake) that scattered the image into a thousand places, only to re-gather it more brilliant than before.

Christopher kept up the conversation, eating hungrily, and passing his cup silently for more tea. She filled it, adding milk and sugar as at home, and broke off in the middle of doing so to sneeze daintily. Sometimes she would halt the desultory conversation and put some formal little question to John, such as:

"Does being a scholar mean you have to work harder?" or "Will you have a cigarette?"

Hypnotized, he took one from her pearl-backed case.

"That's a new departure," commented Christopher, holding his lighter out.

"Oh, don't you smoke as a rule? What a good influence

94

you'll be on Christopher—I know for a fact", Mrs. Warner emphasized smilingly, "that he smokes a very, very great deal too much." She stared at them both, as if the sight of them offered her much private amusement; John, watching her closely, thought the idea of having a grown-up son seemed comical to her, as if she had never got used to it. "Get the bill, darling."

She rose to go to the ladies' room, shaking her skirt free of crumbs, and Christopher stared elaborately about for the waitress, not catching John's eye. A triumphal march began in John's head as he imagined that Christopher was loth to accept his fresh status in John's view, now that there was nothing but common ground between them; he felt as if they had submitted some dispute to a higher authority and the decision had been in his favour.

"I say, Chris, I think your mother's awfully decent," he said excitedly.

"Can we have our bill, please?" said Christopher.

He did not see her again before she left, and on Saturday night Christopher went out and got very drunk with the money she had given him. "What, you in to breakfast, sir?" exclaimed Jack, in soft irony. "You've mistook the time, sir. It's 'a'-past eight, not 'a'-past eleven."

"Sure sign of trouble, Jack. The room's uninhabitable."

And it was till Jack cleaned it up, for which Christopher gave him five shillings. Nevertheless, John's sense of exhilaration persisted. On Monday morning he woke up, had a hot bath, called for a second cup of coffee at breakfast (he had never done this before), and went out afterwards into the gardens for a stroll. The morning was bright, and though everywhere was a tangle of dead stalks and leaves, the wet grass shone as in June. Shadows of great elms lay across the lawn. He sniffed the air: it had that strange, ashen smell of autumn, despite the glittering sheets of light. Now and again a bird called, and it was hard to believe that the garden was in the middle of a town.

To avoid a gardener, he went indoors again and spent some time pretending to decide whether or not to attend a lecture at ten o'clock. Indeed, he came very near to missing it, as Christopher would have done (Christopher still lay in the blacked-out bedroom), but as he himself was up and not, after all, Christopher, he slipped on his big scholar's gown and walked out of the College into the busy streets. For the lecture he decided to be Mr. Crouch, nodding his head wisely at intervals and making a few microscopic jottings, to be copied and expanded later; by eleven, he remembered, the public houses would be open, and he could be Christopher and stand drinking in a bar. He would buy himself a packet of cigarettes and enjoy smoking and drinking. How ashen the air smelt: a quenched smell of an extinct summer.

The lecture room was full of young women in short gowns, carrying bulky handbags and enormous tattered bundles of notes; they smelt inimitably of face powder and (vaguely) Irish stew, and they were dressed in woollen clothes. He soon forgot them and the lecturer as well by thinking of Mrs. Warner. His mind dwelt pleasurably on her uprightness, her precision in handing a cup and saucer, the individuality that caused her to go hatless and show her fine dark hair, that was at once comely and mature. There was something about her that he had never met before, something that made him feel at once both happy and excited, something that made him want to see her again, to live where she lived. She affected him like an invigorating climate.

After the lecture he went and stood in a bar. His high spirits were rising as the sun rose towards the zenith: indeed, he was almost surprised at his own jubilance.

"A bitter, please, and twenty cigarettes."

"These are all we have."

"They'll do nicely," John agreed. He took a paper packet of matches from a holder on the counter and gave sixpence to the blind. Before the grate lay a tabby cat, stretched out as if dead, but something in its mouth and throat suggesting limitless ferocity.

"Likes the fire."

"Hah! S'not the only one."

The woman went on knitting, for the bar was otherwise

96

empty, and John leaned in the shade and blew smoke into the sunlight. Try as he would, he could not make it like Christopher did. By playing off the taste of the beer against the taste of the tobacco, he managed to find each fairly pleasant. The cat yawned and writhed up, stretching on its four feet: John rubbed it with his shoe, and it patiently moved away.

"He's not feeling friendly today."

"Ah, we only keep him for the mice. Don't like cats myself. We only keep him 'cause of the mice."

"You've got mice, then?"

"Any number, yes. These are old houses."

The cat settled down on the other side of the fire, out of his reach.

"He's a good mouser—he'll sit two, three hours over a hole." The woman shook her knitting. "Can't get him away. Ah, these are old houses."

John looked at the cat again, finished his beer and went out into the light. From the stone façades pigeons fluttered down on to the pavements and waddled uneasily about, casting a wary eye at him, but he paid no attention to them. The wind blew and a whole wall of ivy danced in the sun, the leaves blowing back to show their white undersides. So in him a thousand restlessnesses yearned and shook. At the sight of the blue-and-white sky, the flashing windscreens of cars, the square new brick air-raid shelters daubed with white paint, a vigour filled him almost equal to his desire. He wondered whether to go back to the College, find Christopher and suggest they went out drinking.

He was depressed by the sudden reflection of himself in a hat-shop window: he was ashamed of his emaciated suit. It was a blot on him, it did nothing to express his exhilaration, it made him look pinched and underfed. It would be splendid to go into a tailor's and order a dozen new suits, in tweed, with fob pockets and leather buttons. The idea of spending money took hold of his mind, and he began considering what he could buy, something he could wear to show his good humour: a really smart tie, for instance. In fact, a bow-tie. He smiled and began walking quickly through the people.

G

The inside of the outfitter's was lofty and hushed, like a cathedral, and if a tall man resembling a solicitor had not immediately come towards him, he would have turned round and gone out again.

"I want a bow-tie."

"One bow-tie."

This gave John a sudden vision of the bow-tie, lying in a pool of light at the bottom of a lift-shaft, very tiny and distinct. The man went behind the counter and began laying out drawerfuls of ties neatly and quickly, staring beyond John's head into some far corner of the shop.

John went through all the actions of a rich young man (Christopher), choosing a bow-tie in a shop. He would drag one out, then throw it down as if it had deceived him; he would flick them over like the pages of a book and turn from one drawerful to the next. One or two he picked out and twisted, as if to consider their appearance when tied, or carried them over to the door to inspect the colour in a better light. He liked doing this, but he did it quickly so as not to waste the man's time. In the end he chose a pleasant, ordinary one, blue with white spots, and paid three-and-sixpence for it. The man put it into a little envelope, licked the flap and stuck it down.

As soon as he got outside, he went down a public lavatory to put it on.

He was so nervous when he emerged that for all practical purposes he was a walking bow-tie. If all the traffic had stopped dead, he would hardly have noticed it; he proceded with short, self-conscious steps along the dry, sunny pavement, avoiding the eyes of passers-by, his hands clenched in his pockets. He was so preoccupied that he did not see Elizabeth Dowling till she came right up to him: they were walking diagonally in roughly the same direction, and she had a small notebook as well as a handbag, as if she was going to work in a library. Her smart flared skirt and flowers pinned to her jacket made this seem incongruous.

"Hallo, John. Oh, my dear! What—what—what——"

She spluttered in pretended astonishment, and stopped with

her golden head on one side, forcing him to stop too. He muttered a kind of greeting.

"Oh, it's a *too*-heavenly bow," she cried. "But, my dear boy, why haven't you *tied* it properly? My dear, it's *ruinous*."

"Oh—er—isn't it right?" He put his hands up to it uneasily. Certainly it had looked a bit odd in the lavatory. "What's wrong with it?"

"Why, it's all——" She shut her lips, biting back a squirt of laughter. "Here, hold these." She gave him her book and handbag, and pulled the bow undone. Then, starting with an end in each hand, she rapidly retied it, her lips still firmly closed. It was an extraordinary scene, and he could not see any way of preventing it. People passing stared curiously, till he was scarlet, but Elizabeth herself was so unconcerned he could say nothing.

"There, that's more presentable." She stepped back at last. "Not throttled, are you?"

"No—no, thanks very much——"

She took back her book and bag and walked with him for some way. Though they had not met since the afternoon of John's arrival, she treated him as intimately as if they were friends of a year's standing.

"You look much smarter now," she said, the sun showing the dazzling contrast between lips and teeth. Then she left him, running up the stone steps of a library, leaving him standing below in the attitude of a sightseer as he watched her white calves disappear into the inner dusk.

He spent the afternoon asleep on the sofa, with the bow-tie tickling his chin. At dinner in Hall Whitbread grinned across at him in a friendly manner:

"You look a regular dandy. My word, who's been lashin' out?"

He put a whole potato in his mouth, holding his knife and fork like carpenter's tools, and John began to eat quickly in order to finish before he did and to get away from him. A servant brought a plate of prunes and custard, and Whitbread caught his sleeve, asking for more cauliflower.

"Like to come up for coffee?"

John smiled regretfully.

"I'm afraid I'm going out tonight."

So of course he had to go, lest Whitbread should see the light on in his room, or, worse, come to investigate. He put on his overcoat, admired himself in the mirror and walked aimlessly out into the blackness, listening to the hooded Army lorries thundering past at eight-second intervals. There was no traffic but this convoy and an occasional omnibus. Men and women stood silently along the walls of locked banks or collected in little groups that would suddenly explode a few paces backwards in laughter, and then re-form again. He stepped off the pavement to pass them.

As he walked into a quieter part of the town by the river, where there were river-boat offices and shops that sold clay pipes and fishing-rods, his exhilaration, that had sunk into a glowing contentment, began curdling to helplessness. It took him some minutes to discover what it was he wanted and could not get: he conjured up Mrs. Warner and Christopher in turn, and only when he had dismissed them impatiently did he remember Elizabeth, and her friendliness. The soft fumbling of her hands under his chin had aroused a fugitive excitement in him. When could he see her again, as he wanted to?

Christopher was lucky; he could see her whenever he wanted, and touch her, and perhaps kiss her whenever he wanted. He leaned over the stone wall of the bridge, hearing the water chuckling beneath and the shifting trees down the bank. Elizabeth filled his thoughts. Not only Elizabeth, but all that stretched beyond her—iridescent, tingling feelings that had not any obvious cause, shadowy wishes, and more shadowy dreams of fulfilment. As he looked down he could hear the water, but not see it. The day's happiness had gone with the day, and he was left with an uneasy depression, expressed in the thought: where was she now? She was most likely with Christopher.

He wondered where they both were.

About fifteen minutes later he heaved himself upright and began strolling back towards the College, and it was then that quite by accident he met Christopher. As he was passing a tiny street that was practically an alley-way, there came a flurry of feet and a mutter of drunken laughter. Then someone crashed into him, sending him reeling sideways into a lamp-post, which was very painful.

"Oh, God," said a voice. "Sorry, you."

"Bugger the Proctors!" screeched another voice—Eddy's. John called:

"Christopher?"

"Christ, who's 'at?"

"John."

"John? Oh, Kemp. 'Struth, John, ole boy, we've just been nearly progged. What a squeak." Christopher, smelling of spirits, gripped his arm very tightly. "Come an' have a drink. Here, Eddy, where's everyone?"

"Wha'? God knows."

"Come an' have a drink, ole boy. Must do. Where's the nearest, Eddy? The Fox?"

Just then another set of feet pattered down the alley-way, and Patrick Dowling's voice came out of the darkness.

"You there, Chris? You pair of swine. Those progs got us."

"No! What bloody luck. I *am* sorry. I thought we all——"

"Bullers all round us. That's ten shillings down the drain. It's a regular cow."

"Have you got Eddy there?" came Hugh Stanning-Smith's voice. "We heard the bastard yelling."

Eddy was leaning against a lamp-post, singing.

"Now come on, men," urged Christopher persuasively. "We're wasting good drinking time. What about the Fox?"

"Oh, scrub that." Patrick Dowling's voice sounded disagreeably sober. "Scrub that, Christopher. We've been had once tonight, even if you haven't. I'm through for tonight."

A violent sound of vomiting came from the black alley-way.

"Eddy, you sot! Pull yourself together—your Cambridge man's turned himself up."

"Eh?" Eddy stumbled across to the entry, where he could be heard comforting the vomiter. "Let it come up, ol' man. That's right. Christ, not over me, you fool."

"Now, Pat, don't crab everything. Come on, man." Christo-

101

pher returned to the attack. "Just a couple of whiskies at the Fox to round off. Come on, man! The progs'll be in bed by now."

John listened with interest, wondering what excuse Patrick would find to give in; it was curious to hear the full weight of Christopher's personality turned against somebody else. "Christ, lightning never strikes twice in the same place! The Fox is only just round the corner."

"Yes, and so are the progs." John could imagine his lips curling under his long nose.

"Well, you yellow pig. John'll come, won't you, old boy? There, you see, a man who's hardly been in a pub before he came up's got more guts than you. You're coming, Hugh?"

"It's close on closing time, old boy. I've had enough for tonight."

John could hardly believe his ears. Their firm refusals sounded as casual as if the matter was of no matter, instead of a test of loyalty. Their independence excited him and also the fact that instead of being sixth in the group, he had suddenly jumped up to fourth—or even third, for surely the Cambridge man did not count.

"All right, then." Plainly, Christopher had lost his temper. "Come on, Eddy. Can that man walk?"

"Sure," came a husky voice.

"These swine are crying off. It's only across the road. Come on, John."

Eddy followed, singing and stamping his feet, and John followed, too, humming the refrain under his breath. In a moment all his happiness had come bounding back: Christopher's compliments and the fact he had not, after all, been with Elizabeth, combined to send his spirits dizzily high. Perhaps the best of the day was still to come.

They had to force their way into the Fox and Grapes, which was crowded, bright and noisy, with the sound of singing and a piano raggedly audible from another room. Workmen looked resentfully as they entered, but soon forgot them, as it was nearly ten o'clock. John studied his companions in the light: Christopher looked as he did when he came in late at night,

102

pale and determined, but Eddy's mouth was agape and his spotty face flushed and excited. The Cambridge man was a stocky football player, with fair hair, wearing a military raincoat that was splashed with sick at the bottom. He was very white and his eyes were incurious.

"I'll get the drinks," said John quickly. "What are you having?"

He returned from the bar with four tiny glasses, in each of which danced an inch of golden liquid. The bar was so crowded he had to force his way like an explorer through dense undergrowth. The others had been standing silent, letting their attention drift buoyed-up on the chatter and laughter around them.

"That's the stuff," said Christopher, eagerly stretching out a hand. John handed them carefully out, secretly alarmed at the price, and at the prospect of drinking one.

"Not for me, thanks," whispered the young man.

"Oh, hell, it'll warm you up," said Christopher, putting it roughly into his hand. "Take a grip on yourself."

John looked cautiously at his glass. Whisky? Would it make him drunk, would he stagger about and see pink elephants, walk home crookedly and perhaps be sick? If he were sick in front of Christopher he would die of shame.

"Here's to good old whisky," said Eddy loudly, and swallowed what he had, which made John feel affectionate towards him: he seemed so reckless, so aggressively unprotected. John himself carefully sipped a little: Lord! His eyes filled with tears and he gulped furiously: it did not feel as if he had actually swallowed anything, but as if the liquid had soaked into his throat as spilt water soaks into sand. The agony caused him to look impersonally ahead, listening seriously to the sound of singing.

"I like whisky," said Christopher, grinning suspiciously at John as if he guessed his thoughts. "You can feel it doing you harm." His good humour had quite returned. "Jesus, look at the man," he added, reaching out swiftly and giving the bow-tie a rough pull. John had forgotten it for the moment, and Christopher burst into a roar of not unflattering laughter at the

103

expression on his face. "I've been wondering why he looked different. Thought I was tight. Pretty smart, eh?"

Eddy looked at John and then at Christopher. "Cute thing," he said.

John swelled with pride and the noise of the pub drummed in his ears. "You've undone it. God, Chris, you are a swine." He began to laugh happily, feeling the collapsed ends with his hands. "You swine. I can't possibly do it up again." Laughter slowly gathered all his body and began to contract, so that he bent, one hand on his knee. "I—I don't know how."

"You don't?" Christopher was starting to laugh as well. "Then you'll always have to wear it like that—oh, owch, owch, owch." He exploded uncontrollably. "Oh, my God. Owch—owch—owch."

Eddy banged him in the ribs. "Here, shut up, what's the matter? Eh?" He pushed his face close. "You want a fight," he diagnosed.

"Shut up, Eddy. It's that fool John. He can't tie his tie again, now I've wrecked it—oh, owch—owch—owch——" He went off again. John, gripped by silent laughter, nodded dumbly, while Eddy stared at each of them in turn, a puzzled look on his face. He licked his lips and belched. At last he said:

"Then how—here, listen to me—*how?*—di' do it in the first place?"

Christopher stopped laughing. "Eh?"

But John's laughter became more wild and delighted as he hugged the secret to himself. He fought his way to the bar and got four more whiskeys, handing them out like gifts to the other three. It was his moment. He felt extraordinary power over them all, thinking that although he was not the best of them, he was the only one who realized their collective excellence. Both of them gripped him by one arm.

"Yes, you bastard, who tied it to start with?"

John put his whisky down on a side table, too weak to laugh any more. "Elizabeth," he said weakly.

"Who?"

"Elizabeth. You know."

"What the hell d'you mean, Elizabeth?" demanded Christopher, his black eyebrows pulling together in the middle. "What the hell are you talking about?"

John picked his whisky up and tossed it off. His feet straddled. "The merest coincidence," he said, and began to tell of the morning's incident. Half-way through, a crow of amusement half-choked him, and he started to giggle; by the time he finished the end of the story Christopher, tapping his square-faced ring against his glass, was laughing too. They were not laughing at the same things, but that did not matter. Good humour was restored. The Cambridge man said he felt a lot better, and where could they get something to eat? Eddy was whistling. The landlord called time and his wife came out from behind the bar to collect glasses. As she passed Eddy she pushed him aside like a piece of furniture, but he did not notice. John stood smiling, listening to the talk, the loose ends of his bow-tie hanging foolishly down.

John did not feel so happy the next morning as he thought he would. When he had pulled the bedclothes over himself the night before he had thought he would never be depressed again, and went to sleep looking forward to the five more weeks that remained of the term. When Jack called them in the morning, he sat up dubiously. There was a peculiar taste in his mouth. When he blinked, his eyes felt tired. In fact, he felt tired all over. The window-pane was blurred and wet: it had been raining since dawn.

Moreover, when he had forced himself up and had spent the morning attending lectures in chilly rooms, he found he was not free of the worries he had imagined were illusory. After lunch he sat at the desk, trying to make himself work, but continually the thought returned to his mind that one of his shoes had let the water in, that the fire was not burning properly, that he had spent much more money than he should have done. He scribbled a little sum on his blotting paper and found to his

105

dismay that he had about five shillings pocket-money a week left him, after deducting money for a ticket home and a tip for Jack. Then he did a second sum to find out the price of whisky per glass. Half-way through he abandoned it in despair.

He wondered when Christopher would pay him back the pound he owed. He lacked the courage to ask for it.

He was not wearing the bow-tie now, having looked gravely at it that morning and then put it away in his drawer, feeling surprised that he was not more pleased to see it again. The sight of it produced slight shame in him. Now it was three in the afternoon and the taste of the College lunch of sausages and mashed potatoes and cabbage still lingered in his mouth: the rain continued to fall heavily outside without having ceased for a second through the day. An open book lay in front of him, and he held his fountain pen ready above the blank page of an exercise-book; he ran his eye down the page of print as so often before, meaning to gather the main points and note them down. He blinked, shook his head, and read the page again, but the trick would not work. Laboriously he began to read every word, starting at the top of the page, but in a couple of seconds he had lost track of the meaning. He realized that he was due for one of the spells he had been having during the last week when his brain simply refused to assimilate new knowledge; he could hardly read a newspaper intelligently. They caused him a gnawing of alarm. Was he, perhaps, going mad, or stupid?

But it was silly to worry. Christopher never did any work. John got up and wandered to the bookcase, where the file he had bought for Christopher lay under a few newspapers and magazines. He pulled it out and opened it. It was empty, with the price still scrawled in pencil on the first blank sheet. He pushed it back into its place with a sigh. Christopher was out at the moment, to buy some cakes for tea: Elizabeth was coming, and as John remembered this he remembered, too, Christopher's injunction to keep a good fire in, and scuttled over to the hearth. The fire smouldered blackly and John spent a few minutes to draw it up with a newspaper, but the big fireplace was too wide to be properly covered by the war-time newspaper sheets, and he only set light to the thing and had to cram it into the grate hurriedly with the poker. As it burnt it made the fire worse.

Kneeling down gave him a slight headache.

But Elizabeth would be coming, and he gave himself up to wondering how she would look and what she would say and what she really thought behind her square, cosmetic-tended face. He wondered if he could make her like him. Looking at his face in the mirror, he took the comb from his breast pocket and combed his hair different ways, trying to decide which way suited him the best: none of them, he regretfully decided, was conspicuously better than another. Then he sat at the desk again, remembering something Mr. Crouch had once said: "Get into the habit of forgetting everything except the page in front of you. Sit for a moment, concentrating, and pretend you're wiping an ice-cold sponge across your mind, leaving everything quite clear and free. Forget yesterday, forget to-morrow, forget who you are and what you're going to do next. Then start." He frowned. He had always found it rather difficult, and now it seemed impossible: he could not forget yesterday, nor what he was going to do next. The rain poured down outside with a soft hissing as it pattered on dead boughs and leaves.

He was startled when there came a light tap on the door, and Elizabeth looked in.

"Oh, dear, am I *too* early?"

"Oh, er, come in, Elizabeth."

He put his pen down on his exercise-book, which shut of its own accord, and rose to welcome her, as if she were his guest.

"I mustn't disturb you. . . . Are you sure it doesn't matter?"

"No, do come in—let me. Er—can I take your coat? Isn't it wet?"

She let it fall into his hands and he carried it into the bedroom, laying it with cheap insolence across his own bed. In the meantime she studied herself in the glass and sat down on the sofa. She wore a soft brown dress, with a gold chain round her neck, brown shoes and lustrous stockings, and the colours brought out every shade of her dark-gold hair. It fascinated John, who imagined her brushing it, beating it up on both sides till it stood up of its own accord like whipped white of egg.

He found his packet of cigarettes, and she took one.

"I'm afraid they got a bit squashed last night."

"Dear, dear, were you there, too? Patrick is very annoyed about last night." She tilted her eyelids towards the flame. "It seems they'll fine him ten shillings, and it was Eddy's fault for shouting like a *mad*man."

"Yes, perhaps. I wasn't there then."

"I'm surprised you were there at all." She gave him an impudent glance, exhaling smoke. "I thought you were a *sober* person."

"Did you?" He smiled, and kicked the coals nervously. "Sorry the fire's so. . . ."

"And you're not wearing that *lovely* bow, either. I think you should. Where is it?"

"I can't tie it."

"You are mad, you know. Fancy buying a bow when you can't tie it. Bring it here, and I'll show you."

"Bring it——?"

"Yes, I'll show you." She sat up, stretching out an imperious hand, holding the cigarette away from her. He looked into her face and fancied he saw an amused, challenging expression.

"All right." He fetched it from the bedroom and Elizabeth brushed some ash from her skirt, humming a tune quietly to herself. "Here it is."

"Good. Now take your tie off." She twisted it in her hands, holding it away to inspect it critically, her chin doubling slightly. Her rose-coloured finger-nails made the blue silk seem intense in colouring. John awkwardly fumbled with his collar, remembering too late that it was one that had been turned by his mother because it had grown so worn on one side. She approached him, bearing the tie.

"Now then. First, the right end should be longer than the left." She made a movement like putting her arms round his neck, encircling his collar with the bow, and tugging the ends to their correct lengths. "That's right. Now, it's just like tying a shoe-lace—and you do that every day——"

108

He shifted a trifle. She was very close to him. He could smell scented warmth and tobacco on her breath as she talked.

"First an ordinary knot—can you see what I'm doing?"

She put her hands on his shoulders and moved round till he could see her hands reflected in the mirror. Looking at them gave him a queer sensation. Her clear voice might have issued from a gaily-painted loudspeaker in a nursery.

"Now the bow. Fold . . . over . . . double this end. . . ."

As they stood close together, her body seemed bigger than his. He wanted to raise his hands, that hung embarrassed at his sides, and put them on her hips, and pull her against him. A flaring theoretical lust began making it seem more and more likely that he would do this. He wondered what there was to prevent him, and there seemed nothing, and his elbows were beginning to crook when he suddenly caught the expression on her face. He saw in a second that she expected him to do this, that she was waiting for it. His hands dropped. A horrible embarrassment tingled and shuddered inside him, that what he had imagined to be his most secret feeling was almost cynically common. It shocked him deeply. He instinctively moved his head uncomfortably, like an animal at bay.

"Keep still," she said. "There, now it's done." With a lingering, backward gesture at the mirror, "Look at yourself."

He resembled a dog groomed for a show.

"Very nice," he said, covering his confusion. "I must employ you to do it permanently."

She looked amusedly at him and sat down again.

"It's easy."

Through the silence they heard the rain and the sound of approaching footsteps and whistling that John recognized instantly as Christopher's. A quick fear made him stuff his tie into his pocket, guiltily. Elizabeth took up her cigarette again, raising her eyebrows:

"Chris, is it?"

John nodded, terrified lest Christopher should notice the bow he had on and jump to the right conclusions, for he had sensed last night that such a thing might arouse Christopher's sudden violence. But he need not have worried, for as soon as the door

109

opened an outraged coo greeted Christopher, as Elizabeth accused him of neglecting her by being out when she called. Christopher stood grinning and stamping, shaking the wet off his brown pork-pie hat and taking off his raincoat with a stiff, rustling sound. They started a wrangle about this, which John listened to with amusement.

"And when I *do* come, through the *pouring* rain," said Elizabeth, posturing tragically, "you, you *beast*, AREN'T IN."

"I was buying cakes," said Christopher unconcernedly, opening the door of the cupboard, "for you to stuff."

"With my money," put in John jovially. Then he realized he had been very rude, and blushed scarlet. Elizabeth looked at him for a second, and dropped her eyes. After a moment Christopher made another remark, and began laying the table for two with John's cups and plates, which John rightly took as a signal for him to go. He shuffled and blew his nose, replacing his handkerchief in his breast pocket, where he noticed Christopher sometimes kept his, and took down his overcoat from behind the door. Elizabeth had returned to the subject of Christopher's unjustified neglect.

"I've been working, working *all day*, except for coffee and lunch—— All right, I bet that's more than *you* can say." Christopher made a loud baa-ing noise. "I'm literally exhausted. If you only knew what a monster my tutor can be. . . ."

"Oh, come off it." A plate in one hand, he stood grinning at her and suddenly made a playful snatch at her hair. "You spend all your time doing yourself up——"

"Behave!" she cried, swaying back with a little yelp of amusement. They hesitated, smiling at each other.

"I must be going now," muttered John, not looking at them and buttoning his coat. "I—er—late. . . ." He did not know why that little cub-like squabble had affected him as strongly as it had, but it had taken his imagination, and it seemed obvious now that he should not have tried to kiss Elizabeth, whereas a moment before he had been furious with himself. He was content to leave them together. When he looked at them both, he felt like a waiter in an expensive restaurant. Their friendliness to him was like the tips they would give a waiter.

"Good-bye, then."

"Good-bye."

"Goodbye, John."

He went out, filled with a curious sad contentment, as if he had suddenly been changed to another person, and banged the door clumsily so that it did not catch. As he turned back to shut it, he heard Elizabeth say:

"You've trained him well."

Christopher laughed and said "Yes."

"Quite a little gent. And is this still his china? You are a horror."

"That's his butter."

He heard Elizabeth explode with laughter.

"Well, of all the——! It's too bad. He *must* be a feeble sort of worm."

"Mother said he looked stuffed."

"Stuffed! That's *just* the word!"

But I mustn't stop and listen, thought John mechanically, because he'll be coming out to fill my kettle, and he'd be embarrassed. Also he dare not hear any more.

The rain had made the air very chill and all the outer flagstones of the cloisters were wet. The grass was drenched and the stone carvings and gargoyles soaked through. A few of the windows round the quadrangle were lighted.

His face, as he walked to the Lodge, was white, and he felt as if he had been knocked about by a boxer who had known exactly where to hit him in order to hurt him the most.

There was a letter come for him by the afternoon post from his sister Edith, the teacher in Manchester. He picked it up and walked out into the street, starting to open it.

Twenty paces down the road he realized he had not yet begun to read it, and tried to give it his attention. Shelter practice with the children, evacuation, scraps of local news. Old Mr. Reading was in the Infirmary. "I expect you are thoroughly settled down by now," she had written, "and are feeling a terrific 'swell'."

Once they had shown him that he was despicable, he instantly saw himself as fifty times more despicable than they thought

111

him. The past three weeks, that hitherto had been dispersed and vague, sprang suddenly into focus for what they were—an extended, conceited daydream, that had made him irritatingly absurd.

He walked on, the letter in his hand. The College nurse passed him wondering if perhaps he had just received some bad news. He did not see her. The traffic and people in the streets receded as he walked; a column of soldiers whistling a music-hall song marched by on the other side of the road without paying any attention to him; a van was unloading bacon into a grocer's and he had to wait while a huge half-split pig wrapped in sacking was carried in.

He crumpled the letter back into its envelope without reading the last page and pushed it into his pocket.

Oh, yes, of course I use his crocks. He daren't stop me.

Chris, you are awful!

That's his butter you're eating. Spread it on thick.

Oh, Chris!

Mother thought he was a scared stuffed little rabbit.

He must be a pretty miserable specimen.

He sincerely remembered the conversation like this. The original was lost and fresh versions of the different lines kept coming up and overlaying each other. He repeated them carefully in his head. The rain blew in his face. For the moment he was knocked all to pieces, the pieces being different emotions, shame, self-disgust, rage and so on; he had not grasped the situation sufficiently to be able to take up an attitude towards it. All he knew was that his sensibilities were scorched, rather as if he had walked too close to an open furnace door.

It was all so bewildering. Inexplicable incidents came back to his mind, one after the other: Christopher calling him "John", Mrs. Warner including him in her easy smiling, Elizabeth re-tying his bow-tie. As he thought of the bow-tie and saw himself reflected in a shop window, he was carried off in a gust of anger, then bewilderment ebbed back again. What had they really meant by these things, then? But if he picked up each relationship and turned it round critically, he could see that the reverse side was always scorn and derision. He wondered that he could have been so dense as never to have noticed it before. The incident of Christopher and the pound returned constantly to his mind like an ominous, banging gong.

The clocks of the town struck four times: he had been walking about for twenty minutes, the afternoon was coming to its close and still the rain swept up and down the streets. His hair was soaking wet and he was aware that his shoe leaked once more. Busy shoppers pushed their umbrellas here and there about the pavements and a newspaper seller sheltered in the doorway of a bank collected pennies swiftly. A chalked placard told of the news from Albania. He looked around him in a dazed way, wondering where to have tea and noticed the Green Leaf only a few doors down the road. He was there before he remembered its importance, but with an obstinate expression he pushed open the door and went in. His first phase of sheer puzzlement had gone. What possessed him now was a shuddering rage at himself and at all the rest of them; he plunged into the steaming interior filled with the hysterical determination of a man who in sheer fury probes an agonizing wound. The café was two-thirds full and the seat they had occupied was taken, but he managed to sit in the next alcove and wearily pushed aside the used crockery that littered the table.

A waitress came and took his order. She was not the same one as on Saturday. He ordered exactly the same tea as they had had then.

He looked along the alcoves, each with its light, and loneliness began to displace his rage. Loneliness made any emotion he suffered impotent. No feeling he had could possibly affect anyone else.

The tea came and he started eating without pleasure. He was surprised how exactly the taste of each item coincided with how he remembered them from Saturday. The tomato sandwiches were wet and the thin transparent bread-and-butter showed the red tomato lurking within. He stirred his tea and drank.

What was he to do, now that he knew what they thought of him? How should he change his attitude towards them? How ought he to treat them?

H 113

His trains of thought kept snapping off and having to be re-started. He lifted the best cake from the stand and cut it in half. Then he remembered that this habit of cutting food he had picked up from Christopher: at home he had always bitten it.

How should he face Christopher now? And at this thought the last remnants of his illusion collapsed like the last wall of a demolished house. After all, then, he was on his own; he had failed, utterly and ignominiously failed to weave himself into the lives of these people. As he had feared, the door had swung open again and he was alone again, doubly alone. The days would be scrappy, bits and pieces of action. No objects, no continuity.

And still he could not understand why it had all happened, why he had been so obtuse, or they had been so deceitful, what had intervened between them to refract his vision of them all. It was surely not his fault. He lit the fourth of his cigarettes and smoked it slowly. The room filled and emptied again, leaving him sitting small and white-faced at his table. At last the waitress came and scribbled a bill for him, tucking it folded under his plate, whence he extracted it and glanced at the total: three and a penny. He pulled his change out of his pocket and stared in terror at it: one and sevenpence halfpenny. He had no other money. The woman came back, expecting to be paid.

"I—er—I'm sorry—I've come without—I've only got one and sevenpence,"-he blurted, horrified: he spread it out in his hand. In his bewilderment he would not have been surprised had she called the police. "I've come out with no—I'm awfully sorry. . . ."

She looked at him suspiciously.

"Are you a student?"

"Oh, yes—yes——"

He gave his College.

"Just write your name and address on the back of the bill, then: you can pay us tomorrow." She stared at him. "You've been here before, haven't you?"

"Oh, yes—once——"

He wrote "John Kemp" with trembling hands on the bill,

114

remembering irrelevantly that the meals had not been identical because he had forgotten to ask for China tea.

"And the address." Glancing at his shabby clothes, she added:

"Be more careful next time."

He hated having to go back to the College. But night was falling, the bells were chiming six o'clock, workmen cycled along the wet streets with their dim lamps. From farther off came the shouts of urchins who were throwing sticks and stones up at a horse-chestnut tree and along the street windows would be filled with light, then carefully darkened. As he stepped through the gate he sighed: it was humiliating to have to return like a circling boomerang to the place and the person he most wanted to avoid. But he was powerless to make a tragedy of the affair. As he walked slowly across the first quadrangle he could not help noticing the instant peace of the air inside the College, and, his fingers touching his sister's letter, he withdrew it and fitted it properly into its envelope. After all, it seemed, things had been momentarily frozen still with horror were moving forward again.

But he had not expected the rage that flared up at him when he entered their room, where Christopher lay sprawled on the sofa turning the pages of a magazine. For a moment he was blind with anger: the words he had overheard shone in his mind in lacerating detail; for a moment he really thought as soon as he could control his voice he would quarrel with Christopher and get him to change rooms. Then he took off his overcoat and hung it up. Elizabeth had gone and the servant had cleared away the tea-things.

"Been anywhere?" Christopher had forgotten that John had not left the room of his own free will.

John could hardly speak.

"No."

He came round the sofa to the hearth, looking down at Christopher. His big legs were thrust out at ease and though he was not smoking the grate was littered with cigarette-ends. He turned a page in the silence. The electric light was burning. John lodged his sister's letter on the mantelpiece.

"That for me?" asked Christopher idly.

John looked at him intently. "No," he said, "it's from my sister." He cleared his throat.

"Sister?" Christopher folded up the magazine and threw it on to the table. "I didn't know you had one. Is she older than you?"

John saw Christopher's teeth as he yawned. "No," he answered quickly. "Jill's only fifteen."

"Sisters are rather a pest." Christopher put his hands behind his head and leaned back. "I've got two myself. But they're older than I am. At home, is she?"

"No, she's away at school."

Something in John's tone made Christopher glance at him: to his surprise, John was looking at him too. They regarded each other blankly. John picked up a half-written sheet of notes he had been making that afternoon and folded it exactly in half. Then he tore it across the fold.

"Fortunately I don't see much of mine," said Christopher, "though a curious thing happened last summer. Do you know London at all?"

"No."

"Well, it was in the bar of rather a decent hotel in Regent Street one night. I was there with Pat and Elizabeth one night. I think the blitz was on, but nobody seemed to be paying much attention to it: anyway, we'd all had a good bit to drink. Then I happened to notice a girl who was standing near with a couple of Polish officers, and she seemed to be staring at me. I thought it was a bit rum, you know, and I thought perhaps I was imagining it, but, no, she looked exactly as if she was going to come across and speak. I thought it was some super-subtle kind of pick-up, you know." John tore the halves into quarters. "Still, she didn't say anything and I forgot about her. Then, just as we were going out, she suddenly came up to me with a sort of half-smile and said 'It *is* Christopher, isn't it?' And it was my sister Constance. I hadn't seen her for—oh, at least two years." He ended in an oddly embarrassed way.

John gave a short laugh. "People used to call us Jack and Jill."

Christopher made a vomiting sound. "Are you much alike, then?"

"We have the same kind of hair, that's all really." The quarters became eighths. "She will be beautiful. I suppose she is now—and clever, cleverer than I am, probably."

"Bore."

"I don't know. It makes it that we can talk and go about together. We went to London last Christmas, for instance, and this summer we took a cottage in Wales."

"What did you do in London?"

"Oh, saw the sights, you know. Westminster Abbey and all those places. Jill wanted to see the British Museum."

"That's more than I've ever done."

"No, I don't suppose I should have gone alone, but Jill wanted to see it."

"See any shows?"

"I don't remember. . . . We hadn't enough money for much of that. But we saw a Shakespeare play—*Twelfth Night* it was."

"I don't remember that being on," said Christopher, frowning. "Where was it—whât theatre?"

"Oh, I couldn't tell you which one. Jill's got the programme somewhere."

"I really don't remember that being on," pondered Christopher. John had a tiny wad of torn paper in his hand now which he could tear no further, so with a careless gesture he shied it at the fireplace, round which it fluttered like confetti round the door of a church.

"Yes," he continued in the authoritative tone he had been using. "Of course, when I say she's clever, I don't mean clever at everything. She's fond of poetry—that line. And it's funny, she's very sensitive. She had a great friend at school called Patsy—Patsy Hammond. They were really awfully thick. Then a year ago she went back to school as usual after the holidays and found that Patsy had gone to America with her people and wasn't coming back again. She was awfully cut up: hardly wrote for weeks. And when she came home again for the holidays, in three months' time, she just wouldn't touch a kind of bran—a breakfast food we had—just because it came from

117

America. She's always liked it, but she's never touched it, as far as I know from that day to this."

"Just because it's American?"

"I know it sounds odd. But she went off America altogether —everything American—films, books, songs. For a time, you know. Gradually she got over that. Her stumbling-block seemed to be this bran stuff."

Christopher took out his cigarettes. "Where did you say she was?"

"At school, in Derbyshire." He accepted one. "Willow Gables the place is called. It's not very big."

Christopher got up and stretched uneasily, then sat down on the leather-padded fender seat. His head hung forward in a dejected way and his hands were stuffed in his pockets.

"My sisters were at a place near Beckenham. It's queer you should have kept up with yours—I never did."

"There's the holidays, of course." John leant against the mantelpiece, staring down at Christopher's averted head. "And anyway, she's only been there two years. That's why she only had this one friend—Patsy Hammond, who went to America."

Christopher nodded. He seemed to be following a private train of thought. "But you do lose touch with your home if you go to school young," he said. "It's a good thing. It teaches independence, teaches you to stand up for yourself, teaches you how to handle people."

John nodded, watching him. He had heard Christopher say all this before.

"But I regret it sometimes, you know. . . . One sort of loses touch. And one doesn't get a second chance, ever. And we're a pretty rackety family. . . ."

He laid his cigarette in an ashtray and let it burn, staring down at the fire. John saw with gathering amazement that he had said something that made Christopher envious of him— only for this moment, perhaps, but none the less envious. There was a disturbed tone in his voice and even as John watched him, he slowly withdrew his left hand from his pocket, full of money, saying:

"I owe you a quid, don't I?"

118

"Yes," said John wonderingly.

"I'm paying about seven-and-six in the pound at the moment." He grinned and turned the coins over, selecting two half-crowns, a shilling, a sixpence and six pennies. "Here, will that do to be going on with?"

"Thank you." John looked at it and made an effort to count it. "Thirteen to come, isn't that right?"

"Count your blessings," said Christopher with an enormous yawn, pushing the rest of the money back into his pocket. "Here, jumping Jesus, I'd forgotten. What about that essay? I said I'd go to the flicks tonight."

"Mine's on the desk."

"That's awfully white of you, old man. Thanks a lot. I'd clean forgotten."

He sat down at the desk and spread the sheets of paper out, switching on the reading lamp with a careless movement. John was content to be ignored, for he was astonished, both at his lies and at their effect. And they had affected him no less than Christopher: he was excited, filled with tentative little lyrical thoughts, like the mutterings of the orchestra before the overture to an opera. He was not surprised at himself for telling lies, but for telling them so easily: it almost seemed that they had been made up long before it occurred to him to utter them, and the mystery of this kept him silent for a while, wondering that lies could be made up in a dark corner of the mind long before the occasion that called them out arrived. How long had they lain there?

And what were they, that they should have thrown a temporary net around even Christopher? He still trembled from the physical effort of telling them, but so early as this he could touch on the overheard conversation of the afternoon and find that it had in some way grown removed from its first agonizing closeness. Everything indeed seemed altered, as if he had ignorantly twisted his tongue round a magic formula and was watching the world change before his eyes.

Christopher did not get back from the cinema until nearly eleven, but he found John still sitting up when he came in, lying

119

in an armchair without a book. He was ravenously hungry and, taking a half-eaten loaf from the cupboard, hacked a huge slice off and smothered it with marmalade. Munching, he came round and sat on the sofa, beginning to unlace his shoes.

"Watching you do that", said John amusedly, "reminds me of the holiday I spent with Jill in Wales. Girls are funny, you know. At home, she's the last person to have anything to do with housework: you can hardly get her to do a hand's turn. But put her down alone in a cottage and she'll suddenly change into a perfect housewife. Many a time she made me spread a table-cloth or a newspaper when I wanted to cut some bread. Girls seem to take to that sort of thing by instinct as ducks take to water: as soon as we got there she was scouting round everywhere finding out what we'd got—and what we hadn't got, too, which was far more important." He coughed and went on speaking in an authoritative voice. "It was nice down there. Every evening after we'd washed up and lit the lamps (we'd no electricity, of course) we used to sit and read. At first we tried reading Shakespeare aloud, taking the parts, you know, but Jill said it reminded her too much of school, so we dropped that. We used to burn that funny Welsh coal that miners use —it burns without a flame, you know, and lasts all night, just glowing. We'd sit and read till quite late."

"Oh, yes," said Christopher uninterestedly. He threw his shoes over to the door and got up: watching the film had made his eyes tired, and the late nights he had been keeping made him disinclined to stay up purposelessly.

John lingered, putting Christopher's shoes together with his own tidily by the door for the servant to clean in the morning, and hanging up Christopher's scarf. The rain outside had stopped. Then he went to bed, lying wakeful in the dark and listening resentfully to Christopher's heaving breathing, that was on the borderline of a snore. It oppressed him to have this other person so close. From next door came the sound of a piano; there was a rich young man there who played at all hours. John listened. He felt himself spun out very fine along the slender line of notes. The music was slow, with a logical sadness.

Jill came into his mind, as now she would (though he did not know this yet) whenever his emotions were stirred gently. He imagined that it was she playing the piano that he could hear and that they both lived in a big house with gardens. He was on the lawn in the evening; the lawn was in shadow and the sun was so low in the sky that it only caught the attic windows. The colours of the flowers and the striped deckchairs that were still left out had grown indistinct. There was a pile of chipped red flower-pots by the greenhouse. The sound of the piano came out of a large downstairs room, where the windows were open, and he walked towards them, feeling the air to be palpable as if walking on the bed of a transparent sea. He could see her sitting at the piano dressed in white. She bent her head slightly to see the music and her shoulders moved as she played. Her fair hair was controlled with a ribbon; her arms, her whole body, were so slender that the bones showed through softly.

For a time he would be content to watch and listen. But after a while she would draw the curtains and he would go into the house.

The first thing John did after breakfast the next morning was to take his sister's letter out of its envelope and burn it.

He had the idea while lying in bed that morning that if he left a letter from Jill lying about Christopher might surreptitiously read it, and his hold over him (if it really existed) thereby increase. So naturally the letter must be written. He settled himself at the desk: the rain fell outside, splashing the windows and because the sky was so dark and troubled he wrote by lamplight.

It was curious that he felt no hesitancy about what to write. True, he made several drafts, but that was because he found it hard to imitate his sister's hand from the single addressed envelope. It was cramped, like his own, and might suggest immaturity if subtly coarsened. He worked intently, like an

121

etcher or forger, his feet locked together and his hair shining in the electric light. Christopher was lounging in bed in the other room.

When he had finished he wiped his hands on his trousers and grinned.

Willow Gables School,
Nr. Mallerton,
Derbyshire.

Dear John,
You said you would write to me, but of course you haven't, you never do. So I am writing to you instead, so mind you answer.

How are you getting on? Tell me everything about your college and the rooms you have; what work you're doing (remember the bet we made); who your tutor is, do I know him and what's he like? I long to Know All. Give me plenty of details because Maisie Fenton's got a brother at Cambridge and is being just insufferable about him. Still, you don't know Maisie Fenton. (Lucky you!)

I really haven't any news for you; this place is as usual—need I say more? I came top in English this fortnight (pom-tiddly-om-pom) and intend to do so for the rest of the term for reasons which are Secret.

When do your holidays start? Before ours, I expect—for a change!

Much love,
Jill.

P.S.—We're going to some incredible concert thing in Manchester, so I shall post this there if poss. I really don't trust the school box any more after what happened last term. . . .
P.P.S.—It's raining. No hockey!

He had just finished copying the last draft when he heard Christopher getting up, so, carelessly stuffing it into the original envelope, he put it on to the mantelpiece and strolled out. As rain was falling he made for the Junior Common Room, where he sat down in a deep leather armchair and pulled out his battered packet of cigarettes. As he smoked he read an article in the newspaper about the promised British aid to Greece.

122

Outside, in the Fellows' Garden, the trees were heaving in the wind, almost bare of their leaves. Another undergraduate kneeled in the window seat to look out; he had a very finely-made head and black hair. As he stared from the tall windows he slipped a ring off one finger and put it on another. John wondered vaguely who he was: his face was agreeable to look at.

John threw the newspaper aside and took up a magazine: the fire warmed his legs and he stretched them out. He was hardly conscious of the contentment he felt. All of a sudden there seemed nothing to do, nothing but the certain fact that this day would open into another equally empty day, only the soft pattering of the rain on ancient stones. The firelight shone on the brass ashtrays and on certain dark panels. He felt he had been very foolish to trouble overmuch about Christopher Warner; he ceased to long that he himself could order servants about confidently, that he was rich, that he had a blue chin, that he sang dirty songs in his bath. These were very fine things, but they were losing their lustre as ideals. He yawned.

He had made tiny pencil marks around the corners of the envelope where it lay on the mantelpiece, and when he returned to the room he found Christopher had gone and the letter was tucked neatly behind the clock. He caught his breath for a moment, then he remembered the servant came into dust the room in the mornings sometimes and certainly Christopher would never have put it away so tidily. He took it down and after a second's thought laid it diagonally upon the table. It stayed there throughout the day; John shifted its position about tea-time, but Christopher was out all the evening and John went to bed quite early, feeling a drowsiness that was rare with him. Normally at night he was tired, but not pleasantly somnolent.

He did not hear about Christopher and Semple's cupboard till the next day, when Whitbread asked him up to coffee after lunch with a few other scholars. They were a queer little bunch, but John liked being with them and he felt keenly the prestige of being the man who had to share with Warner. They assembled in Whitbread's garret-like room, pulling forward the sofa and straight-backed chairs, leaving the armchair, which was nearest to the fire, for Whitbread himself. None of them would ever take the best armchair in the room or help himself to any foodstuffs without asking or accept an invitation he did not intend to return. All their actions were characterized by this scrupulous convention, and there, up in the little dingy room where Whitbread was assembling cups and saucers and milk, they collected like members of some persecuted sect, as if alien to the life around them. There was no luxury or waste or freedom in their company, and yet John was probably more at home with them than with anyone else, though he did not value their friendship. He was very careful not to show this latter, however, as the one thing they all heartily detested was anyone "of their own class" "trying to get above himself".

"Technically, it's criminal assault. It is, you know, legally."

"The Dean should do something."

"I don't care who hears me say it," said Whitbread, putting a plate of buns he had bought for yesterday's tea on the table. "It's just guttersnipe hooliganism, that's all it is."

"What is?"

"Why, haven't you heard? Warner and Semple. D'you mean to say you haven't heard? I sh'd have thought——"

"I sh'd have thought you'd 'ave been the first to hear," said Jackson, with a laugh. "I sh'd think Warner's pretty proud of himself."

"I've hardly seen Chris today," John explained carelessly. "What's he done?"

"Why, you know Semple? Fellow who goes round tryin' to make you join the Oxford Union. Well, he lives next door to Dowling—you know that fellow——"

"Yes, well?"

"Well, last night Warner and Dowling came in a bit tiddly, you know. They'd had one over the eight——"

"More like five or six," interjected another scholar with a grin.

"—and Semple's suddenly woken up by a tremendous crash. He gets up and finds Warner and Dowling in his sitting-room,

124

beginning to break it up. All his china smashed and all. And when he asks them what they're up to, Warner knocks him down. Just that."

"Haven't you seen Semple's eye?" asked Jackson.

"That does sound a bit——"

"A bit! I sh'd like to know what he thinks he's doing. It's just rank hooliganism, that's all. A fellow like that reckons he owns the earth."

There was an air of hesitant agreement over the company caused by the unadmitted fear that John might report all he heard when he left. But John had no such intention. Studying the tea-leaves at the bottom of his cup ("coffee", with Whitbread, very often turned into tea by a majority vote), he was thrilling to the anecdote and delighting in the contrast of the two worlds he inhabited. Whatever one might think of Christopher Warner, he could not be neglected; one could not pass over these sporadic flowerings of violence. That night he was privileged to hear Christopher and Patrick (chiefly Christopher) relate the story to Eddy after dinner. Christopher had handed out sherry glasses filled with port and was standing on the hearthrug waving a cigarette.

"Well, it all started with us getting back after we left you, Eddy, and going up to Patrick's room because Patrick said he'd got some bread. Not that dry bread is a meal for a man who's had no food since lunch-time—but I was prepared," Christopher said emphatically, "I was prepared to waive that point provided that the bread was forthcoming, so I sat down, and Pat here dragged out a pretty mouldy-looking hunk and cut it in half. One half he bit, the other half he put on a plate and handed to me. Now, mark you, I was devilish sharp set. I was in no mood to quibble about trifles: I was not, shall we say, in a finical mood. But I was just opening my mouth when I noticed what looked to me like mouse-turd on the bread. 'I say, Pat,' I said, d'you keep your bread in a tin?' 'No,' he said, with his mouth full. 'Well, look at that, you rat! Is that fit to offer a guest?' I was aggrieved. I didn't take it in good part. I don't consider myself fussy," said Christopher, with a grandiloquent air, "but there are certain rules, certain laws of hospitality, you

125

know, which I will stand out for till I perish. And one of these is that no man shall offer his guest bread with mouse-turd on it."

"My dear Chris, how was I to know——"

"However, we'll pass over that," continued Christopher, waving the interruption aside. "I was more than compensated by the sight of Pat spitting out his mouthful into the fire. But the nub of the matter was clear to me at once. I was still hungry. I'd had nothing to eat since lunch-time, and then only a couple of pies in the Bull. And apparently this mouse-turd was the only damned thing available!

"Things were grim. Still, I did not, mark you, lose heart. It takes more than a mouse to get a Warner down. I got up and went out into the corridor, where, I may parenthetically state, I proceeded to micturate. Then I knocked at someone's door. They said, 'Come in,' so I came in. There was some little runt working. 'Have you', I said politely, 'any bread-and-butter, toast or cake?' He went as red as a turkey and said, 'No.' I bowed gracefully and went out. Then I fumbled along to the next door. When I opened this one, the room was in darkness, so I concluded that the man was either in bed or still out, and I put on the light and prepared to investigate his cupboard. Now this is the most curious part of the whole business," said Christopher impressively. "I went up to that cupboard. I pulled at the door in a sober and sensible way and the whole bloody thing came toppling over forward, very near maiming me for life!"

"Ha, ha, ha!" roared Eddy, slobbering.

"Well, of course, that made a row. I defy anyone to pull over a damn great cupboard without making the devil of a din, and as luck would have it, the man was in bed. At least, he pretty quickly got up and came out into the sitting-room. He was sporting rather an offensive line in blue-and-white pyjamas, I may add, but I decided to let that pass. 'What the hell are you up to?' he demanded. Now I admit," said Christopher, stabbing the air with his cigarette precisely, "I admit that he had, to a certain extent, right on his side. To find one's cupboard over-turned by a perfect stranger in what must have appeared the

126

middle of the night might conceivably be a shade trying, so I overlooked his tone. 'I'm sorry,' I said. 'As a matter of fact, old man, I was wondering if you had any toast, bread-and-butter or cake handy—you see I've had no dinner——' And I never got any further. It was incredible. There was something in what I said—or perhaps even in the way I said it, though, mark you, I spoke in as gentlemanly a manner as I could—there was something, anyway, that seemed to infuriate him. Plainly something had got under his skin. He burst out into a positive torrent of insults. 'Get out!' he said"—Christopher made a histrionic flourish—"'Get out! I'm sick of your noisy, boozing gang. How dare you come into my room and start breaking everything you can lay your hands on?' And so on and so forth, though I must say I offered to pay for any cups that were cracked or broken.

"But after a while—he didn't slacken, you know: he seemed to warm to his work rather—after a while I began to take offence. He was being just plain bad-mannered, you know: wasn't swearing, just being plain rude. I didn't like his tone. I told him so. I said: 'I don't like your tone.' He told me I could do the other thing. Well, I wasn't going to stand that," said Christopher, in a reasonable tone of voice. "After all, one will only stand so much, and I thought this had got beyond a joke. So I slapped his face—and as luck would have it, I just caught the edge of his spectacles and they went *flying*"—Christopher illustrated the arc—"flying right over to the corner of the room. And he came at me like a tiger. Like a bloody tiger. We sparred for an opening"—Christopher made ludicrous sparring movements across the hearthrug—"then I hit him in the eye. And he went down."

"And stayed down," finished Patrick.

Christopher drank off his glass of port while Eddy mopped his eyes with a gaily-coloured silk handkerchief. "Oh, lord!" he gurgled. "Damn good, Chris! Damn good!" In fact he liked the story so much that when Semple complained to the Dean and Christopher had to pay three pounds damages, he and some friends of his caught Semple unawares and "crucified" him with croquet hoops over his wrists, ankles and neck on the

127

College lawn. This caused a great stir, as Semple lay wriggling on the lawn all night and caught bronchitis, but both Christopher and Patrick had been provably out of College that night and obviously had nothing to do with it. Semple went home and with proper care presumably recovered health.

John basked in all this violence as he would in a hot climate. He was excited and admired Christopher without envying him. The week passed unnoticed and when Christopher poked irritably about for John's essay on the night before their weekly tutorial, John had to confess with a start that he hadn't touched it yet. Christopher took his hand out of his pocket with an incredulous movement.

"Not touched it?"

"No, I'm afraid I really. . . . It's all right, I can cut to-morrow——"

"Can you, hell!"

Christopher approached so that his face came within the immediate circle of the lamp. His expression would have been the same had he detected John in an effort to swindle him out of some money.

"Come on, play the game," he said, in a threatening voice. "What am I going to do?"

John knocked a pencil against his cheek, still smiling, still unable to grasp that the situation was serious."

"Oh, you can hash up something. . . ."

"Look here, Kemp." Christopher's voice was ,harsh now. "This isn't good enough, ratting like this. Don't be a louse."

His broad shoulders filled the light and John, like a swimmer rebreaking the surface after a dive, awoke to fear again. He saw Christopher's face as Semple must have seen it, tightening to deliver a blow. He began talking quickly:

"All right, give me time. What was the subject? I'll have it done by ten. If I work tonight I can get it done by ten."

"Ten? That's damn late," said Christopher, nevertheless backing away from him again.

It took John some time to get the incident into perspective, by which time he had written the essay and Christopher, having been too lazy to copy it, had himself cut the tutorial. It revived in him the memory of the conversation he had overheard. He grew angry with himself and with Christopher. Where there had been indifference to him, there was now resentment. Tears pricked his eyes because he had no means of retaliation—only Jill. He wondered dubiously if that trick would ever work again. The letter had lain around the room for several days, but though John examined it periodically he never found the slightest sign that it had been tampered with. On the evening of the Friday, while Christopher was changing his shirt in front of the fire before dinner, John said ostentatiously, "I suppose I shall have to answer Jill's letter some time," and began to write. "Dear Jill," he wrote. He bit his pen, flushing awkwardly, acutely conscious of the soft sounds of Christopher dressing behind him.

Dear Jill,

Thank you for your letter.

You ask for details—I wish you could be here and see for yourself: it is really impossible for me to tell you everything about this place, and you would enjoy seeing it much more.

He paused again. Christopher had gone into the bedroom to choose a necktie.

I haven't got used to the fact yet that I'm really-and-truly here. Every time I put on my big black gown I feel an indefinable "frisson" at being a life-size member of Oxford University.

Somehow this was wrong. He started a fresh paragraph.

Nobody does any work here—we all live like lords. I can tell you, I often think of you sweating—(he crossed this word out and substituted "swotting")—*away at all your "favourite" subjects while I lounge about here condescending to do perhaps a couple of hours between getting up and going to bed. What do we all do? We are kings in our nutshell. It is so pleasant simply to exist, to breathe the air, to inspect the architecture, to walk beneath the trees, to see the sky reflected in puddles. One could spend a whole morning walking the length of one street—High Street, for instance: "The High," as we call it here. It runs from the centre of the town. . . .*

He broke off and started another fresh paragraph.

First the tobacconists, with their crested tobacco jars, exotic brands of cigarettes, pipes, little wooden bowls heaped with special blends. Then the music shops, with rows of sound-proof cabinets where one is allowed to spend hours playing selections of the most esoteric records. Then the tailors—such tailors!— whose windows are invariably full of bedragoned silk dressing-gowns, velvet waistcoats with brass buttons, flowery ties, fleecy gloves, where one can linger for twenty minutes turning over, say, a selection of bow-ties, choosing one that takes your fancy. Then the bookshops, that sell old prints for hanging in your rooms, as well as all manner of old and new volumes, the old ones rich in their age, the new ones crisp and . . .

But above all this, there is a continual parade of fresh buildings as you progress down towards the river. All Souls', St. Mary's Church, University College, the Examination Schools, Queen's, until you come to Magdalen at the bottom, the last and best. . . .

He tore this second sheet off and turned it over.

As a scholar, one has a certain standing and certain privileges, but also certain obligations towards the less gifted members of the community. Poor Christopher, for instance, with whom I share these rooms, is pathetically dependent on me for his weekly essay. I don't know how you write essays, but I find I tend to plan them out in my head beforehand almost word for word. Yesterday it was after tea and I still hadn't made the least sign of putting pen to paper, so he began to get restless. "Look here, what about that essay?" "Yes, yes, in an hour or so, I haven't thought out the ending yet.' 'Come off it, damn the ending, I want some solid dope!" "My dear Christopher, you shall have it by ten o'clock." "Ten! But I shall be drunk by then!" I pointed out that that was his affair and not mine. To cut a long story a trifle shorter, I drew a line under the last paragraph just as ten was booming out from Tom Tower, and shortly afterwards in stumbled Christopher, fuddled as usual, hiccoughing "Where's 'at essay?" I pushed it across to him, and while pretending to continue reading my essays of Montaigne, watched him covertly as he spelt it out line by line.

When he had finished the first page, he pulled out his fountain pen and then fell asleep. I read for another half-hour, then "turned in", leaving him sleeping at the table like a child. In consequence, he had to "cut" the tutorial this morning and has just received a very sarcastic note from our tutor. . . .

As he reached the end of the page John looked round: the room, to his surprise, was empty. The hands of the clock had fallen to nearly twenty-five past seven: Christopher had taken his gown and gone to dinner. John opened his mouth slightly as panic at missing a meal struggled to control him and failed. He looked at what he had written, correcting a spelling mistake, then added hastily at the bottom:

> *Much love,*
> *John.*

He found an envelope from the drawer and addressed it to:

> *Miss Jill——*

His pen hung over the word "Kemp". He did not like it. He did not, he found, want to connect her with himself in that way. What should he call her? After a moment he finished it:

> *Miss Jill Bradley.*

Bradley was a nice name, it was English, it was like saddle-leather and stables.

> *Miss Jill Bradley,*
> *Willow Gables School,*
> *Nr. Mallerton,*
> *Derbyshire.*

When he had stuck down the flap and put a stamp on, he went out to post it without a hat, coat or scarf. The night was very dark and a huge warm wind whooped boisterously around the streets, streaming out his silky hair, pulling at the letter in his hand. He was trembling when he dropped it into a pillar-box, and leant against the wall a moment, filled with exultation at the idea of thus speaking with nothingness. He envisaged the

131

envelope wandering around England, collecting pencilled
scribbles of suggestions on the front and back until, perhaps a
year or more hence, it came to rest in some dusty corner of a
dead-letter office. How many years would it stay there? Till he,
perhaps, had changed out of all knowing.

He must write again, write dozens of them: dozens of letters
to Miss Jill Bradley must wander through the postal service.

When he got back to the College he forgot he had not eaten,
and sat down and wrote her another letter. This one was about
the incident of his china-crate, which he described untruly:

*I can't say I found any difficulty in making friends here: the
very first afternoon I got here I found an abortive tea party
hanging about in my rooms.*

(They had become "his" rooms; he did not share with anyone now.)

*There were Chris Warner and the two Dowlings (the girl
attractive in a cheap kind of way), an awful ass called Eddy and
another quiet nondescript called Hugh Stanning-Smith, and they
were all wondering what to do about tea. They didn't much want
to go out, because it was late, and they didn't really know where
to go, yet there was nothing in College except bread and milk
and tea and so forth—they had no crocks of any description. So
I was able to play Lord Bountiful and unpack all my new stuff, and
everyone was happy and went away fed. Since then I have been
relatively popular! In any case, it's not every freshman who
holds a tea-party on his very first day in College. . . .*

But at this point, quite unexpectedly, his brain would not
work any more; he could not keep up the run of incidents. He
put the sheet carefully away and stretched himself out on the
sofa. How drowsily content he felt. The warmth of the fire, the
quiet night that rested all around, the complete absence of
worry from his life combined as if to rock him to sleep. He
smoked the last of the packet of cigarettes he had bought on
that sunny Monday morning just over a week ago, and fell
asleep where he lay.

On the next morning after breakfast he went out into the

132

windy, sunny town and bought a large pad of writing paper and a packet of envelopes. The girl gave him wrong change, but he did not notice.

For the next few days in November, he spent most of his time sitting writing in his room, lounging on the sofa or sitting upright at the desk by the window. He wrote slowly, but with ease, covering many double-sided sheets and occasionally folding three or four up and posting them. Often he forgot about mealtimes and failed to appear in the Hall; later he would feel hungry and buy some bread from the College kitchens, hurrying back to his room to eat it and to start a fresh letter. He did not write with any set plan, roving from one thing to another instinctively, describing, relating, falsifying, yet giving on the whole every detail of his four weeks at the University. It was surprising how little he had forgotten. "I was too excited to eat on the journey," he told her, "and when one at last arrives, one is content to stand back and watch the motley crowd pushing for taxis, they are all so unlike any people one has ever seen before." The only incident of importance he passed over was Mrs. Warner's visit; but "The tradespeople are awfully decent when it comes to dealing with the University," he wrote in another letter. "If you haven't the small change to pay for a meal, for instance, you can just sign the bill and pay another time. I have done this often."

Of course, all this had to be kept from Christopher, which because of Christopher's natural incuriousness was not difficult. That Christopher had been the mainspring of the idea had long been obscured.

In the intervals of correspondence he went out for walks round the town, unplanned walks that were merely confined for the most part to the streets. He had grown accustomed to the buildings and did not bother about them any longer: on some afternoons he pénetrated out on to the towpath by the river, watching the continual movement of the sky and the wind on the water, and the swans on the water speeding out of the way of a practising crew, and the grey water breaking in little waves against the banks. He wore his blue overcoat, and indeed was dressed identically as when he had arrived at the beginning of the term. But the expression on his face had changed: before, it had been strained and mistrustful; now, it was relieved and dull. He looked much younger.

At last he began a letter he did not finish. "The other night," he had written,

. . . we came out of the Bull into the dark when Eddy had one of his boring fits of bravado, during which he keeps badgering one to dare him to do something. In the end I said: All right, Eddy, go into the Union there and smash the first glass door you see. All right, he said, and straightway disappeared into porch. None of us had the least idea he'd be crazy enough to do it, but just as we were assuring each other that he'd come out in the end with his tail between his legs, there came the most fearsome sound of breaking glass. (The Union, as I dare say you know, is a seedy Gothic place full of decayed clergymen.) "Holy smoke," ejaculates Christopher, and legs it, closely followed by Patrick and Hugh. I stayed behind to see the fun. Out rushes Eddy: "Come on, for God's sake," he gasped. "Were you seen?" I demanded. "No —but they'll all be out——" Before we could budge half a dozen young men in evening dress came pelting out and up to us they come. "That way!" I cry, pointing with my walking-stick up the dark road where the footfalls of the retreating trio were still faintly audible, and off they go, uttering threatening whoops. Eddy laughed himself sick, and declared I'd saved his life.

But I often wonder why I don't stay in more and read by the fire—do you know, the coal-scuttles here hold nearly a hundred-weight, and we often empty one during a day. Not like the miner's coal! Do you remember how it used to burn down to that glowing mass—and do you remember how if you held a piece of paper over the long glass mantle of the lamp, it would burst into flames? And how your hair nearly caught one night? I often wish——

It was at that point he broke off, with a slight frown, and took a piece of dry bread to chew. After some minutes he added:

—that we were still there, with you sitting in the basket chair——

and then halted again. He got up, wandered round the room;

134

stood idly making bread pellets and flicking them at the photograph of Mrs. Warner, then made up the fire. These sudden pauses were quite usual, but this time he felt that he had reached some insuperable barrier that it was unlikely he could remove. After twenty minutes or so, during which he scribbled faces on the margin of the letter, he put the sheets away and went out into the dark gardens, walking up and down the pitch-black great lawn.

The next day he tried again, even starting again on a fresh sheet, but he could manage nothing but a few scanty reminiscences of their holiday in Wales. Softly, as if in doing so he had given a cursory rub to some old portrait to which the dust was clinging thickly, her face was glowing in his mind. He lay back, surprised, in his chair. It seemed that he had never thought of her before. It was as if he had been talking to her from a public telephone-box, talking interminably, and then had looked up to see her listening in the next compartment, smiling at him through the glass with the receiver held to her ear.

"You——" he began, then broke off again. That sheet he tore up.

Suddenly it was she who was important, she who was interesting, she whom he longed to write about; beside her, he and his life seemed dusty and tedious. With every half-hour that he thought about her, her image grew clearer in his mind: she was fifteen, and slight, her long fine dark honey-coloured hair fell to her shoulders and was bound with a white ribbon. Her dress was white. Her face was not like Elizabeth's, coarse for all its make-up, but serious-looking, delicate in shape and beautiful in repose, with high cheekbones: when she laughed, these cheekbones were most noticeable and her expression became almost savage.

She was a hallucination of innocence: he liked to think of her as preoccupied only with simple untroublesome things, like examinations and friendships, and, as he thought, each minute seemed to clarify her, as if the picture of her had been stacked away waiting in his mind, covered with dust, until this should

135

happen. He spent hours filling up sheets of writing paper not with letters now, but with her address and name, repeated at all angles in different hands (some intended to be her own) and hesitant attempts to draw her face. But he soon stopped this last activity, because every line he drew merely obscured the picture in his own mind, and he had to stop and wait for it to reform.

Under these circumstances it was quite impossible to continue writing to her, and the unfinished letter he sealed up in an envelope and then burnt. Yet he was not content. He began writing about her in the third person, about how she sat playing the piano in the evening, then tore it up. Then he wrote about her getting up in the morning, and tore that up. At last he began to put down what he had told Christopher in the first place, and, page by page, covered with erasures, he managed to evolve a continuous narrative about her; awkwardly, incompetently, he began to build her up outside his life, by describing her own. It was much easier, for all that, than continuing to write the letters: he found his invention put out more flowers than he had expected.

When he had finished it, it was a kind of short story: he had not begun to write with any idea of what the finished product should be, for he had no idea of how writing was done; but on the evening he completed it, he sat down after dinner and copied it all out once more, changing words here and there and correcting mistakes in the spelling.

I

Jill (the story began) would not leap out of the train as soon as it stopped and crowd to the barriers, and she disliked all the girls who did. They were all dressed like herself, in black hats with maroon, blue and white ribands, this annoyed her, too.

When she had adjusted her hat in the glass, deliberately, she stepped to the door and tugged at it.

Heavens! It wouldn't open!

She struggled and tugged, growing red in the face and afraid she would be carried on to Lord knows where.

A bushy-mouthed porter in shirt-sleeves came to her rescue, pulling the door open with a superhuman jerk, and saying:

"There y'are, missy!"

Jill did not like being called missy, and hated not only the porter, but the whole business of returning to school. She put on her blue woollen gloves and handed her ticket over to the ticket collector. Except for one girl who had been sick, she was the last one off the train. This meant that the school omnibus, which stood outside like a patient beast of burden, was full, or nearly full, when she reached it. This was to take them all on the last stage of the journey back to Willow Gables, for the second term of the school year: Christmas lay behind them, and the day was in January, a cold one.

She halted uncertainly. Miss Keen called to her from inside the bus:

"Come along, Jill. There's room here."

Wearily she climbed aboard the 'bus, shaking as cases were dumped on the roof, and sat down between Maisie Fenton and Joy Roberts. She disliked Maisie more than Joy: Maisie was a small dark spaniel-like girl.

" 'Lo, Jill."

" 'Lo, Jill."

"Hallo."

"Decent Christmas?"

"Oh, tolerable, thanks."

"We had a marvellous time," said Maisie Fenton eagerly. "Just ate and played games and slept. Mummy seemed to have thought of marvellous new ways of doing everything."

She went on to tell them how a company of public school cadets had camped near their house, and how her father had known the master in charge and how some of the boys had come to their Boxing Day party.

Jill had not had as good a time as Maisie, but pretended she

137

had. She hated Maisie, and envied her, and hated herself for envying her.

And now the driver started the engine with a shuddering roar: Miss Keen climbed aboard once more, banged her head, but shouted sweetly:

"All in?"

They started, amid delighted squeals. "Off at last!"

Out of the window Jill could see nothing but the frozen fields that the lane ran through, the tangled ditches, the scraps of snow. She had not gone away to school till she was fourteen and even now disliked it. They passed barns with auctioneer's posters half torn down where they had been pasted, a sign-post pointing only one way, a plough standing behind a hedge.

She could hear Miss Keen talking indulgently with the girls who sat beside her:

"So what did you do, then, Phyllis? . . ."

"How perfectly dreadful."

For some reason this irritated her, as did the tradition of raising a cheer as the 'bus turned into the school gates. Jill's spirits sank lower and lower: she was as familiar with the routine as an old convict is familiar with the routine of entering prison.

At the end of the drive was the school, with a stone fountain before it, choked with leaves.

II

"Have you seen Patsy Hammond?"

"No, I haven't."

Jill's face wore a serious expression for she was growing worried. It was nearly an hour later, and she could not find Patsy Hammond, her special friend. Nobody had seen her.

Patsy was indeed Jill's only friend. They were roughly the same age and had each been new girls in the fourth form, which was rather late to enter the school. Patsy was smaller than Jill, with a pale, doleful face, dark hair and expressive hands, and could make Jill sick with laughing. She could imitate almost

138

anybody. Together they had formed an alliance against the rest of the world.

And now Patsy could not be found. Jill had looked in the dormitory, the form-room and the day-room—and nobody had seen her. It seemed that she had not yet arrived, which was queer because she usually came before Jill did. Jill had a feeling of suspense, tinged with alarm. Perhaps she was ill.

"Have you seen Patsy Hammond?"

Joan Carter hadn't.

Wandering along the corridor she met Pat Reynolds, who was the head of the Fifth.

"Hallo, Jill. Decent hols?"

"Scrumptious, thanks, Pat. . . . I say, you haven't seen Patsy, have you?"

"Patsy Hammond? Is she coming back?"

"What?"

"Well, Matron seemed to think not." It was like Pat to call her Matron instead of Rummy. "I don't know."

There was nearly ten minutes before the tea bell would ring and Jill dashed along to the Matron's room, where Rummy sat at her table, surrounded by girls who liked her. She had a jolly, red face and wore gold-rimmed spectacles. Her table was covered with letters and certificates.

"Hallo, Jill. Had a good Christmas?"

"Oh, yes, thanks. I say, Matron——"

"M'm?"

She was nervous because the twelve other girls in the room were all listening.

"Is—is Patsy Hammond coming back this term?"

"Why, no. Her father's gone to America and the whole family's gone with him. Patsy'll go to school in America. Didn't she tell you?"

"No. . . ."

The little gas fire made a faint whine as it burned.

"Oh, didn't she? I thought you two were great pals."

"Oh, I knew she might go . . . I wasn't certain." Jill pulled herself together and began trying to lie. "I knew it was possible. . . ."

As she backed out of the room she suspected a faint titter, and one of them whispered, "*Sic transit* a beautiful friendship." Jill heard her and blushed crimson. That sentence foreshadowed the mocking amusement that would greet their parting. People had always regarded their exclusive friendship with faint hostility.

She walked blindly down the passage, beginning to cry. This made her cross with herself, and she stooped, pretending to tie a shoelace, trying to control her sobbing. Then the bell rang and the passage was filled with girls, clattering, chattering; they knocked against her and one nearly pushed her over.

"Tell you later."

"Sit by me."

"Don't *run* in the corridors. *Walk.*"

When they had all passed, she rose and followed them into the dining-room where tea was laid. Her first paroxysm of tears had ended, leaving her calm with the calm of desperate unhappiness.

III

She had been betrayed, she felt, and half her misery was due to that feeling, but in addition there was the more lasting pain of having lost Patsy. Neither of them had liked being at school: they were girls who found it unpleasant simply to sit in a class and be able to be asked a question. Jill lived entirely on the defensive except when she was with Patsy: that was the only time she could expand and be herself again. Now Patsy had gone and she was quite alone.

How *could* she have gone like that?

Her form mates, when they took any notice of her, made amused comments because they thought her stuck-up: if she was made a fool of in class, there was no one to console her afterwards; there was no one to sit by at meals and discuss the food with, no one to wait for in the corridor. And it was no use trying to feel splendid and alone when being alone made you miserable.

Even the mistresses noticed her:

140

"That Bradley child, always moping about."

Being alone made her look out for someone else who was lonely, and this was when she first noticed Minerva Strachey. Minerva Strachey was a Sixth Form girl, and a prefect, and supposed to be very clever. She had a small study to herself, which was unusual, most studies being shared by two or three girls. Jill had never noticed her till one morning the Head-mistress announced that Minerva Strachey had won a University scholarship, and in accordance with tradition had asked for a "half". Everybody clapped, glad to prolong prayers and excited by the novelty, staring round open-mouthed towards the back to try to see her. This Jill refused to do.

It was not until later that she discovered who the girl was when by the notice-board one Sixth-former called out:

"Congratulations, Minerva!"

"Thanks," said a low voice, and turning in curiosity Jill saw a dark slender girl with books under her arm walking away towards the studies. The girl who had spoken first waited till she was out of hearing, and then remarked to a friend:

"*Toujours* the lone wolf."

Jill, suddenly excited, took a couple of steps after her and then stopped; it would not be proper for her to approach Minerva. But her interest was aroused and she kept a look-out for her.

She noticed that Minerva hardly ever attended any classes, but spent her time working alone in the library. How clever she must be! When she was not working, she went for solitary walks or sat reading in her room. There was no one with whom she seemed particular friendly.

She was not pretty, but Jill decided her face was "interesting". It was oval and pale, with very dark blue eyes; her expression was grave without being in the least stodgy. Jill noticed that she never "moped about", for all her loneliness; she simply went her own way, quietly and pleasantly, making no demands on anyone. Jill felt with a rush that she wanted to be like her.

"To look at Minerva", she told herself extravagantly, "is like reading a page by a Stoic philosopher."

141

One day Minerva left one of her notebooks behind in the library, and Jill found it and read it eagerly. She practised Minerva's signature till she could do it perfectly, and read all the essays and notes Minerva had made on literature:

Thus we see that in creating the character of Shylock, Shakespeare's original intention was deflected, and instead of a comic money-lender he produced a figure of tragic significance.

For days Jill tried to nerve herself to give it back to her and thus to part with it, and in the end she handed it in to the English mistress, who promised to give it to Minerva herself. She privately supposed Jill was too lazy to do so.

Jill could imitate Minerva's handwriting, her bearing and the way she folded her hands, but it was all of no avail. Minerva's remote indifference she could not capture. If she failed to construe a sentence rightly, her cheeks burned, and she hated both the mistress and herself.

All she could do was to watch for Minerva at the end of school, and look up sometimes from the dusk in the playground to see the light burning in her room.

IV

She measured everyone, including herself, by the standard of Minerva, and found them all wanting. The girls in her form seemed strident and lumpish, and, despite all her resolutions, she felt impelled to quarrel with them. She was unable to ignore them as Minerva would. Particularly she disliked a plump, jolly girl called Rosalie Marston, who was the centre of a group of casual acquaintances that formed the third estate of the fifth.

There was no reason why she should find Rosalie irritating: she was good-natured, friendly in a cursory way, shallow, but good-hearted. She had fluffy hair, excellent white teeth set a trifle wide apart, and eternal ink stains on her fingers. It seemed she could not touch a pen without getting inky.

Among her friends were several spiteful girls whom Rosalie was too dense or too casual to dislike.

Jill often imagined herself quarrelling with Rosalie, but never

142

thought it would ever really happen. Nevertheless, it did, in a most unlikely way. It started with Minerva's half-holiday. Jill had promised herself to dedicate Minerva's half-holiday to Minerva by spending it walking alone in the country, but one morning the Headmistress announced that it would be utilized to allow the school to watch the hockey match against St. Bride's School. which was the most important one of the season.

"But we're always *given* a half-day to watch that!" exclaimed Jill. It was a downright swindle.

To her astonishment and fury she found that nobody saw it from her point of view, all being excited at the prospect of witnessing the match. Their gullibility made her angry, and at break she loafed in the washroom, sulking. Rosalie and her friends were also there.

"Whoops, girls," said Rosalie, rubbing her face with wet palms. "No school this afternoon. Bit of a twist, messing up our games day."

"Don't look a gift horse *au bouche*," advised Molly Vine, retying her hair ribbon. "You should be thankful you're going to watch the match and not going to be chased about getting your fat down."

"All hail to the Badger. Agreed. Poof." Rosalie groped for a towel, her eyes tightly shut. There was something in her mole-like groping that made Jill snap irritably:

"It's a swindle. We always have the day off to watch the St. Bride's match."

"Then the more often I'm swindled," said Margaret Wolsey, "the better I shall like it."

"But we haven't been given a proper half at all. We shall all be marched down to the field as usual to watch the match. . . ."

"Well, don't you want to watch it?"

"What *do* you want to do?"

Jill flushed.

"That's not the point. If we're given a half-holiday, we ought to be able to do as we please with it. That's what a holiday *means*."

"Oh, come on." Rosalie had found the towel and was

143

rubbing her red cheeks till they shone. "Rally round the old school. Come along and give 'em a yell."

This sidetracking infuriated Jill.

"Oh, don't you *see*? It's only an underhand way of not giving us a half-holiday at all. We——"

"But we've *got* a half-holiday——"

"But we *haven't*. You are thick. You're all as thick as wood. She's taken you in like a pack of kids. What's the good——"

"Oh, don't niggle. We've got a half to watch a match, haven't we? Watch it and shut up."

"Shut up yourself. I'm not niggling."

"Yes, you are. You're splitting hairs. Can't you have the decency to back up the school?"

"Oh, damn the school. I'm not talking about that. If you're too dense to see the Badger's swindled you——"

"Tripe. Tripe. Shut up and stop quibbling."

"I really don't see what you're bothering about," said Rosalie placidly, replacing the towel. Jill turned on her quivering with indignation.

"Then you must be *damned* stupid!" she said, and walked out.

She was furious all through lunch. She would *not* watch the match. She stole glances at Minerva, to strengthen her resolve, and when lunch was over she hung about the lobbies till the match was due to start. Then she slipped into the library, where she planned to stay the whole afternoon. Going out was too risky, and then, of course, Minerva herself might always come into the library.

Despite her courage, she could not help feeling a little nervous, and she chose a seat not directly in line with the door. It was forbidden for any girl below the Sixth to enter the library except at special times, and she listened nervously for footsteps, sitting with *Bleak House* open on her lap. From the distance came faint cheers and moans.

About three o'clock she heard someone coming and held her breath. The footsteps stopped at the door and came in. Jill was petrified. The person moved along the shelves till she suddenly came in sight—it was Miss Keen.

"Good heavens, Jill! What are you doing here? Are you ill?"

"Oh, no, Miss Keen."

"Then why aren't you out on the field? Go at once."

Jill breathed hard. "But——"

"Well?"

"I thought I could do as I liked on a half-holiday."

To Jill, it did not sound particularly rude. But Miss Keen became angry.

"What do you mean? Don't be impertinent. How dare you frowst in here. Get out on to the field at once."

"If this is a half-holiday, I can do as I please."

"No, you certainly cannot. You are excused school simply to watch the match against St. Bride's."

"But I'm excused school because Minerva Strachey——"

"Don't stand there arguing and contradicting me. It's disgusting to loaf about indoors instead of supporting the school."

"I can stay in if I want to."

"I think you'd better come and see the Headmistress."

Jill's heart gave a horrible lurch.

"I don't see why——"

"Perhaps she will convince you that when she gives an order she means it to be obeyed."

With a scared face Jill followed Miss Keen to the Headmistress's study, where she was told to wait, as Miss Badger was among the crowd watching the match on the field. Miss Keen went off to find her, and Jill sat wretchedly on a hard chair, watching the Headmistress's secretary typing. She occasionally sipped a cup of tea that stood beside her. The room was strange to Jill, and that added to her nervousness. She had not the least idea what she was going to say.

In about ten minutes the Headmistress came and was met outside the door by the maid with the afternoon post.

"The letters, and a telegram, ma'am."

"Thank you," said Miss Badger, striding in. She took not the slightest notice of Jill, but went into her study by the inner door, holding the letters. She was a tall woman, with a strong and simple face that was almost peasant-like, and still wore a mackintosh and scarf. The secretary followed her, closing the door, and Jill was alone, staring miserably at the fringe on the rug. She had to sit there for two or three minutes before the secretary came back.

"The Head will see you now."

Jill walked with trembling knees through the half-open door and closed it behind her. Miss Badger was standing by the fire in the marble fireplace, with the opened telegram in her hand.

"Come in, Jill. I'm afraid I have some bad news for you. Your father is very ill and your mother suggests you go home at once."

v

Six days later Jill travelled back by train to the school. In the meantime her father had died and she had attended the funeral, which she could not forget. The wind had heaved restlessly about as they stood in the wet churchyard, throwing handfuls of rain, making the women hold their black hats and skirts. It was awful to see the coffin going down into the grave. Jill was too terrified to cry.

Not till the train was slowing down into Mallerton did Jill remember her quarrel with Miss Keen, and it seemed so far away that it was not worth bothering about. She knew nobody would ever mention it now, but she tried not to think of it because it seemed to be bound up with her father's death. Every time she thought of that she felt sad and frightened—sad, because she had not done so much for her father that she should have done; and frightened, because never before had she come into contact with death. She, too, must die like that, and her mother and everyone she knew.

It was nearly dusk when she got out of the train at Mallerton, and the porter came along the platform with a lamp, to take her ticket. She handed it over dumbly.

And there, in the tiny booking-hall, stood a girl—Minerva Strachey—under a light, her hands in her pockets.

146

"Are you Jill Bradley? Miss Badger asked me to meet you. There's a taxi outside."

Jill stared at her, trying in a moment to bridge the gap of six days back to something she hardly remembered.

"Oh," she said. "I see."

They slid together into the broad leathery back seat of the taxi, Minerva saying through the open glass partition:

"The school, please."

"Got to go slow, Miss. Fog's coming on."

"Very well."

The taxi crawled off down the main street of Mallerton, past the Corn Exchange, the driver honking his horn—an old, bugle-shaped one. Jill wondered what Minerva would say to her.

"A good journey?"

"Oh, yes, thank you."

"I've some chocolate, if you feel hungry."

"Oh, no, thank you——"

"Go on. There's plenty. I'm not crazy about it."

Jill took off her hat and accepted the chocolate. It was a kind she liked. Her confusion and unpreparedness for this meeting were being slowly overcome by the grace and calmness that Minerva spread about her.

Minerva said directly:

"I hear you've had some bad news. I'm very sorry; if there's anything I can do to help, I should be only too pleased."

Her voice was so soft and clear that Jill never thought about crying.

"Thanks—no, there's nothing to do, now."

"I'm very sorry," said Minerva again.

"It was all very unexpected. He had 'flu—and it turned to pneumonia—and it seems he hadn't any strength to resist it. He's been overworking."

"That's very sad, very sad indeed."

Suddenly Jill burst into tears. She turned her face away and looked down at her lap. Minerva paid no attention, only saying after a pause:

"You must be feeling very miserable: I'm sorry I brought the subject up. But you will have to get used to it, you know."

147

"Oh, it's not that. You don't understand. I know everyone has to die. It's the thought of having to waste one's life in awful places like school. . . ."

"Oh, don't you like school?"

"No!"

"Have you no friends?"

"No."

"Not one?"

"Not a real one." Jill stopped crying and looked at Minerva wretchedly. "What am I going to do?"

"I don't know. Stick it out, I should say. Things will get better."

"Everyone thinks I'm stuck-up."

"Everyone thinks *I'm* stuck-up."

"Oh, but they don't—and you aren't! No, you're different!" cried Jill impulsively. "And, anyway, it doesn't matter with you—you're so far beyond them, you can get on without anyone else—but I can't, though I've tried; I've watched you and tried——"

Minerva raised her eyebrows.

"What a queer thing to say," she said coolly.

Jill suddenly swallowed her emotion and bit back more open confessions that were to follow, recognizing instantly that Minerva had administered a gentle rebuff. She was ashamed of herself. She saw that Minerva had indicated that her detachment, even though it was admired, must still be respected; that loneliness was not to be abandoned at the first chance of friendship, but was a thing to be cherished in itself. She sat silent for the rest of the journey. Once Minerva offered her more chocolate, which she took.

The stone gate-pillars loomed through the fog, and they began to put on their hats. "I hope you get on all right," said Minerva, smiling pleasantly at Jill. "Let me know if there's anything I can do for you, won't you?" The taxi stopped. "And tell Miss Badger you've arrived—I must stop and pay the driver."

Jilll got out of the taxi, glad to stretch her cramped legs. Taking her small suitcase in one hand, she walked up the steps to the front door and went in. Minerva turned to the driver, with money in her hand. Seeing Jill hesitate at the door, she smiled and waved briefly. Jill remembered that her father was dead.

But on reading it through a day later, he was disappointed that it was so little of what he had desired. It seemed to present nothing of the Jill he knew; indeed, it blurred her image rather than anything else, and thinking what it lacked was intimacy, he searched through all the stationers in the town till he found a diary for the current (though almost spent) year. This he began to keep for her, concocting entries day by day, not surprised at the ease with which he wrote them.

TUESDAY. Oh, a horrid day. Horrid and hateful! Now the novelty's worn off (and it wears off damned quickly in these days) I'm getting to hate it as much as ever. All my kirbi-grips had vanished for a start this morning (yes, and WHO took them?), so what with searching for them and trying to find a slide, I hadn't time to get my hymn-book before prayers—and of course the Badger had to choose today to inspect them, as she said she'd seen too many girls sharing recently. I suppose she thinks I *like* sharing with Molly. Anyway, the upshot is I've got "Eternal Father Strong to Save" to write out three times. Then Jennings put me on in Latin just at the very line I'd broken off to listen to Jackie talking about her sister (the actress) and got a black mark for that—"You *least of all*, Jill, can afford to waste time. . . ." Then, oh well, then it was sausages for dinner, which I'm convinced give me spots. And object drawing in the afternoon, with the highly-inspiring object being a pair of steps. I rubbed mine out so much that Miss Shore said: "Well, *underneath the dirt*, Jill, I dare say it's an excellent drawing, but not seeing, can't say." Everyone laughed, so I said: "I think the paper is of rather cheap quality. . . ."

149

WEDNESDAY. This is supposed to be a half-holiday, but I was roped in for compulsory-voluntary-compulsory gardening, in consequence of which I have a blister on my hand which is why this writing's so bad. That's the trouble with this place—nothing is private. This ghastly spirit of keenness—always rushing to or from a place, getting marks for this or stripes for that or prizes for the other. It keeps me continually on edge, ready to fly out at anybody. "Our little spitfire, Jill," as Jennings puts it (I must get so that I can say that *quite calmly*).

THURSDAY. I must be honest and say I don't like Keats as much as Dowson. The O to A, for instance—"their *clammy* cells". . . . Ugh! People's hands. "Wailful choir"—"hilly bourn"—so *old-fashioned*, which is a silly thing to say, I suppose. And then "burst Joy's grape against his palate fine"— apart from reminding me of Joy Roberts, always makes me think of dentists and false teeth.

Must stop now. I always think it's a good comment on this place that I have to write my diary locked in the lavatories. . . .

FRIDAY. Today we were messing about in the Hall during break because it was raining, and I caught sight of myself in the glass of one of the pictures. Quite a shock—just another tunic, blouse and tie. Me from the Outside. And this is Me from the Inside? No, on the whole I don't think so, not the real me; not like when I'm riding Toby in a "wordless ecstasy", or listening to the Faery Song from the *Immortal Hour*. . . .

SATURDAY. Another loathsome day, all through Delia. Why the hell should we have to sit in alphabetical order? I hate her more than I've ever hated anyone else in my whole life. I hate her stupid fat face and her fringe. I hate her clumsy untidiness —the way she can't write without bending her forefinger concave on the penholder. In Maths today we had geometry, and she hadn't got a pencil. She asked me for one—I'd only got a new Venus, and said so. Before I could stop her, she said "That'll do," snatched it away from me, broke it in half and gave me back the half without a point. I tried to hit her in the face, and we scuffled a bit so that old B. peered round and chanted some kind of warning to us. Why can't the old fool keep order? I was absolutely trembling with fury and couldn't see for tears. I hadn't got a penknife to sharpen the bit I had, and I knew that I should burst out crying if I asked anyone to lend me one, because it was a special pencil out of the box Daddy gave me for last Christmas, and I'd really brought it back to do some sketching. I just sat staring at the page until old B. came round and saw that I hadn't done anything. Then the fat was *au feu*. I told her I hadn't got a pencil, and she said that was no reason, I could have borrowed one. I said I didn't feel well. "You were well enough to be fighting ten minutes back," she said. "I *wasn't* fighting," I said, and burst out crying, raging and loathing myself and wanting to kill the whole crowd of them. Luckily the bell went.

LATER. She—Delia—'s kept *on* at me. She's noticed I spend ages in the lats every night (writing this, of course, but she won't believe that) and goes about telling everyone. I wish this place were burnt to the ground with everyone in it.

SUNDAY. The day of rest, I don't think. Too furious to write more.

MONDAY. Got told off today, and really nobody seems to think I shall get my school cert. I don't myself. Why can't one go and live quietly away from this pack of guttersnipes and fools?

TUESDAY. A queer thing happened today. Miss Fairfax had a class of babes to look after as well as us, and they were in the next room, sewing. She told me—ME!—to go in and read to them, and literally put me in charge of a whole class of twenty babes. I was so surprised that I was hardly nervous at all, and read them a fairy story about a woodcutter's daughter who lived in the Depths of the Woods (lucky beast). I put loads of expression into it, so that they were quite thrilled, and every now and then I had to tell them to get on with their kettle-holders and hair-tidies and pin-cushions, they were just listening with open mouths. But they got their cottons into such hideous tangles that I had to keep stopping to help them, and in the end I just let them sit round and listen till the period ended. They were entranced. At one point I felt a horrid pang for my own lost youth and salad days—but really I'm not sorry at all. I mean I know things will get worse and worse, but I don't mind because they'll get better and better too. I wouldn't go back, not for millions. . . .

They weren't so bad today.

Then he was troubled because the rest of the diary was untouched, and he began trying to fill in the whole year with entries, hoping secretly to create one year of her life, that he could amplify with little poems about spring and autumn and letters of thanks for birthday and Christmas presents. But it meant transposing the story he had written, and this tired him, and then he grew confused about chronology, and suddenly the whole thing seemed vapid and uninteresting. He had not moved one inch nearer creating an independent Jill; all he had done was to model himself on her image. And doing so had pushed the image from his mind. Try as he would, he could not coax a picture of her to materialize, though at first they had come so easily.

The final possession came one day at lunch, when he was quietly eating bread and cheese and listening to casual talk among the scholars, some of whom were discussing the sinking of the *Jervis Bay*. He sat spellbound, holding his knife, his heart beating loudly. The sensation he had was of looking intently into the centre of a pure white light: he seemed to see the essence of Jill, around which all the secondary material things formed and reformed as he wrote them down. He thought he saw exactly what she was and how he should express it: the word was *innocent*, one he had used dozens of times in his own mind, and yet until that moment had never understood.

He rose, leaving a crust of brown bread and some cheese still uneaten, eager to get back to pen and paper, but as he reached the door another student came up to him and began talking persuasively about the activities of some political club. The young man had red hair and enormously broad shoulders. John shifted in suspense, longing to get away.

"But I don't know anything about——"

"Then you're exactly the kind of person the club is meant for. You see, this is the way we look at it. We students have certain advantages here—advantages that we've worked for, perhaps—

but at any rate advantages that put us in the position of being able to get a grip on affairs. A lot of fellows of our age are working in factories or in the services, and have no free time at all. We have, and I think you'll agree that it's up to us to put it to good use. We've got libraries, a good supply of speakers, and even in the short time we get up here now it's possible—I know it's possible—to learn enough about the past and present in order to avoid making a mess of the future when the time comes for us to be citizens."

"Yes, but——"

"We have the central club, you see, the main club with meetings every week to discuss questions of immediate general interest, when we get a speaker of pretty good reputation, as a rule. You'll have seen the posters——"

"Oh, yes, but——"

"But in addition to that, we try to do something on our own. So many clubs just meet every week in order to be talked at—I won't mention any names, but you probably know the kind I mean. Now we subdivide into college groups—each college, you see, has a discussion group and every term each group takes a certain question and examines it from all angles. Different members take different aspects. Let's suppose, for the sake of argument, that our College group is discussing India. Then I take, say, the administration; you might take the aims and methods of the Nationalist Party; someone else would take the different religious bodies and their different political attitudes, and so on and so forth. In this way we get what is virtually a team of experts, each one making it his business to know all he possibly can about his particular subject. And we all pool our knowledge by reading a paper to the rest of the group each."

"I——"

"Already, you see, you're not just a rank-and-file member of the club—for that term you are the specialist on whatever particular subject you've been studying, and can pull the speaker up at club meetings if he goes off the rails. You have some sort of a position already. You see, we try to *do* something."

"Yes, I see, but——"

"And after all, who is going to do it if we don't? When this

153

war's over, there's going to be an enormous demand for well-informed, intelligent people to run groups and hold meetings in order to see that the politicians don't go and make the same old mistakes all over again. A sort of advance-guard of the new world order."

"Er—I——"

"Now, won't you come along to the open tea meeting this afternoon? We're very lucky—the President is coming along to talk to new and prospective members."

"Well—it all sounds most interesting. . . . Where will it be?"

"In my rooms—you know. You might like to bring along pencil and paper, or think up some questions to ask. The half-term subscription is two bob."

"Yes—if I can—but I've got to go now—appointment——"

And he managed to slip away, half running out into the quadrangle before he realized that of course that extraordinary clarity of perception that had been vouchsafed him for a few moments had gone, utterly gone. When he had pencil and paper in his room, nothing presented itself to his mind except a flat dullness, like a grey stone wall, and sighing he put them down and lent back on the sofa with his hands behind his head.

Shortly afterwards Eddy looked in, wearing a tweed cap, which he took off and threw on to the table.

"Chris not in?"

"I think he's playing squash——"

"Ah," said Eddy, settling in the armchair. "Mind if I wait."

He put an unlit cigarette between his loose lips and stretched his legs, so that one of his feet knocked against John's ankle, an action for which he did not apologize. John put away Jill's diary and, having buttoned up his overcoat, went wearily out, not knowing where he was going or for how long. In the College lodge there was a letter for him from the Dean of the College, inviting him to tea at his house on Sunday: John noticed an identical envelope for Whitbread also. He put it away in his pocket.

Everyone at the cinema seemed in twos, threes or fours and, despite himself, when the lights went up, he was thinking about

154

Christopher and Elizabeth, half excusing the casual conversation he had overheard. He found it hard to recall the exact words, but had they, after all, been so insulting? Hadn't they had some friendliness in them, patronizing, perhaps, but a certain good-humoured toleration? Elizabeth had not been round lately, for both she and Patrick had been occupied with some cousin who was staying in the town, so Christopher had occasionally chatted to John in a friendly manner and John had answered him quite affably and humbly. Perhaps the way they had spoken about him was the way they spoke about everybody; not significant of anything, but amiable amusement.

He felt as a child feels who has in a fit of temper run out of a game, and, looking round, watches the game still going on despite his absence, and is filled with a desire to rejoin it.

As he sat drinking tea in a cheap and rather dirty café, however, he experienced such a pang of absolute self-disgust that he wondered how he was going to live another hour. It was impossible to make friends with Christopher and Elizabeth, and that was the only thing he wanted to do, now that he had awoken hopelessly from his attempt to build a world around Jill. He knew that one more world had crumbled to bits under his hand. He paid a waitress in a grubby overall pinned at the hip, and walked out.

His footsteps turned naturally towards the College, but he remembered in time the political tea-meeting and stopped short. Ancient buildings were all around him; a few people in overcoats hurried this way and that; a girl on a bicycle fled by, as if escaping. A few cars were parked down the broad street and a dozen lights showed from a nearby college. A Negro passed him dressed in an enormous fur coat, wearing gold-rimmed spectacles and carrying an ivory walking-cane: John stood and stared vaguely after him, the wind stirring his hair, then with a sudden useless decision, he pushed open the glass-panelled door of a large bookshop, hoping to find something cheap enough for him to buy, and ready to enjoy the smell of the books, the electric light shining on glossy pages and the subdued tapping of a typewriter from behind an office door. He moved

155

thoughtfully from shelf to shelf, here and there taking a book to inspect it, not enviously, but with a distant curiosity. From the desk came the clink of coins and polite murmured inquiries.

Then as he was absently fingering the edges of an uncut page with a transient sense of frustration, his glance wandered along the aisle where he was standing and he received a shock that could not have been greater if a brick had been thrown through the plate-glass shop-window.

He saw Jill.

She stepped out from behind an alcove, working her way slowly along the shelves, moving eventually in his direction. For a moment she bobbed back into the alcove for a second look at an unseen book, but then reappeared, shifting gradually along the cases.

It was not a question of thinking: that girl is something like Jill. There was nothing casual in the resemblance: it was so exact that for a second his mind could not remember who it was, this over-familiar face. And he was too bewildered to think as the realization came upon him.

It was her hair, the colour of dark viscous honey, her serious face, her wild high cheekbones. Little hollows appeared and reappeared under these because, as John saw when he approached, she was whistling very softly. Her winter coat hung open and blue woollen gloves were stuffed into the pockets. Instead of stockings, she wore little socks, and her hands, now that she had taken a book down and was turning the pages—were small, bony and not well-cared-for. As John drew near to her, she glanced up at him and backed a few paces absently to allow him room to pass.

An interval elapsed, during which time John, making no effort to pass, stood staring at her. It was absurd, laughable, unbelievable. Then for a second time she looked up and met his wide eyes with her grey, utterly strange ones. Both of them, both so young-looking, stared at one another.

"I——" John began hurriedly, then paused. "You—er—— Haven't we met before, somewhere?"

She gave a tiny frown and said quickly:

156

"No, I don't think so, not as far as I know."

He did not realize she was nervous, imagining her to be snubbing him curtly. He blushed, flustered.

"Oh, then, I'm sorry. . . . I thought. . . ."

She gave a quick half-laugh.

"I'm sure I don't know you," she said, and lifted her book to close the argument.

Nobody had noticed the incident. John, still standing there, knew that he had to apologize and move away. Yet it was only on the reflex of his embarrassment that he did so, because it was all so ridiculous, he wanted to make her admit she knew him, to confess he hardly knew what. The sight of her awkward girl's body afflicted him with a fearful longing, like some call of destiny. He had been ready for anything except non-recognition.

From behind another case he took stock of her again, hastily making sure by shutting his eyes and opening them again, that his impression remained undisturbed. This made his emotion all the keener: from wanting to laugh, he passed naturally into wanting to cry, to sob with a kind of relief. For above his astonishment, his humiliation, a grander feeling surged: that of thankfulness. He felt like a sailing ship running home into the estuary of a river after a long sea-journey.

. But she was drifting away. She had slid the book back carelessly on to the shelf and was dragging slowly down the aisle between the shelves, her eyes on the titles of books, but her hands pulling out the blue woollen gloves in preparation to go for good. He lurked behind her. Architecture did not detain her, nor did cookery, nor music. John pushed all other questions aside in his resolution to follow her. She drifted to the door and pulled it open: outside in the November dusk a horse and cart were going by and down the street several shops had lighted windows before closing up. She walked away, doing up her coat and pulling her gloves on, and he followed, fifteen yards behind, trying to interpret every swing of her step. Once he had fallen into line behind her, he felt absolved from all decisions, satisfied by this mere act of devotion.

She walked slowly up the street, not looking back. He

157

quickened his pace till her fawn coat was within ten yards, anxious to reassure himself by the sight of her face that she remained who he thought she was, that it had not all been some fantastic trick of light. But it would be silly to get too close to her. What with eagerness and fear, his heart beat steadily and he found he was sweating under his clothes, as if he were hunting some rare and sensitive animal.

What actually happened had the deliberate tantalizing quality of a dream. She crossed the road to a cycle park which was arranged along one side of a small churchyard, bent to unlock the padlock from the back wheel, slipped the chain and lock into the saddlebag, screwed the flashlight till it came on, and scooted away into the dusk before rising fully into the saddle. He saw her pass the Martyrs' Memorial, glance quickly about her for converging lines of traffic and pedal away out of sight. She was a hundred yards away in a minute.

He automatically ran after her, pelting as hard as he could go up the north-going road, knocking into people who were walking home after shopping or a day's work. He ran fully three hundred yards up the road leading out of the town towards Banbury, between the lines of residential houses built in the last century, with gardens and trees overhanging the road, then he slowed down to a walk, brisk and useless. He knew it was useless. But what else could he do? He nourished a hope that she might turn back for some reason or have paid a call at one of these houses, so that he would see the bike waiting outside and be able to wait himself. In any case, he was too excited to go quietly home to sit in his room.

As he walked he turned the matter over in a bewildered mind, illogically, taking first one aspect of it and then hastily rushing to a different standpoint, making no effort to connect the two. Here, then, she was. Disconcertingly, the idea that he had concocted out of the world's sight had suddenly showed itself as ordinary flesh and blood, as real, calling for real action on his part. What was he going to do?

She was real, then, and had a name and address. How was he going to find them out? He looked about him. The gutters were

158

filled with leaves and an absence of traffic allowed a stillness to brood over the front gardens, where there still remained a few Michaelmas daisies and late dahlias. Any one of these houses might be her home: he stared at them enviously, and the lighted front room with sometimes a white table-cloth laid for tea. There was nobody about, except for a maidservant who came out to post a letter, running to a pillar-box with a coat slung over her shoulders. In what crescent or deserted avenue had she at last jumped off her bicycle, opening the wooden gate carefully so as not to let the dog out?

He stopped under a tree, looking this way and that. And if he found her name and address, what then? He would not dare to approach her again after his rudeness that afternoon. All that would remain for him to do would be to discover her real life, to follow her about and not be noticed, to make lists of the clothes she wore and the places she went to, to make her the purpose of his life once more, now that he had just begun sniffing enviously again at the society of Christopher Warner and Elizabeth Dowling. In this quest his loneliness would be an asset: it would be mobility and even charm.

He was awake before daybreak next morning, lying excitedly in bed and looking forward to the day in front of him. As he dressed, he took pains with his appearance, tied his bow and put some oil on his hair. There were kippers for breakfast, a circumstance which Whitbread greatly appreciated, and he showed great skill in dissecting his own portion, talking to John as he chewed.

"It's a knack, you know," he said. "I've an uncle, now, who can get every bone out of a kipper in a hundred seconds. I've timed him, while he did it. And you couldn't find a single one afterwards, large or small, not after he'd been through it. You just have to know where to look."

John removed a handful of bones from his mouth.

"There's the Bursar," continued Whitbread, as the don entered the Hall by the upper door and sat down at High Table. A wartime regulation caused many of the dons living in College to breakfast communally, and the Bursar availed himself of the provision with almost defiant regularity. "He looks as if he had a thick night. Too much S.C.R. port, I'll lay."

"That reminds me," said John hurriedly, "I've a note for you. It was in the lodge last night and I wasn't in to dinner. It's from the Dean—most likely an invitation to tea. I'm sorry I forgot it."

"Oh!" Whitbread took it and put it unopened into his inside pocket. "I know you won't take this in the wrong way, Kemp, but do you mind not meddling with my letters? Things get lost like that. I know you meant it as a kindness, but it might have been important, and I should have been late getting it."

After breakfast he put on his overcoat and strolled nervously out into the town. There had been a sharp frost the night before and lorries that had been out all night had white roofs that sparkled in the sun. The sky was remote and blue: everywhere an atmosphere of briskness prevailed. John watched large trays of loaves and buns being carried into a confectioner's shop from a van; already shoppers were out and students cycled past with books tumbled carelessly in the basket at their handlebars. Other students wearing gowns hurried past on foot. In the entrance hall of a cinema a woman on her knees was scrubbing the linoleum: she wore an apron of sackcloth and a bucket stood by her side. From the booking office came the sound of money being counted.

He felt like a detective, single-handed, and indeed slightly at a loss to know how to begin. Instinct led him first to the bookshop where he had seen her the day before, but it was practically empty, and he did not stay there long. The difficulty of his task began to oppress him. It might be that she would not come into the town that morning; indeed, she might be only a visitor to the city, and by now be gone; in any case, supposing that she did revisit the shops, the chances that he would happen to see her were extremely slight.

To judge from her appearance, she was fifteen or sixteen years old. And yet was she at school? The time that he had seen her was roughly five o'clock. If she were at a local day school, she could have been home and then come out again, particuarly as she had the bicycle, but surely if she had only wanted to visit a bookshop she could have done that on the way home. Unless, of course, it did not lie in her way. In any case, what about tea?

The main point was that if she were attending school, his searching the town for her during the morning and afternoon was sheerly a waste of time. He drifted along the main street, looking eagerly about him at the faces that passed; at nearly half-past ten he went into the coffee-room of a large store and sat at a corner table. The room was nearly empty, but as eleven o'clock approached parties of people came in and sat smoking and talking, drinking coffee and wasting time. He had never visited this place before, but he had heard it spoken of as the place where the most people could be seen in the shortest possible time, and as the room became fuller and fuller, he saw how true this was. After a time tables were moved together and extra chairs carried in from the luncheon room next door to accommodate larger parties. He saw Christopher Warner come in and Tony Braithwaite and Patrick: later they were joined by Elizabeth and a dark Jewish-looking girl he had never seen before. Tony Braithwaite, he had since learned, played the piano in the University dance band. At every fresh advent he felt a painful twinge of apprehension till he had seen all the faces of the new party. With his fair hair and pale face he looked like a fanatic, but his eyes were not bright enough.

The coffee cost him fourpence and it was a remarkably cheap way of carrying out his search. After three-quarters of an hour, he moved to another similar café, where he sat till a quarter-past twelve. Many different people came and went, but not the one he was looking for. In the interval between his leaving the café and returning to the College for lunch, he visited several bookshops and large emporiums, where he concentrated on the departments that might be expected to interest her—the material counter, the shoe department, the soap and perfume corner. The shop girls regarded him suspiciously, but did not interfere with him.

When lunch-time came, it was not surprising that he felt depressed. He felt physically tired, for one thing, and the amount of energy and enthusiasm he had expended to so little purpose was disquieting. He had not realized till now that his intense desire to see her was no reason for her to appear to him; he had not realized till now how great even one city was, how impossible it was to observe even the few main streets adequately. And the crowds of people made his search seem no less urgent, but less significant.

Yet he could not rest. In the afternoon he made his way round the straggling, peaceful area of North Oxford, crossing the parks, where the faint cries of hockey players were carried hither and thither on the wind, along the river walk and through into the respectable tree-lined roads that intersected and curved into each other. It was odd that no sooner had he chosen a place where she would, in his opinion, probably be found, the place seemed empty and a search of it useless. Before he turned any corner he looked behind him lest she should appear too late for him to see her. To the casual observer it looked as if he thought he was being pursued.

The sun, a red ball burning frostily, sank lower behind the leafless trees, over the house-tops and gardens as four o'clock came nearer. John walked quickly back to the town by the main road, looking intently at every approaching cyclist, and, on reaching the centre once more, went for tea to a large café. Here, if anywhere, she might appear, he thought, looking round at the little tables with their white tablecloths, the pleasant artificial flowers and cigarette-ash trays and the trio of middle-aged people playing musical comedy selections on a piano, a violin and a 'cello. It was with scenes like this that he was beginning to associate her. And yet she did not come. He ate the toast and jam and cakes and drank his tea and stared restlessly about, but fruitlessly; the trio of musicians paused, sat about for six minutes, then began another selection. In his present mood of impatience, he found the music irritating in the extreme. People came and went. At last, in despair, he called for his bill and paid it, feeling how bitterly he had failed.

Despite his knowledge that he was wasting time and money in a most unprofitable way, he spent the next day in this manner

162

and also the one after that. Quite simply, he could do nothing else. He admitted to himself that it was unlikely that he should ever see her again; he knew, too, that even if he did, he would have no way of finding out her name, no way of making himself known to her. At the thought of their first clumsy encounter he could cry with rage. It had not only been embarrassing, it had also prevented any recurrence of an attempt at friendship. At tea-time on the third day he sat at a glass-topped table in a different tea-room, watching the people eating and the reflection of the vast room in the mirrors on the walls, waiting for the food he had asked for to be brought. When it came, he looked at the tray the waitress carried to see what cakes she had chosen, and some instinct lifted his eyes beyond their immediate object to the far door. Jill stood there. The waitress came to the table, blocking his view and began setting out the things. John, with an inarticulate mutter, tried to crane his neck to see round her, failed, and struggled to his feet. By the time he was up the doorway was empty and a quick look round showed that she had not advanced into the room, but simply retreated into the street as if she had not seen anyone she knew.

"Two and eight, sir," said the waitress, tearing off the bill.

He paid it, and ran out into the street, leaving his overcoat behind. She could not have gone far, her whole attitude had been casual; her hands in the pockets of her coat, she had looked at the room with complete unconcern, as if it had nothing to do with her. He looked this way and that. There was no trace, no sign. The people formed and re-formed, crossed and altered even as he looked at them; in ten seconds she could easily have been concealed in the shifting street. He fetched his overcoat from the café (there were people sitting at his table) and set out among the dusky traffic, knowing that she must be somewhere near, tantalizingly close, and that if he was quick he would almost certainly find her again.

He did not. After he had searched the immediate streets, he suddenly remembered that obviously she would have gone to another teashop, having found the first one full, or unsatisfactory in some other way, and he began entering every one he came to, standing for a moment in the door as she had done and then hurrying out. He visited every one he could think of, even the large café of a cinema, but it was no good. She was not to be found and he gradually lost heart, becoming not so much depressed as angrily disappointed.

It was the wasted chance that annoyed him, for he had come to realize how rare these chances were going to be, if indeed another one occurred.

The next day was a Sunday. Would she, he wondered, go to church? And despite his disappointment and fury, he could not help feeling thankful that at least he knew she existed and that he was following correct tactics if he wanted to see her again. He sat in the Common Room turning over a Sunday newspaper without interest, while Christopher and some second-year students talked loudly in one corner of the room. Patrick was there, too, and after a while demanded that Christopher should pay back the two pounds he owed him.

"Two quid? What is the man talking about?" inquired Christopher, irritably.

"The two quid you owe me."

"I don't owe you two quid."

"Oh, yes, you do," said Patrick, pulling a little leather pocket book from his waistcoat. He opened it and began to turn the pages.

"You're a liar."

"I am not a liar. I lent them you the day before we left London. October the ninth."

"I don't remember," said Christopher obstinately.

"I don't wonder. You were boozed as hell. Anyway, it's down here, if you want to see it."

"I don't want to see your damned Doomsday Book," said Christopher rudely, groping in his pockets. "I can't pay you all of it. Will a quid do?"

"I should say it would do for the moment," smiled Patrick, taking the folded note and making another entry in his book. By accident John caught Christopher's eyes and the latter thrust his hand into his pocket again.

164

"God, all right, don't tell me, I owe you something, too. What a bloody life. Here, take that to be going on with."

He held out two half-crowns with the action of tipping a porter. John blushed sharply.

"That's all right—if you're short——"

"Take it."

"No, it's quite all right."

"What the hell d'you mean? Take it. I don't want you to give me money."

He accented, or so John fancied, the words "you" and "me", and flung the two coins down on the open book John had begun to read. John sat silently, red in the face, not touching them.

"When you've lived as long as I have, Chris," said one of the second-year students, "you won't pay men who don't want to be paid. Your fine sense of honour will have become dulled. In any case, I was relying on you to stand me a flick this afternoon."

Laughter released a more general conversation, and, unnoticed, John picked up the five shillings and pocketed it, because, after all, as he ashamedly thought, he was glad to get it, having spent more money in the last few days than he could really afford. Then he got up and left the room, overwhelmingly conscious that Jill and all she represented must be kept hidden away from Christopher, absolutely at a loss to remember why he had ever mentioned her name at all.

This was the afternoon that Whitbread and he had been invited to tea at the Dean's house, so he idled about in his room, writing a letter to his parents, until it was time to set off. He had arranged to meet Whitbread in the College lodge at four o'clock, and carried the letter with him. The two of them set off along the road in the bright afternoon sunshine, neither wearing hats. Under his overcoat Whitbread had on a black jacket and a pair of striped trousers that made him look like an office-boy.

"Do we pass a postbox?" inquired John, knowing that Whitbread could be relied upon to know such things.

"We can do. You could have posted that in t'lodge."

"Is there a box there?"

"Yes, of course there is, man. Have you never seen it?"

John confessed he hadn't. An old man hobbled along the pavement picking up cigarette stubs from the gutter. Whitbread walked along with an air of satisfaction.

"Ay! The Dean only asks scholars to these little do's. Shows what he thinks of us. It gives you a chance to make a good impression."

"I don't know him well," said John, resenting the intimacy with which Whitbread addressed him.

"He's O.K. You'll have to show him you're not tarred with t'same brush as that fellow Warner—Dean's had a bit of trouble with him already. I don't know what he comes up here for. If it's just drink and women he wants, he might as well stay in London. After all, he doesn't want a degree—he hasn't got to earn a living."

"Not that he'd get one," said John, with sudden spitefulness, glad when Whitbread laughed and agreed. They walked on, up the Banbury Road, passing young married couples who strolled slowly along, attended by tottering children or pushing perambulators. Wet leaves struck to the dry pavement. The tree trunks had white rings painted on them about three feet from the ground. In the distance a brass band could be heard playing a simple hymn tune and a single aeroplane crawled along the very top of the sky, so high it was practically invisible.

"This way if you want to post that letter," said Whitbread, turning to cross the road. "It just means we come into the road where he lives by the other end."

The silence of the afternoon was remarkable, and they reached the pillar-box in an entirely empty avenue.

"That's the house," commented Whitbread, nodding towards one fenced house in a row of others. "Not bad for a junior fellow's screw."

He opened the gate and stood aside for John to pass through. As he did so, Jill cycled slowly by, with the deliberation of a mirage. One hand rested on the handlebars, the other was in the pocket of her loosely-belted coat; she lounged on the saddle, pedalling negligently, whistling once more. Her hair tumbled in

166

the wind, the sun tinting it with a bronze shade he had not noticed before.

John was paralysed. The habit she had of appearing just at the moment when he was unable to follow her—as now, when Whitbread had rung the doorbell and was waiting, pulling down the points of his waistcoat and listening for the steps of the maidservant across the hall—this habit seemed part of a dream-like frustration. He took a step back through the gate, seeing her sailing away like a small boy's model yacht, irretrievable into the distance.

"Come on!" hissed Whitbread, as he hesitated. "Here, Kemp, stop wool-gathering."

It was no use. Before another ten seconds had passed, she had turned the corner and was lost to sight, and the maid was just opening the door.

Two days after this, during which time John had seen no more of Jill at all and was beginning to prepare himself for the realization that she had gone for ever, Christopher sauntered in after lunch and sidled up to the mirror, rubbing his jaw in an interrogative way that suggested he was about to shave. In this, as in other physical habits, he was not regular. Leaning forward, he protruded his face critically, inspecting his jaw from several angles, then, with a dissatisfied grunt, he took off his jacket and put on his scarlet dressing-gown. Lodging the kettle on the fire, he lit a cigarette.

John was working quietly at the desk.

When the kettle boiled Christopher slopped a little water into one of John's teacups which had lost its handle, placed it steaming on the mantelpiece and fetched his shaving things from the bedroom.

"My barber tells me", he said, working up a froth, "that the secret of shaving is to lather for eight minutes." The foam grew around his jaw. "That's what he says."

167

John raised his attention from his book. "I thought you shaved yesterday. What are you shaving today for?"

"True. I did shave yesterday." Christopher laid down his cigarette, lathered his upper lip, then replaced it. "I did indeed. . . . And for a very good reason, I may add." He frowned at his reflection. "I went to tea with Elizabeth."

"Well, and today——?"

"Today Elizabeth is coming to tea with me."

"Have a good time," said John, with a nervous laugh.

"Oh, I shall." He gave an exclamation and paused again, this time to stop water trickling down his right wrist and up his cuff. "Oh, I shall indeed. Trust a Warner." He wiped the butt of his shaving brush on the towel slung round his neck and continued lathering. "We shall be having the *ne plus ultra* of good times unless I'm mistaken." John, taking a few seconds to grasp the implications of this, gave at length another half-hearted laugh. "Unless I'm very much mistaken indeed." He gave a grin, which on his lather-covered face seemed particularly disquieting. Then he dipped his safety-razor into the water. "And I don't think I am." The brittle sound as he began to scrape played on the silence. "Oh, we shall be sporting the oak all right."

John said nothing, continuing to smile. Christopher chanted, rinsing the razor:

"*One more river, and that's the River of Jordan,*
One more river, there's one . . . more . . . river . . . too—oo. . . ."

He manipulated a delicate turning. "Of course, if it weren't the first time I shouldn't be taking all this trouble," he said in his normal voice.

"The first time?"

"First time with her. That surprises you, does it? You aren't the only one. . . ."

"Well, really, I did think——"

Christopher threw his cigarette away, blowing out a cloud of smoke that fell downwards till it was sucked up the chimney, and began to shave under his nose. "No, the first time," he said with a sigh. "Girls are queer about that sort of thing, as you'll find out, my lad."

168

"Then how d'you know——"

There was curiosity in John's voice, but there was a troubled note as well. Quite to his surprise an agitation was beginning to fume up inside him as if he were being threatened in some way.

"Oh, well, I don't know," Christopher drawled. "It'll be all right. . . . She'll come up to scratch, not a doubt about it. . . ."

"But has she said——"

"One doesn't *say* everything in this life." Christopher lathered his face for the second time. "There are some things that don't need saying. . . . In fact there are some things it's definitely advisable not to say. If I asked her she'd say no. All right. I shan't ask her. . . .

"Matter of fact," he continued, scraping a different way from the first time, "I did ask her once. Last September that was, in London. . . . I'd only known her about three weeks. She said no.

"Of course it's possible she'll jib. There's something a bit queer about her and Patrick. I told you Patrick suddenly turned Catholic, didn't I? Well, that's very odd, look at it as you please. And Elizabeth. . . . She had a terrific purity ramp at one time; well, when I knew her first. Wouldn't think it to look at her, would you?"

"No," John admitted. He got up and walked about the room. Christopher's words made him uneasy. He knew that he lacked the other's confidence.

"I'd better go out, then," he said.

"Well, in the circumstances, old man, I think your presence might be a drag on the conversation," said Christopher waggishly. He dried his face on a towel and lightly shook talcum powder into the palm of his left hand. "Here!" he said over his shoulder, "there's no need to go yet."

But the door closed. John had slipped on his overcoat and was walking round the cloisters, looking up at the sky from which rain had ceased to fall, where the wind was blowing patches of cloud away, revealing blue distances. He wanted to walk and be alone: he was actually trembling, shaking at the knees, and it was some time before he could come to grips with his perturbation. In the meanwhile he had turned out of the College and down some dirty streets leading away from the picturesque part of the town : here there was the hospital, cheap lodgings, fish-and-chip shops, shops that sold second-hand furniture with the price scrawled in white on the mirrors. It might have been a street from his own home. Some children played around the entrance to a cinema and broke off their game to ask if he were going in. He did not answer.

What shocked him (for he felt shocked) was the enormous disparity he had stumbled upon between his imagination and what actually happened. When he thought of Christopher in his dressing-gown, legs straddling, his hand steadily working the razor and talking reflectively about what was going to happen, he knew with a sickening certainty that he could never sustain that position; that he would, in fact, turn and run long before it came. Even now he had turned and run, run away from that room, although he knew that he would think of nothing else all day, and in all conscience it had little enough to do with him. If this was what his quest for Jill was leading to, he would give it up without a second thought.

He came out of the allotments at the end of the town and following the path across the fields soon reached the river, which he crossed by the wooden bridge. There was a clear walk then for a mile or two, along the towpath, and he followed it, going out into the country, where cows strayed near the path and a pair of horses stood facing different ways; at a distance rose the dark slopes of a wood. The wind whistled in the bushes, the choppy water was the colour of steel, and a swan, with a tempestuous beating of wings, half rose out of the water as if to break into flight, but then thought better of it and subsided back again.

By this time he had arrived at a different conclusion. It would be all right if he could keep her away from Christopher. He must keep them apart. If he could make friends with her he must push her back into her own life, where he himself could follow. Never must she be allowed to go outside her own life. And then through her he might enter this life, this other innocent life she led. He was glad of the conversation with Christopher. It had brought him down to earth a little and forced him to

170

consider the facts he was dealing with. He recognized first of all (with a certain shameful relief) that it was not likely he would ever get to know her, but if he did, it must be away from his present surroundings that they must move. And as he knew that he would lack Christopher's rather brutal self-confidence when the time came (what was the time?), he must also see to it that the time never did come.

Pleased with his reaction into decisiveness, he continued his walk till he came to a village at the end 'of the towpath and waited at the 'bus stop. His agitation had died down and though his thoughts still circled the room cautiously, he no longer felt stronger aversion from it than he would feel from a room where a delicate and unpleasant surgical operation was taking place. Indeed, he had convinced himself that it was actually as rare and accidental as that would be. It was not connected with him any more. He would return to the centre of the town by 'bus, and, entering a café, have tea. He would skirt the College till after six, for he remembered that Christopher and Elizabeth were going to the theatre at that time.

After a while the 'bus came, and when it moved off at last he eventually recognized the extreme north end of the town, the unbroken lines of houses with quiet avenues leading off. The day had clouded over as a mirror clouds when breathed upon. It was Jill territory, and out of habit he kept a watch for her. And presently he saw her: he was sitting upstairs on the offside and the 'bus pulled up at a stop to let an old lady alight. An avenue led away on the other side of the road and down this Jill came running at full speed. The old lady had edged over the platform, gripping both handrail and silver-banded stick, and was preparing for the descent, cautiously extending one foot in the direction of the ground. The conductress waited with her hand on the bell. Jill came nearer, and, with a slight swerving in her direction so that she aimed at the back of the 'bus, showed John that she was trying to catch it. But nobody had seen her because she was approaching from the off side. The old lady, half off, was nerving herself for the final severance. Hardly had the situation grasped him than the bell rang twice, there was a second's sickening pause and then the 'bus lurched

171

forward. Jill had just reached the opposite kerb and as the 'bus drew away was lost to sight. And while he was still twisted in anguish in his seat, there was a quick patter of feet up the stairs and, flushed, breathless, but smiling from a remark exchanged with the conductress, Jill appeared, holding her handbag, looking for a seat. It seemed that the impetus of her great last effort to catch the 'bus had carried her on up the stairs.

She sat at the back. He dared not look round for fear she should recognize him. There was something about having her behind him that changed their roles: he became the one that was hunted, and it made him uncomfortable. He did not hear what fare she paid, so himself paid to the terminus so that he could alight at any point she chose. It was not likely that she would get off again so soon, but every time the 'bus stopped he turned his head very slightly so that out of the corner of his eye he could make sure the fawn blur of her coat was still there.

As she had been so eager not to miss the 'bus, she must either be late for an appointment or be going a good distance. Though he did not know exactly what time it was he imagined the second alternative was probably correct: it was not the time of day to start going far and most likely she was wanting to get into the town before the shops shut to buy something, some small urgent thing. It was certainly too late to be going out to tea and too early to be going to the cinema or theatre. But wherever she was going, he determined that this time she should not escape, this time he would run her to earth and follow her back home, even if he missed tea and dinner and breakfast next morning to do it.

The 'bus ran into the broad St. Giles', where lighted windows shone through the leafless trees on either side, and as he expected when the 'bus began to slow up for the stop at the other end she rose and he saw her fawn shoulders disappearing down the stairs. This was a popular stopping place, and in the general crush it was some moments before he could get clear of the people, and in that time she had gone some twenty yards, briskly alternating her fast steps every now and then with a little skip. Her very direction puzzled him. It was not towards the shopping centre, unless indirectly, nor the cinema. It was

towards the quieter precincts of some colleges. He was so surprised by this that he very nearly got himself run down. And
when she led him along under the walls of his own College, his
astonishment began to curdle, and when she disturbed a group
of students who lounged talking at the gate and stepped inside
so that she was lost to view, he stopped dead, his heart having
come suddenly up into his throat. Then he ran, the sweat starting out all over him as in a dream. He came panting into the
porch to hear the porter giving her directions, and they were
the same ones that nearly six weeks ago he had himself listened
to. "Staircase fourteen's on the right-hand side," the porter
was saying. "You can't miss it."

Thanking him, she set off quickly across the gravel quadrangle, swinging her handbag by the broad strap. A few tilts of
her head set her hair roughly back into place. John grabbed at
the porter's sleeve as he was turning away.

"Where's she going?" he demanded excitedly.

"Why, your room, sir; your room she's going."

"Does she want me?"

"Couldn't say, sir," said the porter, giving him a cold look,
which John disregarded on account of the sudden terrible
remembrance that was spreading over him. "But she can't go
there," he exclaimed. She vanished through the archway. "She
can't," he repeated, breaking into a run after her. "She can't,"
he echoed in the archway to the cloisters, hearing the tapping of
her shoes going round the far side, the two different-sounding
scrapes as she mounted the steps, and then through the gaps
in pillars he saw her throw off her hesitation and plunge inside.
His mouth dried and he felt almost sick, as if he had seen a
person unwittingly enter a room full of poisonous snakes. For
all that nothing happened: three rooks flew across the square
of the sky and the distant sound of jazz could be heard as
usual. What he expected to happen he did not know, but he
felt the suspense of one who has lighted a powder trail leading
to an ammunition dump.

Without meaning to, he followed her to the arch of the staircase, then, realizing that after all that there were several sets of
rooms she might have entered, yet not caring, too agitated to

173

consider things reasonably, driven forward by an emotional compound of fear, curiosity, a desire to save her and the pure desperation which when he was most at a loss seemed to push him into action, he knocked on his own door and opened it.

"John!" said Elizabeth, in a surprised voice. They all looked round again.

"Hallo, old man, didn't expect you in," said Christopher, with false joviality. John smiled suddenly.

"How do you all do?" he said.

"Will you put that kettle on," said Patrick, in the concentrated voice of one who has stood as much as he is going to stand. Christopher stuck the kettle on the fire without answering. "Oh, you don't know these people," he said casually to John, indicating the dark girl and Jill. "This is my better half, John Kemp. This is Evelyn and this is Gillian, who has the misfortune to be a cousin of Elizabeth"—Elizabeth made as if to throw her cigarette at him—"and Patrick."

He could do nothing for a moment but look at the six people in the room, noticing what they were doing. Christopher sat on the fender seat shaking the teapot with a dubious smile; Patrick and a dark Jewish-looking girl faced each other in two armchairs; Eddy sat on a plain wooden chair tipped perilously back against the desk; Elizabeth and Jill sat on the sofa. Tea was just finishing and dirty plates and cups littered the hearthrug. In a corner was a pile of coats, Jill's on top. Slightly bowed she sat, with her hands in her lap and her hair falling forward, the shape of her small shoulder-blades showing through her jacket.

"Oh?" John smiled still, the smile buckling under the weight of his astonishment. Evelyn nodded to him and Jill gave him one swift glance, hardly letting her eyes meet him. "Pleased to——"

"There'll be tea in a moment, if you can find a cup," Christopher went on. "Is there another one? I think I took the last one for Gillian. You've both come at the unfortunate time between kettles."

"I'm *sorry* I'm late," Jill repeated softly, twining her fingers together, and John found he remembered her voice.

174

To cover his confusion he went to the cupboard and found the cup without a handle Christopher had used for shaving and put unwashed out of sight. He took it outside to the tap, and as he was going Christopher replied, "Oh, that's all right, only there doesn't seem a frightful lot to eat. Not anything, as a matter of fact," so when he had washed out the rim of small hairs he ran over to Whitbread's room, which was empty. Books lay open on the table. Pulling open the cupboard, he found half a cake and stole it, running back to staircase fourteen with it under his jacket. "Here, where did this come from?" said Christopher, finding it with surprise a moment later. "Why, John, you old pirate. Good stuff. Now Gillian can be fed." He looked round for a clean plate and whacked a large slab on to it.

"Oh, that's far too big—I suppose I'd better not ask where it came from!" she said, biting and laughing. Imagining she spoke directly to him, John caught his breath. Gillian, she was Gillian, her name was Jill.

"Well, as a matter of academic interest, where did it come from?" said Christopher, arching an eyebrow at John, who was happy at being included in the conspiracy.

"From Whitbread."

"Who? Never 'eard of 'im," and Christopher went off into a roar of laughter.

"Give me some of it," said Patrick, leaning forward with an eager expression on his face.

"Oh, he's an awful man," said John, joining in. "Have all you want."

"Is it good?" Patrick asked Jill. She had a mouthful and could only nod for a moment. "Yes, lovely, but you've given me far too much. I've had one tea already. She doesn't know I'm having tea here." She blinked round shyly.

"Why shouldn't you be here?" demanded Eddy, as if scenting a personal insult.

"Well, don't talk as if she was going to vanish away into thin air at any moment!" Elizabeth protested, slipping one protective arm around Jill and pulling her against her. "Aunt Charlotte is only a bit strict. She thinks her two devoted cousins are

175

going to the theatre alone. If she knew all you louts were coming along, she'd have kittens."

"How did you escape?" said Evelyn, speaking for the first time since John had come. "By a rope of sheets from your bedroom window?"

"Or a file in a loaf?"

"She has to sit reading *East Lynne* to the old girl," said Elizabeth, looking round. "Just think, in this day and age."

"Oh, it isn't as bad as that," exclaimed Jill, putting her cup down. "Only *Sorrell and Son*." She gave a hard little laugh as if at the sound of her own voice.

"Who?" said Eddy. "I say, let's go and give the old girl a jolly-up. Pity Guy Fawkes night and all that's over. But we could give her a few carols——"

"Don't be an idiot," said Elizabeth crossly.

While they talked, Jill finished her small tea. She paid attention to everything that was said, transferring her look from speaker to speaker, turning her head so that delicate tendons showed in her neck. It was the knowledge that she would look so at him if he spoke that kept him from saying anything. All the joy he should be feeling at having her contented in a room where he was had been neutralized by the fact that he had only run her to earth in the very centre of the place he most wished to avoid—neutralized into a kind of wondering bewilderment. He helped Christopher put the black-out up.

"Alas, we must fare forth," sighed Elizabeth at last. "Get Gillian's coat, Christopher. You might behave like a gentleman, even if you aren't one."

"Ha, ha, ha!" roared Eddy, tying his muffler. Patrick and Evelyn broke off a private conversation they had been holding and looked round amicably. John went to the door, sensing that when Jill had been helped into her coat by Christopher, she would drift in that direction, and struggled in vain against the rising distress he felt at their going. She did, shying away a trifle and looking at him uncertainly. John's face became extraordinarily tense.

"I hope you enjoy it," he said.

176

"Yes—oh, yes, I expect we shall. Do you know what it's like?"

"No. I wish I was coming with you."

"Aren't you?" she said, as Elizabeth and the rest came up and swept her from the room, clattered out and down the steps. He was left alone, with the diminishing sound of their footsteps. After a second's pause he crossed to the sofa and drank the cold dregs from Jill's cup, putting his mouth where hers had been.

So many different things dismayed him. When he had followed them to the theatre and lacking the courage to go inside leant against the wall in the dusk, he occupied himself with stacking them in order of importance in his mind like a pack of playing cards. The most important was that Jill and Elizabeth were cousins. Even after an hour's steady effort he could not bring himself to anything more than a theoretical belief in this. And yet with even a theoretical belief came a dreadful sliding fear that perhaps they were much more similar in character than they looked, and certainly the knowledge came that Jill was absolutely under Elizabeth's control. Then there was the refusal on her part to recognize any relationship between them. This was uncanny, as uncanny as if he had approached a mirror, raising his hand in salute and the reflection had made no answering sign. Then there was his recollection of his decision made that afternoon that it would be all right if he could keep her away from Christopher.

He crossed the street and paid for a cheap seat at the cinema, close up to the screen. The enormous shadows gesticulated before him and he sat with his eyes shut, hearing only the intermittent remarks of the characters and the sounds of the action. It was curious how little speech there was. A squalling childish voice said something and everyone laughed: this was followed by a long interval of banging, scraping and rending, interspersed by studiedly familiar noises—the tinkling of glass against decanter, the slamming of a car door. He opened his eyes for a moment, saw a man and a girl driving through the country, and shut them again. When he thought of Jill being so near, only across the street, with people he knew, yet where he was not with her and could not see her, his breath came faster and a curious physical unease affected him and he wanted to stretch. He looked at the film again: the man and the girl had gone, and in their place a different man sat at a desk answering a telephone. It was obvious that he was intended to be funny. Shortly another telephone rang and he held it to the other ear. Replies intended for one caller were misinterpreted by the other, and the man, becoming more flustered, entangled the two flexes till he was practically bound to the chair. The audience was rocking with laughter. John became interested in the film for short spurts, but remembering every now and then that he must not forget the time and let them get away from the theatre unobserved. To avoid this he left a quarter of an hour too soon before the film had finished and went out still without knowing its title. A queue of people eyed him as he emerged.

The street was lightless, full of soldiers and airmen in search of eating-houses and bars. Shouts echoed up and down. When the first house began to pour out of the theatre, John found it was impossible to keep proper watch without half-entering the foyer, and when he had got so far he noticed a second exit he could not hope to cover. In his anxiety and eagerness he craned his neck into the light and received a blow in the ribs from an unexpected quarter. Christopher, Patrick and Eddy, their overcoats loose, were grinning at his elbow.

"Hallo, old boy, come to meet us?"

"No—no! I——" He started back in terror. "No, I just wondered . . . I wondered if I could get in for the second house——"

"Good idea! Good idea! It's well worth while, eh, Eddy?"

"Damned good show," affirmed Eddy, hiccoughing. He tried to repeat a joke that occurred during the performance and covered his failure with immoderate laughter.

"But there's no time to lose," said Patrick.

"No, I should get your seat now, old man. . . . There's bound to be something left. . . . Here, come and see."

They whirled John away to the brilliantly-lit square of glass

178

that was hung around with prices. As Christopher bent before it, the light showed the unnatural smoothness of his chin, recalling to John that he had shaved that afternoon.

"Where's Elizabeth and the others?" he asked Patrick in an undertone. Patrick stared at him without replying with a contemptuous grin.

"Yes, you're all right, old boy! Stalls left, seven and six. Forward seven and six! You're lucky. First house was pretty near packed out, eh, Eddy?"

"God, yes."

"Where are the others, Chris?" John asked desperately, handing over a ten-shilling note as if paying for information. They all reeled away from the window, John clutching a blue ticket and half a crown.

"Here, let's go for a drink," said Eddy. "Damned if I want any supper. We can eat after they close."

"But somewhere quiet."

"Lord, Pat," said Christopher with contempt, "can't you ever forget the progs?"

"Bugger the Proctors!" screeched Eddy, and a lot of people looked round. John noticed the commissionaire coming towards them. He was a big man with an unpleasant scarred face.

"Are you comin' in or goin' out?"

"Eh?" said Christopher, turning in genuine astonishment.

"Because, if yer comin' in, yer'd better keep yer mouths shut. Yer make a row and yer'll be in the street before yer know where you are."

He stooped his shoulders and put his face close.

"You mind your own damned business!" said Eddy indignantly, throwing back his head so that the weak, shaded light made deep hollows round his eyes and nostrils.

"What's that you say? Eh? What did yer say?"

"I said, mind your own damned business," repeated Eddy, deliberately and with insolence.

"And piss off," added Christopher, edging forward. His voice was commanding and he made no attempt to moderate it. The man gave no signs of increased anger.

"Now you go on and get out. Go on, get out. We don't want your sort 'ere. Get out, if you can't be'ave."

John, fearing a fight, managed to slip away and in desperation gave his ticket to a uniformed girl, going into the auditorium, which was slowly filling, though still three-quarters empty. Immediately regretting this, he put his folded overcoat on his seat, and, smoothing his soft hair, returned to the foyer, hoping that the girls would have reappeared. But now there was no trace of them and the commissionaire stood talking amiably to the usherette who took the tickets. He ran out on to the dark steps and heard the hoots of cars that crawled past, the halloo-ings and clatter of the town at night. They were nowhere. Turning back to the auditorium, he felt hollow with grief, as if there were a great well of aloneness inside him that could never be filled up. The lights were going down: one by one they went out and the imprisoning darkness returned.

He sat through the play. There was nothing else to do. When he came out the moon had risen and the railings round the little churchyard cast a grilled shadow on the grass and graves. There were huge masses of shadow, cumbrous, swallowing, but here and there façades, whole sides of streets would rise up in the pale light, their detail picked out, quietly showing their gracefulness. The wind swelled and subsided through the arches and many intricate spires. His knocking at the gate was the only sound in the street. Then the clocks began to strike a quarter to eleven.

Apart from the fact that the fire had gone out, the room was exactly as he had left it: Christopher was not there, nor by the look of things had he been back. John relit the fire with a fire-lighter fetched from the servant's cupboard, and, having washed his hands, sat down on the sofa with Christopher's months-old American magazine to read. Surely, wherever he was, whatever he was doing, he would be in by midnight. Where could they all be? The thought of the six of them laughing and enjoying themselves together caused him acute suffering as tangible as toothache. He put his head on his hands, the palms pressing the eyes, and thought how utterly tired he was of waiting. He could hear the ticking of the clock and the new flames flickering.

180

Always he had known himself to be ineffectual, but never before had he seemed quite helpless, paralysed, outpointed. He got up and poked around the bookshelves for a book connected with all the work he had left undone, noticing as he did so the file he had bought for Christopher. He did not bother to see if it were still empty.

The clock said five to twelve. Until ten past he sat expecting the sound of footsteps, for the gates were finally locked at midnight, but none came. He lay back and closed his eyes.

When he awoke Christopher was walking about and the clock showed a quarter to one. The bright light bewildered him so that he had forgotten the reason he was sitting up. The expression on Christopher's face was an angry one, and, sitting down, dropped his shoes off with a clatter.

"Just lost eighteen bob," he said.

All John could think of was that he had laid a bet that he would seduce Jill and had failed.

"Lost a bet?" he said stupidly.

Christopher scowled. "Three hours of poker with Robin Scott and Max and that fool Patrick. My God, I wonder sometimes why we put up with that man. D'you know, the swine won eighteen bob and then started crabbing about giving me a cigarette?" He threw the stub of it into the fire. "The lousy rat."

Having said this with extreme vehemence, Christopher put on his slippers and went into the bedroom: in a few moments he was swearing at the top of his voice, having broken his tooth glass. John hurried in, his mind growing clearer.

"Then you've been in College all night?"

"Ever since they closed, yes. Mind, there's a bit under there."

"But the girls, what happened to them?"

"Oh, Elizabeth rushed off with her kid and Evelyn hadn't got a late pass. . . . I'm getting sick of Elizabeth." Christopher slapped his belly vigorously and rubbed the front of his thighs, then put on his pyjama jacket and crawled into bed. He lay, exhaling heavily. John began to undress.

"And what happened this afternoon?"

181

"That's right. Lord, what a day. Oh, that was all mucked up by that blasted little cousin of theirs."

"How was that?"

"Oh——" Christopher stretched out his arms in weariness at having to remember it all again, his gesture being caught up in a yawn. "Oh, well, you see, Elizabeth had a couple of free seats we were going to use, she got them ages ago. Then this old bitch of an aunt gets to know that she's got them and makes her take Gillian. Then Gillian, the silly little fool, tells Patrick, and Patrick wanted to come and bring Evelyn, so of course the whole thing turned into a family party, properly bitched up."

"And you didn't get a chance to, well, pop the question?"

"No, but I'll tell you something, Elizabeth's turned all stand-offish again, I've noticed it all night. She's gone all motherly and protective and pure over this little fool Gillian. What do you think about that? I'm getting a bit tired of it. Christ, perhaps I won't knock it out of her when we get back to London. . . ." He gave a laugh and turned over on his side with a great rustling. "Well, anyway, I shan't have to shave tomorrow. Oh, God. Put the light out, can you? I can't be bothered."

For some reason this conversation gave John a sense of reprieve, and when he awoke in the morning he felt not despair, but happiness, his mood having changed overnight as the wind might swing completely round. It was only half light when he took his towel and went for a bath, and a few stars were still shining among the towers. Smoke from newly-lit fires poured from chimneys and was whipped away. Wind, warm and blustering, tore along under the overcast sky: in half an hour it would be an ordinary dull morning. But John did not see it like that; this half-light, this standing as it were on a prow coming over the edge of a new day, all seemed to represent the imminence of something new. And what could that be but Jill? The wet green grass in the quadrangle, the brooding of the cloisters,

182

the trees with their dripping twigs, and, above all, the wind—these felt like the agents of some great force that was on his side. He felt sure that he was going to succeed. Emerging flushed from his bath, he felt sure that if once they met again, something as strong as the wind would blow away every suspicion, every unsatisfaction he had ever suffered. He could not think why he had ever doubted the fact. They had only to meet.

What did it matter, after all, if she was Elizabeth's cousin? Whitbread had been suspicious of John simply because he shared rooms with Christopher; she was as he was: herself, no more. Everything which had contributed to his character had slipped away like an eroding cliff. When he discovered a letter from his sister in the College lodge asking why he had not answered her last one he felt too great a weariness to read beyond the first page. Bird-calls from the gardens soothed him as he dressed. His face watched him from the mirror.

At midday, after a morning of coffee-drinking, he looked into the Bull and Butcher and found Eddy Makepeace sitting alone with a glass of beer at his side. He had unfolded a newspaper and was reading the racing forecasts with an attentive look on his face. As John came in he coughed and lifted his glass to his mouth.

"Good morning," said John.

"How do." Eddy returned to his paper, but John came and sat beside him, breaking open a packet of cigarettes. "Have one?" he said.

"Ah." Eddy produced his lighter, taking one. An item of news in the column that he was reading caught his eye and his mouth opened slightly. "Great God on a bicycle," he commented to himself, extending the flame.

"Good show last night."

"Eh? Oh, the show, yes. Yes, damned good show."

"Some good lines."

"Oh, yes, some damned good lines." Eddy tried once more to reproduce the joke that had pleased him, and wheezed gently with laughter, in which John joined. He could see the back of Eddy's head reflected in a mirror.

"Where did Elizabeth get to, by the way?"

183

"Eh? Oh, Elizabeth. When, d'you mean?"

"After the show."

"Why, she went home. That's right, she nipped out quite early, before 'The King'. Don't like people to do that," said Eddy, wagging his head.

"She had that other girl with her, I suppose?"

"Who, Evelyn? Not on your life. They loathe each other. Or d'you mean that kid, that Gillian kid? Yes, she had."

"She's Elizabeth's cousin, isn't she?"

"Sure thing."

"She can't be very old."

"Just left school." Eddy changed the position of his legs and folded his newspaper away into his pocket. Then he blinked several times. "Don't feel very well this morning," he said.

"Hang-over?" inquired John knowingly. Eddy started to given an incoherent and boring account of a party he had returned to on the night before. "Here, where is everybody? Is Christopher coming in this morning?"

"I expect he'll be along."

"But you ought to hear Jack tell the story. There he was, going across the lawn with a glass and bottle, when he sees the Dean coming along with a torch. What do you think the silly sod did? Lay down for cover, like playing at soldiers. Up comes the Dean and shines his torch on him—lying there, you know, with a bottle in one hand and a glass . . ."

John laughed.

"Lord, I wish I'd seen it. Here, where is everyone? Here, Charley, has Mr. Warner been in here this morning?" Eddy called.

Charley said that he had not. Eddy drank off his beer and John bought him another.

"And how long is she staying?" he asked as he brought them back.

"How long is who staying?"

"This kid—this Gillian—— What's her second name?"

"I don't know. I don't know anything about her. Her mother's convalescent or something, and she's staying with an

184

aunt. The kid, I mean. I wanted to go and give her a jolly-up, but Elizabeth crapped on it pretty sharp."

"Why, where do they live?"

"Banbury Road way somewhere. Here!" Eddy stared at John, turning his cigarette between his fingers. It had gone out and, noticing this, he groped again for his lighter. "Here, you're not thinking of starting anything, are you? Don't be a silly fool. Elizabeth'd eat you."

"What's it got to do with her? Anyway, I wasn't," laughed John nervously, the muscles of his mouth contracting as if he has tasted something sour. Remembering a favourite retort among Whitbread's friends, he added: "You've got a crude mind."

Eddy blew out fresh smoke and drank a little beer.

"Don't be a silly fool," he repeated, and John understood he meant not only that John was stupid for trying to attract Jill to him, but stupid to be attracted to her in the first place.

"Well, damn it, what's it got to do——"

"Try, and find out." Eddy looked at his watch, an expensive one: his father was an official in India. "Damn baby snatcher." He added a comment of exceptional indecency, which made John flush and sit very still. "Hell, where is everyone?"

As if in answer, at that moment Patrick came in, first putting his head round the door. He wore a dark overcoat and carried a walking stick, coming up to them with a foxy grin. "Who's buying the next round?" he inquired.

"Hallo, Pat," said Eddy. "Three milds, that's the order."

"There you are, John, you heard what the gentleman said." Patrick hooked his stick round a chair and drew it towards him, then sat down. "Well, go on, boy! Don't sit there as if you were stuffed."

John took Eddy's outstretched glass, going to the bar.

"And you might tell Charley to put a gin in mine," called Patrick. John pretended not to hear. Eddy grinned.

When he returned, they were talking about the previous night. "No, really, Chris is a shocking loser," Patrick was saying. "We were having a hand of poker with some second-year men and Chris went down badly. And didn't he show it. He's

185

just a kid, you know, when it comes to taking the rap. Are you seeing him, by the way?" he added, turning to John. "I shan't be in for lunch. Elizabeth sent me a message for him."

"What is it?"

"Well, it was to me really, but Christopher would do as well." He flicked his cigarette. "Will he go and tell cousin Gillian that Elizabeth can't meet her for tea? She's ill or something."

"Like her bloody cheek!" said Eddy emphatically. "Why the hell can't she run her own damned errands? That's the trouble with her, she thinks nobody's got anything better to do than run about for her all the time."

"Well, they aren't on the 'phone or she'd have rung them up," Patrick explained. "They were going to the Green Leaf. Elizabeth had lost a watch strap there and was going to fetch it."

"Well, there's a chance for you," said Eddy, grinning broadly at John, who felt what was coming like the imminence of sea-sickness. "Here, know the latest? This man's got a letch on your kid cousin."

Patrick's grin spread wider, and he tilted his chair back, laughing up at the ceiling, disregarding John's amorphous denials and gestures. "Don't pay any attention to him," he was saying. "He's got a crude mind. I'm not a damn baby snatcher."

"Well, I wish you luck," said Patrick, his amusement dropping down at last. "Here's your chance, then. All you've got to do is take it."

"Chance to get clean through on the rails."

"Strike while the iron maintains a reasonable temperature."

"Lord, it's cut and dried, isn't it? Cut and dried," said Eddy, belching.

They poked him in the ribs with their laughter, slapping him on alternate shoulders to keep the joke going, buying him another drink. "Here, give him a gin in it," said Patrick again. "Give him a bit of Dutch. Go on, Charley put a gin in that last one." And he drew a new pound note from his wallet with his first two fingers.

"Now drink it down," said Eddy, bearing it brimful back.

"You are a couple of—— Look here, don't play the fool," said John indignantly. "I never said anything——"

186

"Lord, the man was giving her the once-over at tea yesterday all right. Eh, Pat?" Eddy winked.

"Foam dripping from his jaws," nodded Patrick. "Slavering at the chops." Confronted by their two false faces, John was without words. "There you see, he knows what we're talking about all right. Well, I'm damned. And here's the chance of a lifetime served up on a golden bloody plate. Now what you want to do——"

"Have you got the doings?" interrupted Eddy, leaning his bulging eyes forward. "That's what you'd better think about."

"Yes, you must get it all clear in your mind," said Patrick, also leaning forward, with his stick between his knees. One on each side of him, John cautiously responded to the rhythm of their laughter, for his true feelings had shrunk away and he had seen them safely locked up. "Whose room can I have," he laughed.

"You can have mine," said Eddy. "With pleasure, old man, and here, listen, here's an inside tip—let her get in first, there's a sod of a bump near the wall."

"Now let's get it all straight," said Patrick, wagging his right forfinger in the air before them. "What you do is call for her——"

"No, damn it, Pat, that's no good; surely he picks her up at the Green Leaf where she can't get away. What he does is come along and say: 'Sorry, Elizabeth unavoidably detained but here's unworthy self in her place——' "

"All right, then. Then at tea you put in the groundwork. Then after that suggest walking round to see Eddy——"

"Say you've left your cigar-piercer on my grand piano," cackled Eddy, scratching himself.

"And then you can get to work—sport the oak—put the black-out up——"

They were standing by this time, buttoning up their overcoats, bending over him to pat him on the shoulder again. "You'll feel like a million dollars tonight," Eddy assured him. Their breath clouding the cold air, their feet clattering on the paving stones, they proceeded up the yard towards the gentlemen's lavatory, over which stood a leafless tree.

He seriously could not connect what they said with any desire of his own, yet he knew it was a chance for all that, a chance like a piece of bread thrown among a weaving crowd of gulls and one sleek-headed, quick-beaked bird swooping it off with a slight deflection from its course. And he must be that bird, because the news was out, the hunt was up. It was incredible to him that the secret he had guarded should be parted in fifteen minutes between Eddy and Patrick, who in their turn would reveal it to Christopher and Elizabeth, from whom it would fork out in a delta of casual acquaintances. The news was screaming silently across the heavens, he realized with a feeling of panic, and he must reach Jill before it did. For this reason he must take the chance. The door to the different world had been left half ajar and swiftly, lightly, coolly, calmly, he must slip through it and be for ever safe.

A flower-seller offered him a flower on his way back, but he pretended not to see.

Yet, if Christopher had been in to luncheon, John would probably have passed the message on out of sheer servility. But he was not and John ate his curried rice with that resigned queasiness he always felt when external circumstances determined his actions for him. Whitbread, bitterly complaining, left most of his meal: it was the first he had not finished since coming into residence.

As he lay down on the sofa to wait until the time came for him to go out, the fire smothered under a load of fresh coal, he pulled his writing pad on to his lap, thinking it was time he sent his long-overdue letter to Mr. Crouch. "Dear Mr. Crouch," he wrote, "I am sorry I haven't written to you since I arrived, but I have had a good deal to do." The two lies lay quietly on the page waiting for him to add to them, but he could not. Crouch and the world of his boyhood lay tidily behind him: all the sense of continuity that made days, weeks, months, slip away like the perspective of a street, had broken up, and all seemed a crowd of gulls, circling, crying, recircling, suspended, between the sky and the shore.

He was dreading this afternoon of definite action like a visit to the dentist's. The drink he had had still confused his mind. It was strange, everywhere there were young men like himself planning their afternoons, their evenings, all they would do now and for ever more: no one felt this lapsing, lifting, turning and returning motion like a crowd of gulls. Knowing their desires they went straight for them. And although he knew his, going straight for them was like firing a gun in a dream: things locked and jammed, every possible bewildering mistake interfered.

When it was time for him to set out he tore the sheet of note-paper from the pad and burnt it before leaving the room. He was starting early because he dare not run the risk of missing her, and he had to slow down his nervous steps deliberately. The wind could hold off the rain no longer: drops fell, then a fine unified rain came down, whole blocks of it blowing about like the sudden turning of swallows. It swept against windows, blew horizontally up the street, diagonally across the lawns; from every tree, bush and wall of ivy there came a faint hissing. The streets began to reflect the grey sky. Once more the old buildings dripped. And John, rejecting two half-formed inclinations—one to walk down to the river and the other to walk anywhere as long as it was far away—stood for three minutes to shelter on the steps of All Saints' Church by the 'bus stop, looking at the lights in the upper windows of the shops opposite.

He wished he was rich enough to give a party, a party for Jill, with the furniture pushed back, a white cloth on the table and barrels and clean glasses making the room like a bar. A fire of logs roared. There was gin the colour of morning mist and whisky like fairy gold. He wore a ten-guinea suit and smoked with an amber cigarette-holder. Everyone came: Christopher hung his pork-pie hat on a stag's antler, cracking jokes; John punched Eddy in the ribs and raced him through the first pint; danced with Elizabeth and felt her breasts pushed against him. Bottles were recorked and sent floating down the river with messages inside them. The radiogram played without being attended to. And the dancers became fewer, one by one they dropped out, till in the end only Jill stood where she had stood all the evening, dressed in white, in

189

a corner, turning and turning one tiny unemptied glass in her two hands.

Descending the steps with two discontented skips, he pushed through the people, elaborating and economizing the story, so intent on it that even when Jill herself came out of a shop ten yards away his stride carried him up to her before he realized she was there.

His surprise articulated itself into a greeting and she looked round quickly, her face wary and without expectancy. "Oh, hello!" She just about recognized him. Dressed in a fawn raincoat of military cut (with a belt and flaps to the pocket) she wrinkled her nose at the rain and held an umbrella ready for opening with both hands, a trifle gingerly. "Gosh, isn't the weather foul," she said, with a kind of undirected petulance.

Slowly, exasperatingly slowly, he thought of something to say:

"What have you been buying?"

"Christmas cards." Her voice was surprised. "This is a good place."

"Is it?" He continued looking at her. "Isn't it—rather early, isn't it?"

She instantly checked a movement to look at her wrist watch, answering:

"Well, it's only a month till Christmas."

"Is that all." He laughed. "Look, as a matter of fact I was looking for you. Elizabeth is ill or something. She can't come."

"Ill, is she? Oh, dear. What, really ill?"

"Oh, I don't think so—she just sent a message saying she was sorry——"

"She did have a headache last night, I remember. . . . Thank you very much for telling me."

John looked at her intently, collecting the half-dozen shuddering words together:

"Will you have tea with *me*?"

"Oh——" She was caught off her balance, almost literally, for she took a step down on to the pavement away from him. "Oh, I don't think I will, thanks. I must go back if Elizabeth's not well."

"Oh, do. It's only half-past three." Beyond her head he could see a clock showing twenty to four. Now it was happening and her real quick body was edging away from him, the precariousness of it all made him speak urgently. In theory he wanted to take hold of her.

"Oh, I don't think I'd better, thanks. Thanks very much all the same. I'd better go back."

He took a step after her. "This the way you're going?"

"Yes. . . ." She gave him a doubtful look. "I've got another errand."

It did not seem bad-mannered to fall in beside her as she set off up the street again, the way he had come, because there was nothing else to do short of the impossibility of leaving her there and then. She had opened her brown, small-sized umbrella and the spread of it kept him a foot or so from her. Her Wellingtons made a lolloping sound as she walked. Now that he was not talking, he had less excuse to look at her, but when he did his admiration was unhindered; he blushed quickly as if on the point of tears. She raised her left hand and drew back a wet strand of hair, tucking it behind her ear.

"This is my shop. I want some braid."

He followed her through the swing doors, to the thick carpets, hanging dresses and the stacked-up material that filled the air with silence. There was a smell of cloth. A young girl dressed in black, with a white collar, came to serve her; they were of the same age and height and John compared them as he stood back by a table of handbags and leather belts. The girl's mouth fell open as she listened, and she went to a drawer behind the counter: Jill followed, twisting the umbrella nervously. Because of her fair hair and her pale raincoat contrasting with the dark dresses of all the assistants, the light seemed to be drawn down to her, to single her out. The girl stretched her hands apart and between them was bright brick-red braid. Jill bent forward, touched it: John heard her ask a question. It amused him to see her finger the stuff so seriously. Then lengths of it were carelessly stretched against the brass yard-measurement at the edge of the counter, snipped off and wrapped in a twist of brown paper. In the meantime she paid the bill and dropped

191

her umbrella. The presence of John standing in the front of the shop with his shabby blue overcoat and feet planted apart, seemed to unsettle her.

"Are you finished? What about some tea now?"

"No, I must go, I must catch a 'bus."

"Where?"

"Round the corner."

This was very near and John was suddenly filled with the dread of losing her. "Don't go," he said desperately.

"What?"

"I wanted to say . . . It's really the strangest thing——"

A perambulator and some women parted them, and when they rejoined the edge of her open umbrella tapped him on the head twice.

"Before I met you—— You remember, the first time I asked you if we hadn't met before——"

"Well, we hadn't, surely——"

"No, but we did. And in a way we had. Excuse me." They pushed through a gossiping crowd on the street corner. "I knew you, you see I knew you quite well——"

"What?" An immense Air Force transport lorry and trailer was taking the corner and every interstice of silence was filled with a complaining din. "I'm sorry, I didn't quite——"

"I mean, your face was familiar to me." John looked at her, longing for some other medium than speech. "Long before I saw you I knew who you were——"

"Do you mean Elizabeth had——"

"What? I mean, I beg——"

"Had Elizabeth——"

"No—I mean, it's hard to explain." They looked all ways, crossing the road to the 'bus stop, staring round as if bewildered. "It seemed I knew you—I knew your name was Jill——"

"It's not Jill!" During a lull in the traffic her voice rang out perhaps more sharply than she had intended, and she turned, for the first time a laugh broke over her face, drawing back her mouth, heightening her savage cheekbones. "I'm sorry, that's just a thing with me. I told you yesterday—oh, no, you weren't

192

there. No, I won't be called anything but Gillian, please. . . .
But do go on. I feel I vaguely interrupted you."

"It all sounds so silly—you see, I had a letter from my
sister," John was beginning when a big red 'bus came splashing
up, causing the little crowd to stir and tighten. "A letter came,"
he repeated as they moved. "Look, I must tell you all this
properly. Come and have tea with me tomorrow."

"I must go now. Good-bye."

"Will you come and have tea with me tomorrow?"

"Yes, all right, good-bye."

"Will you come about four?"

"What? Yes, all right." She was on the step and did not look
back. "Good-bye."

He stood back, watching the 'bus load up and move away,
dazzled by the sudden pyrotechnical ending to their meeting
and her promise. He was so overcome he walked straight home,
the noise and the wind and the hiss of tyres on the road bearing
him up like martial music, walked home and sat in his empty
room. But almost immediately he got up and went out again,
too excited to sit still. He could not believe that she had given
her word to come and see him. It was as if he had been walking
at a brick wall, knowing it to be brick and impenetrable, and
had suddenly found that he was wrong, finding that he could
go straight through it, that it was only a pattern of light. He
was through it! An almost physical sense of emergence possessed him.

Without knowing where he was going he made his way to the
canal, that stands through the town nearly unnoticed past coal-
yards, railway sidings, the backs of houses and gardens. He had
never walked by it before, and its novelty coincided with his
unfamiliar mood. The wet gravel stained his shoes. The rain
had stopped, and the water was quite still, disfigured at times
by scum, weed and rotten wood, all drifted to a standstill. A
brightly painted coal barge was moored to a wharf on the other
bank: on his side there was a hedge dividing him from allotments and the railway lines. The hedge was wet, smelling of
damp wood and leaves, but the nettles under it were dry
and soft-looking, with occasionally a single bead of water

193

lodged between leaf and stem. A packet of chips lay half hidden in the ditch.

From this side, the west, the sun began to struggle through, a yellow light making every twig glisten. The air seemed to freshen at once and the only sound was the squelching of his shoes; ducks swam cautiously away from him and farther on a single swan drifted sulkily on the water. The dropped head, the neck's magnificent curve and the webbed feet giving every now and then a stroke backwards expressed disdain and scornfulness. Because of the nearness of the coal yards and the telephone wires and dirty water, he did not think it beautiful at first. But something about it fascinated him. And as he watched, an express train hurtled past twenty yards off on the shining rails, and the long stretch of coaches racing away awakened nothing like regret in him, as they once would. He was glad to see them go; glad, simply, to be where he was, and to see them go.

Out of the fullness of his heart he invited Whitbread round for some beer when they had finished dinner in the half-empty hall (it was a meatless night, and many members of the College distrusted the chef's experiments).

"Eh, that's nice of you," said Whitbread, clasping his own gown near each shoulder as they stood up. "If you don't mind, though, I prefer coffee."

"Coffee, then," said John, laughing. They walked out together: the Head Scout watched them distantly.

Whitbread had never been in John's rooms before and looked about him with interest, rubbing his hands before the fire and appraising everything. "Ay! this could be a real nice room. Expensive in the old days, I reckon. You wouldn't have had this room in the old days."

"No, I suppose not." John laid out cups and saucers. "There's having to share——"

"That's a drawback, I know." His eyes fell upon the crockery, and he made a pleased noise, changing the subject. "That's a nice pattern. Yes, I like that. Yours, is it, or——?"

"It's mine all right. Chris hasn't got any."

"Hasn't he? What does he do, then?"

"Uses mine," said John, with a grin, but also with a very slight trace of embarrassment.

Whitbread looked deeply indignant. "Eh, I wouldn't stand for that; no, I wouldn't!" he exclaimed. "Eh, I think that's going a bit far! D'you mean to say he just——— Eh, I wouldn't stand for that, not for a moment!"

"It doesn't matter," said John lightly. This was one of the moments when the thought of Jill came over him with a little ripple of renewed pleasure. "It doesn't matter at all. Sugar?"

"Ay, if you can spare it." He looked at John with honest, covetous eyes. "How are you off?"

"Go on, take what you like."

He held the sugar bowl out to Whitbread, liking him for his quaint politeness, which was so different from Eddy's "Where's the sugar, Chris, you mean hound?"

Whitbread took four lumps.

"Here," he said, leaning forward confidentially, stirring his coffee. "I hope you don't mind my asking, but have you a lock on your cupboard?"

"No, I don't think so."

"No, nor have I. I'm thinking of having one put on. There's *thieves* in this college."

"Thieves?"

"Ay, thieves. Only t'other day I lost a cake from my room, only a third eaten. A lovely cake it was, too—from home. That's no joke. To my mind, a lot of these fellows are pretty light-fingered, for all their cash."

He slept at last: and woke at last in the morning, lying for perhaps five seconds wondering what there was to remember until he remembered it. It was as if the world lay silent as an orchestra under the conductor's outstretched arms. Then the moment of remembrance set every nerve in his body trembling, as a movement by the conductor might send a hundred bows to work. For one curious transient second he thought he knew how a bride feels on the morning of her wedding.

He watched Christopher's face very carefully as they got up.

195

If Eddy and Patrick had spread the ribald news, he would sooner spend the day twenty miles away. But Christopher made no reference that could be construed in any way as bearing on Jill's promised visit. He had certainly spent the night before with Eddy, but all he said was, sitting semi-disconsolately in his bath robe, with a towel around his shoulders as if he was at the barber's, that they had met a very interesting man who repaired organs. So John dressed in his best clothes—his suit, that is, his bow, and a clean shirt. He put some oil on his hair to help part it, and immediately disliked the effect, so undressed and went to wash his head in the showers.

It was Saturday once more, busy, yet full of pleasure. The town was as gay as a landlocked swimming pool. Ancient buildings lay petted in the sun: roofs where the sun had not yet reached were white with frost. As John came out of the College at about ten o'clock to buy food for tea, it seemed impossible on such a day that anyone should be short of five minutes or five pounds, or be unable by entering the next café to find handfuls of his best friends. He inspected the crowded shops. He bought here and there a number of fruit tarts, a jam roll and a sponge cake filled with jam, and a fruit cake. He carried them most carefully and watched the clean new bags for any stain that would show that the jam was crawling out. As soon as he could, he took them back to his rooms and arranged them on plates. The daily pint of milk had just arrived and he set that with them at the back of the cupboard.

At this point he noticed that his hair since washing had become far too fluffy, and he spent some time in front of the bedroom mirror with a comb and hair oil, smearing drop after drop along the teeth of the comb in an effort to distribute it evenly. This made it look better, but he still was not satisfied, though there was nothing else he could do. He went out a second time to look for radishes and lettuces, for he had noticed them in the shops and it occurred to him that they would contrast pleasantly with all the sweet things he had just bought.

The market was the best place to buy them, a stone-paved maze of semi-permanent stalls covered with a glass roof right in the centre of the town. John had already visited it several times before: he had discovered that to step into it from the streets outside was to enter an unexpectedly different world, a world he found he liked. It smelt of chrysanthemums and vegetables; all around the butchers' shops sawdust was scattered on the stone flags, naked electric bulbs shone on boxes of fruit, and always pools of water were slowly draining and drying away as if the place was sluiced down with a hose-pipe every hour or so. At this time of the day there were lines of women queueing for meat, dressed in dull clothes and carrying baskets. They straddled round as they stood, talking patiently, exchanging traditional unquestioned comments on things that affected their daily lives. As he slipped past them he heard them say things their parents must have said, things that women like them said in every country, and looking at their fat or withered faces, their hair tucked into old hats, and the worn purses in their hands, they seemed to him the oldest thing in the city he had seen.

John, because of experience at home, could choose lettuces with sound fresh hearts, and radishes that were not fibrous; the newspaper parcel he carried away was light and damp. For a moment, attracted by the large vases of flowers, he was tempted to buy a dozen blooms to decorate the room, but turned aside instead to a tobacconist's, where he selected a packet of semi-expensive cigarettes and was momentarily alarmed at the price of them. As he left the shop he noticed from his reflection in the window that his hair was just breaking prettily out of place, half-way between wildness and precision, and this pleased him.

When he he had hidden his purchases away in the cupboard and washed his hands, it was time for lunch. He was too nervous to eat and almost immediately after leaving Hall began to feel hunger.

He considered his nervousness gravely as he walked round the gardens in this suspension of time before two o'clock. It seemed to have no significance.

Christopher was lazily collecting his football clothes, for a match had been arranged for the College XV that afternoon and this would take him out of the way—so propitiously that

197

John suspected himself of having known the fact beforehand without consciously recognizing it. Smoking a cigarette, Christopher packed up his little case full of jerseys, shorts and a towel and announced his intention of borrowing Semple's bike for the afternoon. Since Semple had gone down, his bicycle had lain unused in the cycle sheds until Christopher had discovered it: he had since bought a padlock to keep it locked.

"Who are you playing?" John asked idly.

"An R.A.F. crowd."

He glanced at John, making no comment on his appearance, and though John was relieved, a sense of depression also overtook him at the thought of how little he could alter even his outward semblance. When he was alone, he studied himself in the mirror, and after careful thought removed the fountain pen from his breast pocket, tucking a clean handkerchief there instead. Then he went to the bedroom to find Christopher's nail scissors, and trimmed where his eyebrows met in the middle. His own nails he had thoroughly brushed that morning.

Now it was time to consider the food. The lettuce should be washed, he decided, turning it about on its dirty newspaper, and filled the crested washbowl for the purpose. Plunging it in, he pulled off the outside leaves one by one, shaking them and putting them on his towel, which he spread across the bed. But once he began to pull it to pieces, it seemed to grow larger, it was enormous, far too big for two. Here was enough for a hutchful of rabbits. In the end he threw away all but the centre, the succulent pale green heart: this he shook in a towel, as he had seen his mother do, to drain it.

The radishes should have been brushed, but he had to be content with rubbing the mud off by hand and snipping off the tails. He put them all in a saucer, ate two, and immediately was afflicted with a kind of nervous hiccups, which lasted while he was making fumbling attempts to cut thin bread and butter. Time and time again the knife came through with only half a slice wilting down on to the plate, and big buttery crumbs falling out of the middle. The failures he ate, and in time the hiccups stopped. When he had a successful plateful, he bundled the depleted bread and butter back into the cupboard.

He came aware that the room was not very tidy, and he put the food on to a side table while he rearranged what was lying about. A small phalanx of empty bottles belonging to Christopher he straightened, but did not remove, as he thought they might look impressive: the wine bottles he put at the front with their labels showing. He erected the books on the shelves. The gowns he hung up, also within sight, emptied the ashtrays, plumped the cushions and straightened the things on the desk. The hairy tablecloth was covered in crumbs and, failing to brush them off with his hands, he took it off bodily and gave it a shake. At each flap several loose sheets of notes went sailing into the hearth.

There were several improvements he could still make, he thought, and he set about improving the general effect rather than correcting isolated details. Christopher's battered, tape-bound, but expensive and athletic-looking racquet he laid at a careless diagonal on the window seat. The wine list Christopher had stolen from one of the restaurants he propped up in a more prominent position on the mantelshelf. On the table he placed the two most scholarly books he had out at the moment from the College library and beside them a half-finished sheet of notes in his own writing, annotated and underlined in the way he had learnt from Mr. Crouch. The fire he stoked skilfully so that in about an hour there would be a bright comforting blaze. Then he shut his eyes, opened them, and tried to decide if the result impressed him in any definite way. It did not, but then perhaps he knew it too well.

When he had laid a tablecloth and the food, cups and saucers and knives on a small occasional table by the sofa, the whole looked daintier than he had imagined possible, and even appetizing, though he did not by this time feel hungry. But there was no salt. He had forgotten about this, clutching the salt-cellar in a desperate way, remembering that the kitchen was shut. There was nothing for it but to go out and buy a packet from the nearest grocer; it was far too large and cost more than seemed right, but he did not argue, recalling irrelevantly the *gabelle*—one of the causes of the French Revolution.

And when he got back, panting, the afternoon post had

come. There was nothing for him, and at this moment, with the hands of the College clock pointing at twenty to four, a definite unease began swerving about his bowels. She was going to come. Up till then he had not believed she would, or he could not have gone about the preparations in such a methodical way. All his actions had sprung from a kind of theoretical assumption, as a farmer might prepare against the winter, and he had been placidly expecting a note from her to say that she was very sorry, but the visit was impossible. Now this had not happened, and was not going to happen. In a half-hour she would probably be here. The last barrier had been taken away.

Salt in hand, he walked diffidently back round the cloisters, and he found the room looking so different because of his scene-shifting that it looked unfriendly, and a small hysteria seized him. He must get away before she came. He would leave a note pinned to the door. The idea of her standing there, taking her coat off, expecting to be entertained, sent him shuddering to the window to see if there were any signs of her. There were not. He could sport the oak and slip out the back way, through the gardens, and run no risk of meeting her. That was what he would do.

But with an effort of will he filled the salt-cellar, resigning himself to whatever should happen. For, after all, he did want her to come, he knew he did. Whatever happened, they would be together; even if they sat in miserable silence, out of this single circumstance some virtue could be distilled. Even the fact of meeting would be a point that with the passage of time might spread out fanwise behind her into a new country, somewhere free of himself. Though he knew he had been stupid in aiming dumbly in this direction with no regard for his incapacity to control any situation that might arise through doing so, he was still not really sorry. In a small outlandish way he was proud, seeing it as an act of bravery, like a soldier without weapons charging a machine-gun emplacement.

He rocked backwards and forwards on his heels in front of the fire, hands in his pockets. All was ready—too soon, of course.

But his thoughts were interrupted by the sound of a girl's

quick steps round the cloisters. Eight minutes at the very least early? Compliment or accident? He sat down, stood up. No, perhaps it was no one for him. They drew nearer. He fixed his eyes on the door, seriously, his hand moving in surprise round the bow tie he was wearing. The feet mounted the steps, approaching the door.

Two knocks.

"Come in."

Elizabeth entered.

He blinked. His first thought was that she had called to see Christopher, and that he must get her out of the way as soon as possible. But she did not seem surprised to see him. She released the doorknob, and holding her handbag in both hands, addressed him:

"Oh, hullo, John. I just wanted to talk to you a moment. . . . Gillian said you asked her to tea."

"Yes, I——"

"Well, I think it would be better if she didn't come." She paid no attention to the tea table, keeping her eyes fixed on him and speaking rather more loudly than usual and without her customary trailing vowel sounds. "You see, her people are really awfully strict and would be very annoyed if they found out. I thought you knew all that."

"But—she said——"

"Well, she's only a kid, and didn't want to hurt your feelings. Really, you ought to have known. . . . I thought you knew how things stood."

Cold air from the door reached John's face.

"Well, I—I'm sorry. . . ."

"When she told me, I thought it was some kind of a joke you or someone were trying to play. . . . But even if it isn't, I'm afraid it's not possible for her to come. I should have thought you'd have guessed that."

And in the hesitant interval after this she suddenly turned and went out, closing the door behind her, with no farewell.

In a couple of minutes there was a fresh noise of six stumbling feet outside, and the door burst open to admit Eddy Makepeace, Patrick Dowling and Tony Braithwaite. Tony and

201

Eddy gripped him jovially by the arms and slapped his back. Patrick went round the sofa to the little table that held the food.

"Bad luck, old man!" cried Eddy. "Bad luck. A damn noble attempt. We saw her come in. Did she take your pants down and smack your bottom?"

"What did she say?" asked Tony. "I knew she'd jump on it."

"But you should have let us in on it," protested Eddy. "I didn't hear till lunch-time. If we'd known, we could have fixed everything, got her out of the way and all the rest of it."

"I thought she was ill," said Tony.

"Supposed to be." Pat's mouth was full. "Not too ill, it seems."

"The interfering sow," said Eddy indignantly. "You know, Pat, all respects, but your sister is the hell of a bitch. A nosy bitch, that's what she is."

"Still, it was a sound attempt," said Tony Braithwaite. "We must try it again sometime. I think it would be wonderful if we could really get her right from under her nose."

"I like annoying her," said Eddy. "I don't know why, but I love it."

"Tony, put the kettle on," Patrick directed. "Don't forget to fill it, either, like last night. We might as well help John out with all this stuff—lettuce, John?"

He extended the plate. John opened his mouth and made a queer noise: it began as a polite refusal, but owing to the fact that he had been breathing unusually, it ended as a semi-articulated cry, shaken with a curious blubbering vibrato. He had not meant to utter it, but once he had done so it was of course impossible for him to remain in the room, and he crossed to the door and went out, leaving Patrick staring after him in mock (and the other two with real) surprise.

It seemed that the next few days passed quickly, but the lengthening of time only increased the pain he felt, as if each day were a weight added to a load slung from a hook in the flesh. He spent them in trying to enlarge the periods during which he forgot the events of that Saturday afternoon. He did not succeed very well. All his life he had imagined people were hostile to him and wanted to hurt him; now he knew he had been right and all the worst fears of childhood were realized. He was used to humiliating memories, but these seemed different, they had really existed. Because of them his daily habits turned completely round: he made every effort to avoid finding Jill, not to go in any place where she might be. He even kept out of his own room, but in any case it had grown loathsome to him. The memory lay on his mind like an enormous boulder, and he felt that the passage of time would erase it hardly as fast as such a boulder would be worn away by the continual dripping of water. The weight of it stunned, drugged him. He went about, as people thought, in a dream.

It seemed impossible that anything should shift it, yet, at lunchtime on the fourth day, Whitbread did so, a few casual remarks by him making it seem as flimsy as a paper decahedron. Whitbread was the only person John had regularly spoken to that week, and then it was at mealtimes, and usually about food. And now, having placed sufficient cold meat and salad in his mouth to last him for a minute or two, Whitbread wheeled his large dormouse-like head in John's direction, blinking, as if uncertain how to start.

"D'you hear the one o'clock news, Kemp?" John looked round, startled, and Whitbread repeated his question. "No," said John. "No, I didn't."

"Oh." Whitbread paused to manœuvre the food in his mouth. "I thought perhaps you had. They dropped a packet on your town last night, it seems."

"What, you mean on Huddlesford?"

"Ay. I think it was pretty serious, from what they said."

"What, you mean a real air-raid—like Coventry?"

"A heavy and concentrated attack, they said. It has to be pretty strong before they mention it at all." Whitbread's eyes widened slightly as he swallowed, and he collected some more food together with his knife and fork. John had stopped

203

chewing. "I thought perhaps—if you have anyone there——"

"My parents are there——" John turned to Whitbread. "What did they say? Tell me what they said!"

"Oh, it was the usual stuff, you know. . . . Heavy and concentrated attack, damage to schools, hospitals, churches, residential areas—like they always say, you know. . . . The fires are under control——"

"Did they say whereabouts was damaged?"

"No, well, they never say that."

"Not at all—no hint?"

"Residential areas. . . . I expect they went for the station and factories and the centre of the city. . . ." He looked doubtfully at John. "Do you live anywhere near the station?"

"No, not at all."

John got up, leaving his food, and went trembling out into the sun. They said a thousand people were killed outright in a raid like that, not counting the wounded and those that died afterwards. It was not possible for his parents to have escaped. What was he going to do? An icy pocket of misery had suddenly enveloped him, cutting him off from the pale lemon light of the sun that slightly warmed the air, and the pigeon waddling across his path. He remarked the soft silky grey feathers. His mind was struggling under the impact of the news, as an unwary bather caught by a wave will be swept along with waving arms and legs. Each time he thought his parents were dead, he believed it a little more. And it was all over now, settled one way or the other, and he did not know. How could he find out? He longed for confirmation.

The first thing he thought to do was to go to the Post Office and send home a telegram of inquiry. The girl behind the bars counted the words as if it were an ordinary message. As he paid he asked when it would be delivered. She did not know.

"It depends, you see, on the telephone services. . . . They're out of action. They might be out three or four days, it all depends."

"There's no quicker way?"

"Not at present, no."

He pocketed the change, thinking of his telegram arriving at his wrecked house, and being undelivered, wandering perhaps like his letters to Jill. In the midday sunshine the first edition of papers was being sold, and he hastened to the corner to buy one, but the last copy was bought just as he arrived. The chalked placard read *Heavy Raid on Northern Town*, and when he found another paper-seller who had also sold out, hers said *Heavy Raid on Huddlesford*. The knowledge that Whitbread had told the truth settled down like an iron mould on his mind; he walked back to the College filled with dread. Everyone was just leaving the Hall, coming out into the sun with their hands in their pockets, the sharp sunlit folds of their trousers creasing and uncreasing. As they deployed they carried on their conversation in shouts. The porter, Herbert, stood watching from the lodge door.

"Herbert, who's got the key to the shed at the bottom of the rugger ground?"

"Can't hear you, sir!" The porter put one hand to his ear and when the young man came up, continued: "Didn't they learn you to come and ask what you want to know properly where you was brought up?"

Whitbread caught John up as he was walking wretchedly into the cloisters.

"Here, Kemp, if I were you I'd get leave to go home for a couple of days."

John was touched by the concerned note in his voice.

"D'you think I could?"

"Of course you could, man. Go and catch Rivers now."

"I've just sent a telegram. But they say it won't be delivered for days——"

"No, the lines will all be taken up with official calls."

"They may let me know."

"I should go and see for yourself."

"Yes, but——" John was conscious of being badgered towards action he did not want to take.

"Well, hang it, man," exclaimed Whitbread, "you've got to *know*!"

"Yes, I suppose so."

He had to know: if they were dead, he had to know as soon

205

as possible: if he delayed, and then found that out, it would be unbearable. Yet he felt a great unwillingness to do anything: he had learnt that action usually left him worse off than better.

"I should go and see Rivers now, and get there tonight."

John licked his lips unhappily.

"No, it's too late to go today. I'll wait till tomorrow morning, and then go, if I've heard nothing."

"I should go and see him now in any case. He might be able to help."

Reluctantly, John fetched his gown and paid a call on Rivers, the Senior Tutor. He was out. John drifted up to Whitbread's room, which was on the same staircase, biting his lips.

"Well?"

"He wasn't in."

"Oh, wasn't he?" Whitbread had already sat down at the desk where his books were, though the clock showed only a quarter to two. "Try again in an hour's time. You can bring your books and work here, if you like."

"I say, would you mind? Shouldn't I interrupt you?"

"It'd take more than you to do that," said Whitbread, with a grin, squaring his elbows.

So John fetched some books and crouched in the tiny window seat, moving after a short time to an armchair near the fire. He kept quiet, but did little work. Three times he called on Rivers and each time he was out. Once he went to the lavatory. Whitbread worked on steadily and imperturbably: his calm was encouraging: he worked exactly as John used to work at school. Outside, the clear November day clouded. John went to see if there was any post for him, but there was not.

At half-past four they brewed strong tea and toasted bread on knives before the fire. "You know, what I like about Oxford is that there's a place for everyone," said Whitbread. "You and me, now. My dad was always saying that if I got to college I'd have no friends, everyone'd look down on me. But I used to tell him I knew I'd find some decent fellows—like yourself, now— fellows in similar circumstances who'd be prepared to be friendly. I used to tell him, all over the country there are fellows like me trying to better themselves. There'll be enough of them there." He turned round the piece of bread he was toasting. "But he wouldn't have it, you know. Said they'd all be Eton and lah-di-dah." He laughed.

"Well, Warner——"

"Warner!" Whitbread sat back scoffingly. "*He's* nobody. *He* hasn't got the breeding of a back-streeter."

"Well, he's rich enough," said John.

"Is he? I never see him throwing much money away, and he cadges a good deal. He'd cadge off anyone—he'd cadge off you, if you were fool enough to let him, and I'll wager he wouldn't pay you back. Oh, I've got no time for his sort."

John spread some beef extract on his dry toast. "He's decent enough."

"Well, I've no time for him." Whitbread spoke impressively. "I get sick of his sort. It's not as if he were any real class, either: now, someone of consequence, from Eton or Harrow, say—I can respect them. Someone of breeding. Money makes a difference, and it's no use saying it doesn't. But these fellows like Warner, trying to jump into the class above them, coming from tinpot public schools like Lamprey, where they only learn bad language and dirty habits——"

"He rather amuses me," said John, lamely.

"Ay, well, maybe he does. But bad manners don't amuse me, I've seen too much of the real thing. Him and his actress mother and shady father."

"Is she an actress?"

"Yes! Was at one time, anyway. But what does it mean, him coming here?" Whitbread interrogated the air with a piece of bitten toast. "If he'd had to do what I did—if he'd had to do a quarter of what I did——"

He went on to describe his schooldays, the struggle he had to stay on after taking the School Certificate, the hours of study, the hostility of his two elder brothers (both electrical engineers), who said he was a drag on the family, and was trying to get above himself. One night they had torn up some of his notebooks. After that he always kept a second, skeleton set of notes and references, for fear they should do it again. "They never did, though. And when I got my scholarship, we all shook

207

hands when they came home from work, and they apologized. Nothing succeeds like success." Whitbread grinned gnomishly. "Eh, wasteful! You're burning that bread. Give it a scrape."

John obeyed. "You had a harder time than I did. I should never've thought of trying for a scholarship, if it hadn't been for my English master." He paused, thinking. "Why, I should never have dreamed of it."

"Ay, well, that's your trouble, Kemp," said Whitbread. "You don't push yourself enough. It's no good being clever if you can't put yourself over. Now, I'm not that clever, but I'm going. That's my philosophy. And I've got this far, anyway." He stared proudly round the small garret.

"Mother and Dad were decent about it, too," said John. He looked into the fire, chewing, and his face went hard as he remembered. Putting down his empty teacup, he got up. "I think I'll go and see if Rivers is back yet. Thanks awfully for the tea—I hope I haven't been a nuisance or anything——"

"Not at all!"

The Senior Tutor had just at that moment come in and was hanging his hat and overcoat in a small closet. He washed, listening to what John had to say through the open door, and came back, rubbing his hands together and switching on the reading lamp that stood on his desk. He was a tall, stooping man, and with an air of vagueness and inattention, and his deep voice was uneven in clarity.

"You mean you want leave of absence for one night," he said, pulling out his fountain pen and taking up a printed form. "Are you sure that one night will be enough?"

"Oh, I hope so; yes, sir."

Rivers filled in the form roughly, disregarding the dotted lines. He handed it to John with a smile of extreme kindness.

"Well, if you find it isn't, send me a wire or something. It will be all right."

"Yes, sir. Thank you, sir."

"When are you going? Tonight?"

"Tomorrow."

"Right." Rivers's cheek twitched in an embarrassed way, but he did not say anything more, only smiled, so John withdrew. He walked back to his room, examining the pass: Rivers must consider the air-raid as serious, for such passes were notoriously difficult to get. Now that it was all settled, he felt resigned and to a certain extent relieved. There was nothing to do now but wait for the morning. He looked apprehensively at the darkened sky. The servant had put up the black-out in their room, and there John found Christopher just back from the cinema, crouching on the fender-seat to warm his hands. The gold signet ring he wore glinted intermittently in the firelight.

"Hallo, brother," he remarked softly. "How's tricks?" He made no mention of the Huddlesford raid, and for this John was glad, though, as a matter of fact, Christopher had not heard about the raid, and if he had would not have connected John with it. When he had warmed himself, he went into the bedroom, whistling loudly, to change his shirt and tie.

"Care for a drink?" he suggested casually when he returned.

"I'd sooner not leave College, thanks," said John stiffly. "I'm expecting a message."

"Well, let's have one here."

Christopher took out a bottle and a pair of glasses. John, sitting on the sofa, watched him fill each small glass to the brim, the light shining through, and thought how often he had sworn to hate Christopher for ever. It all made no difference. Such things were no more than the wind blowing first one way, then another. Nothing was altered by them. He took up the glass.

"Cheers."

"Cheers."

After Christopher had drunk, he chuckled, and offered John a gaudy packet of cigarettes. "Go on," he said, "they're Cuban —soaked in molasses. I got the last couple of packets from the George today. There'll be no more for the duration. They'll knock you back. I gave Elizabeth one this afternoon and it nearly did for her. I say, you got across her last week, didn't you?"

John had to think for a moment before he recollected. "Oh, yes," he said. "Yes, I suppose I did."

"Well, I told you how it would be." Christopher chuckled again, boyishly, in high good humour, and drank some more

o

sherry. "She's an angel with a flaming ruddy sword. Of course, she wants to keep in with the old woman. Pots of cash. You should see her when she goes to tea there—all dressed up like a Mother Superior. Black dress, white collar and cuffs—Christ!"

John laughed, smoothing his hair.

"I thought there was something."

"You bet there is. I say, you don't mind, do you? I mean, it would have been a damned good joke. Eddy wanted to try it himself. As long as you weren't serious——"

John drew in smoke, and burst out coughing and laughing, the smoke arising round his head in a halo. "Lord, no. No, it was only a passing thought."

"Well, it would have been a damned good joke. Elizabeth's such a rotten hypocrite. . . . We ought to have worked it better, planned it beforehand properly."

John finished off his sherry, wondering idly what might have happened if this alternative set of events had come to pass. He did not care much.

"I suppose she'll be going away soon?"

"Gillian, you mean? As a matter of fact, she's gone—for the week-end. She'll be back next week, till the end of term." Christopher yawned. "I owe you some money, don't I?"

"Eight shillings."

"As much as that? Crikey. Will you take five and another drink?"

"All right."

Christopher up-ended the bottle. There was just enough for two nearly-full glasses, though the wine was clouded. John drank quickly, looking at the foreign printing on his cigarette. In the distance seven o'clock struck.

"I think I'll go to the Lodge and see if there's any message," he said, getting up. "It's just possible there is."

"See you later," Christopher assented, subsiding on to the sofa. John picked up his gown and crossed the dark echoing quadrangles, feeling his way and wishing for a torch. He drew strongly at his cigarette to get a light from that.

There was nothing in the Lodge. The Dean of the College was standing inspecting a sheaf of letters from his pigeon-hole, holding them into the dim light, and the porter, who had been chatting with an auxiliary fireman, came out from the inner room rubbing his hands and saying:

"The sirens have just gone, sir, in London."

It was long and depressing, the journey north the next day. As the train left Oxford John had a pang of regret and also of fear, because he seemed to be leaving a region of unreality and insubstantial pain for the real world where he could really be hurt. The raid had been too large to ignore and the morning papers had gone to the other extreme, extracting every ounce of horror and pathos they could. John had looked carefully at the gaunt windows of churches, the rescue parties among the debris, the little children clutching hot mugs of tea, before he started, The dominating picture showed an old man gazing fiercely up at the sky: it was captioned

THEY'LL GET IT BACK!

The impression they gave was that the whole town was a heap of wreckage. John was certain that the worst had happened to his parents, he knew they were dead; it was obvious, he deserved to be punished in this way. Since leaving them, he had pushed them to the back of his mind, had sometimes felt ashamed of them, had not bothered to write to them regularly, he had done things they would have been sorry at. Now he could only think of their goodness. The very things that in the past had most irritated him about them—his father's deliberate way of hooking on his spectacles: first one ear, then the other; or the noise his mother made when she swallowed—these very things turned suddenly round and became emblems of their most lovable qualities. And when he remembered how recently they had been getting old, being increasingly sleepy after meals, more cautious in coming downstairs, he was tormented with thinking the worst had happened, they had been killed because he treated them lightly. There was no reason why he should remember all this if it were not to make his pain the more agonizing: he deserved it, twenty times over, but it was unbearable that they should have suffered because of that.

211

It was twenty-past three when the train arrived at Kilbury Halt, a tiny junction three miles from Huddlesford Central, and as it would go no farther all passengers for Huddlesford had to get out. In a sombre line they clumped over the wooden footbridge, John last. He nerved himself for any shock when he got into the street, but everything was quite undamaged: a baker's van stood at the kerb, a sweetshop was open.

Pulling his thoughts together, he started off. Kilbury was some distance from his home, and it would take three-quarters of an hour's quick walking to reach it. If his house and parents were untouched, he would stay the night: if not—well, it hardly mattered what happened if they were not. He had heard that the wounded had been taken to hospitals in surrounding towns.

He had never walked this way before, never in his whole life. Under the sour sky and occasional unwilling sun the streets seemed menacing: for five minutes he saw no damage at all, then all at once he saw a bombed house, nearly the first he had ever seen. He looked at the broken bricks, lurching floors and laths sticking out like delicate broken bones. The front gate, blown off its hinges, had been propped neatly against the hedge. The bomb had gone straight through the roof and exploded inside.

This was the first of many, and as he came nearer the centre of the town, where disused tramlines were still in the streets and there were warehouses and shops, ruins all at once appeared on every side. Many streets that harboured delayed-action bombs were barred off, and in these streets the tiles and broken glass remained unswept, littering the road, not in tidy heaps in the gutters. He had sudden perspectives of streets that had been completely wrecked. There were very few ordinary pedestrians about here: groups of men and boys in helmets and blue overalls stood chatting at street corners, and among one such group John noticed a boy who had been at school with him. In his anxiety he at once crossed the road and went up to him.

"Hallo, Fred, is——"

"Johnny! Well, I don't know. Fancy seein' you in these parts. Made a bit of a mess, hasn't it?"

"What's it like up my way?"

"Where's that?"

"King Edward Street—by the Stadium."

"I don't know about that." The boy took the chinstrap of his helmet into his mouth.

"Does anybody know?" John appealed to the four or five others. "Have they had it badly round the Stadium?"

No one seemed to know: they all lived close by and their interest did not extend outside this particular district. "They had it badly round the hospital," volunteered one of them. John turned away impatiently.

"Well, nowhere's had nothing, that's a sure thing," said Fred. "But I don't think it's any worse round the Stadium than anywhere else. I'd go and look, if I were you. But you can't go through the centre. They're dynamitin'—what's left of it."

"They are?"

"Yes, there's a barrier at one-mile radius all round the Town Hall. You'll have to go round Swanmill Park way. There!" A dull explosion sounded from the distance, and Fred grinned, his hand lifted.

"What's it for?"

"Stop the fires spreading. I say, Johnny!"

"Yes?" said John, turning ten yards away.

"How y'getting on at Oxford?"

"Oxford? Oh—all right."

As soon as he was out of their sight he broke into a quick shamble, filled by the other's words with a desire to know the worst. He ran down a side street, leaping over pools of a curious red mud compounded of brick dust and hosepipe water. It seemed utterly deserted here: here and there a house, a mere shell, would be standing, but on the whole it seemed like a city abandoned because of pestilence or a migration of humanity. Only a cat pushed against a front door, pushed and mewed, rubbed its head and looked up and mewed again. John crossed from street to street, streets he had never been in before, streets he had only known of by hearsay and never traced. Several times he thought he was lost. Everywhere, though all else had gone, evidence of destruction appeared: a burnt-out shop, the window-frames charred, the inside a pile of smouldering rub-

213

bish. A thin stalk of smoke still trickled slowly up into the air.
Nearby a house had fallen on a car, and though the rubble had
been shovelled away the car still remained, crushed and covered
with white dust, the leather seats full of bricks and glass.

There was another muffled explosion, like a funeral salute of
guns.

And now the sun was going down, after he had hurried
several miles through all this, panting and sweating all over.
As he at last reached the bottom of the long road off which his
own street branched, he saw the sun behind the dark grey
clouds, no more than a wrathful disc behind a row of factory
chimneys. It had a monitory, baleful look; it was spreading a
curious warm dusk which made even this most familiar spot
grow strange: it stared apocalyptically down over the back
entries, rickety sheds, straight dirty brick houses and rubbish
tips, like one hostile eye. He was filled with dread. As he went
stumbling up the long hill, noticing half-bricks driven by fierce
explosions into the hedges, the years reeled back and he was
praying for his parents like a child and fervently. He gasped
aloud that he would do anything, promise anything, if only it
would be all right. Any attempts at a personal life he had made
seemed merely a tangle of a hypocritical selfishness: really he
was theirs, dependent on them for ever. Everything would be
renounced, if only everything was all right. And if the worst had
happened, he prayed for enough strength to stand it.

The globular white lamp still hung over the corner shop,
surprisingly intact. He turned into King Edward Street.

It stretched unbrokenly, two lines of poor houses without
front gardens, just as it had always done. He could see his
house, number forty-eight, standing in line with the rest, just
as it had always done. He walked to it.

There was a note pinned to the door in his father's writing,
saying they had gone to Preston, to the address of an uncle's
house.

He walked a few steps away, hardly knowing what he was
doing, he was so thankful. Relief streamed over him as palpably
as if he had been swamped with a bucket of water: he was
smiling, looking up at the sky and down along the street, seeing

how the dying sun made the brick houses glow just as through all his childhood. It was if he had just come home from school and was having to go up the entry road to the back door because his mother was out shopping. The key had been under a loose stone and later under a flower-pot. He turned and read the note again: then examined the house carefully, walking round to the back to make sure it had not even been scratched. The garden had been dug over, and a huge alien lump of concrete lay embedded in the freshly turned soil. He stood staring, touching the creosoted fence with his hand, walking round to the front again, unwilling to go away. Bending close to the window-pane, he looked into the front room: it was tidy as usual, there were ornaments on the mantelpiece and the clocks showed the right time. There was a pile of newspapers on the table and behind a glass vase he could see the half-dozen letters he had written home all put neatly together. It was strange, like looking into a doll's house, and putting his hands against the window frames he felt as protective as a child does feel towards a doll's house and its tiny rooms. He wanted to make some signal to show that he understood that all was well.

Now, with this great load removed, it was the strangeness of everything that occupied him. The town had been so familiar and so intimately wound into his boyhood that its destruction became fascinating. Dozens of places he knew well had been wrecked: the local dingy cinema, a fish shop; great gouts of clay had been flung against posters. As he walked he looked at the ruins, tracing the effects of single explosions on groups of buildings, great tearing blows that left iron twisted into semi-interrogative shapes. Darkness fell very quickly: a few cyclists swept home from work along the lanes cleared in the streets. The moon, by day a thin pith-coloured segment, hung brilliantly in the sky, spilling its light down on to the skeletons of roofs, blank walls and piles of masonry that undulated like a frozen sea. It had never seemed so bright. The wreckage looked like ruins of an age over and done with.

Light-headed with hunger, he picked his way back to Kilbury Halt, not knowing what he was going to do except that it would be best to try to get back to Oxford. On inquiry he found that there would be a south-going train in half an hour.

"And is there a pub near by?"

"There's the Brandon Arms over the road. Can't say if they're open."

John went across to find out, his shadow preceding him in the moonlight. The building was all in darkness, but he found a door ajar, and, going in, he found a small bar lit by candles and half a dozen men sitting round the wall. Three candles were in sticks and one in a bottle: the landlady leant with her elbows on the counter, in silence. The room was bitterly cold and she wore a coat with a fur collar. All was silence. Every time the wind blew outside the candle flame danced and flapped.

He asked for a pint of bitter. "And have you anything to eat?"

"There's not a thing in the place, love. And there's only bottled dark. Will you have that?"

"Yes, please."

He watched it, black and rich-looking in the candlelight, come glistening up to the brim of the glass. To drink it on an empty stomach would make him ill.

"Are you sure there's nothing to eat? I've had nothing all day."

She looked at him apathetically, dragging herself upright. "I'll see if there's anything."

In three minutes she came back with a thick sandwich on a plate and a packet of potato crisps. The sandwich was two slices of dry bread with a bit of cold bacon in between.

"Thank you—thank you very much." He paid her, taking up the sandwich.

The assembled men watched her put the money away in silence, then they watched John as he ate. They did not show any personal interest in him: they seemed more as if they had to have their attention occupied all the time by one thing or another. Four were workmen, two looked as if, like John, they were awaiting a train.

The woman aimlessly rubbed the bar down with her dish-cloth. "I thought I'd open as long as there's anything to sell," she said. "Can't have everything going on strike, can we?"

"That's right," said one of the men.

"How's yer 'usband, Mrs. Page, 'ave you 'eard?" another said, stirring to speak. He was heavily built, with a moustache, bowler hat and overcoat stained with mud; like the rest of them he looked as if he had been sleeping in his clothes.

"No, I 'aven't—and I shan't, neither." The woman settled her elbows on the bar again. "I'm not worrying, though. There's no good worrying."

"No, there's no use worrying."

"And 'e always 'ealed quick."

"Ah, a quick 'ealer, like," said the bowler-hatted man, as if helping her to find words.

"Oh, he always 'ealed quick, yes."

"That's a blessin'."

"That's right. And it's only 'is leg. Lots 'ave 'ad worse. Be thankful, I say."

Another man let his breath explode emphatically in assent and took up his beer. A third man, sitting with his elbows on his knees, looked up and broke excitedly into speech. He was under thirty, with a fresh face beginning to grow lined, fair wavy hair and a clipped moustache: his clothes were smart, but grubby, his oiled-stained camel-hair coat being fastened by a belt without a buckle. A soiled trilby hat lay by his beer-glass.

"I've had a time, I have. I don't hardly know what I'm doing, why I'm here or anything. I came over from Manchester on Wednesday to see the branch here—Fowler's, you know; business trip, firm's petrol, bring the wife, expenses found. We was putting up at the King's Head. Just started dinner when that little lot starts coming down. Well, there was a lull in the middle, you remember there was. We came out of the cellars and I told her to go up and pack a case and meet me round the front in five minutes, while I got the car out."

He paused and drank, keeping his eyes fixed on the landlady, who still leant and stared back, a half-polished glass abandoned in her hands. The paper in the windows flapped. The men had their heads lowered, as if in church: they seemed to recognize the young man's need to speak without being over-much interested in what he was saying.

"Of course, as soon as I get round to the garages a copper comes up and tells me not to be a b.f. The streets were all blocked—couldn't get a wooden horse through them, let alone a V8. But I stand there arguing. Then we hear one coming down. The noise they make!—it gets the hotel fair and square, that was the one that hit it first. Now all yesterday and today—can't get near the place, can't get anything out of anyone. Don't know a soul here—don't know a soul here, except the manager of Fowler's, and they say he's copped it. Can't get near the works, anyway. No one seems to know anything. I don't know what to do."

He stopped as abruptly as he had started, staring down at the ground between his feet. A very old man piped up in a trembling voice:

"They hit a shelter down our way."

There was a pause.

"I reckon they'll do this to everywhere," said the young man, looking up again. "Everywhere. There won't be a town left standing."

His voice had a half-hysterical eager note as if he desired this more than anything.

"But they'll get it back, the papers say," said the bowler-hatted man, wiping his nose.

Nobody spoke, sitting half-listening in the silence.

John walked back to the station, which was hardly more than two platforms by a level crossing, and leant against a wooden fence to wait for the train. He was tired, and what he had seen made him feel as negligible as a fly crawling over a heap of stones: it made life seem like an unsuccessful attempt to light a candle in the wind.

He was travelling all night. At Birmingham he managed to get a meal which left him with two and threepence and the return half of his ticket. Most of the travellers were soldiers, clustering loudly about, dumping their kitbags like corpses on the floor of the waiting-room. Their necks were red as if scalded. The train ran slowly, cautiously, through the darkness. He grew very tired and slept.

The dirty yellow light spread over his face and hands, showing them relaxed, and his pale silky hair. His shoes were stained with red mud, so were the bottoms of his trousers and his right sleeve. The galloping wheels insinuated their unrest into his dreams, and he saw once again the scarecrow buildings, the streets half heaved-up by detonations, the candlelit bar. It no longer seemed meaningless: struggling awake again, rubbing his eyes with chilled hands, he thought it represented the end of his use for the place. It meant no more to him now, and so it was destroyed: it seemed symbolic, a kind of annulling of his childhood. The thought excited him. It was as if he had been told: all the past is cancelled: all the suffering connected with that town, all your childhood, is wiped out. Now there is a fresh start for you: you are no longer governed by what has gone before.

The train ran on, through fields lying under the frost and darkness.

And then again, it was like being told: see how little anything matters. All that anyone has is the life that keeps him going, and see how easily that can be patted out. See how appallingly little life is.

He yawned and grinned, clasping his hands between his knees. What a mess he had been making, when it was all really so easy: he could hardly believe it. He had been a proper fool, worrying and bothering himself. But he'd show them. Stretching full length on the carriage seat, he did not bother to formulate any particular promises; light-heartedly, he simply repeated that he'd have done with it, that it was all over, that now they'd be seeing something. It was cold, and he pulled the short flaps of his overcoat as far as they would go over his knees. In his position, half-awake, shivering and imagining things to himself, he spent the rest of the slow journey through the night, squinting round the blind as they stopped and restarted. He was aching when at a little before five in the morning they drew into the long, almost-deserted station. It was frosty, and he wished for gloves. Rows of lamps spread pools of light along

219

the platform. Here and there there were milk churns and a pile of parcels. From the end of the train came a banging as porters threw luggage in and out of the van.

He left the station and walked slowly through the streets. The shops were all locked up, every entrance being chained and barred. His head rang with fatigue. His body was weary to hysteria, inventing dance-rhythms and figures for the echo of his footsteps. Now and then they became suddenly hollow as he passed an arcade or deep shop door. In the gutter the wind rustled an invisible bit of paper.

There was a faint starlight in the open, but he had in the alleys to feel his way along rough stone walls, encountering cold moss with his fingers. Above him soared the elaborate-shaped colleges. And as five began to strike, his exalted exhaustion took one more queer twisted impulse from them. He leant against the wall, sobbing dryly, as the numerous bells discussed the hour in the darkness and the frost. Their age was comforting: he could wrap himself in it like a cloak.

It was easy to climb over the wall near a chestnut tree, and he did so, scratching his hands. Then he made his way quietly back to his own room.

He did not wake up till after two the next day. The black-out was taken down, the room cleaned and Christopher's bed made all without disturbing him. For some minutes he lay staring at the ceiling, reviewing the thoughts and memories in his mind, arranging them in an orderly way: then he heaved back the bedclothes and got up. He drank a glass of cold water and stretched his arms.

There were voices coming from the sitting-room, so after slipping on his overcoat and hanging a towel round his neck, he pushed open the door. Christopher, Eddy and Patrick were sitting round an enormous coal fire drinking bottled beer and smoking cigars. The air was hot and smelt richly.

"Oh, come off it," Patrick was saying contemptuously. "You don't know anything about racing."

"All right, then!" Eddy sat indignantly upright. "I bet you I'm up on the month—on the term, then! I bet you I'm up on the term."

Eddy was wearing a yellow waistcoat with brass buttons, which made his flushed face look very pink. The ash from his cigar broke and fell.

"Hallo, John," said Christopher, sitting with his back to the door and twisting his neck to look round. "Have a drink."

"There's none left," said Patrick, filling up his tumbler again and throwing the bottle away into a corner. It thundered on the boards without breaking.

John found a full bottle under the desk, and, pouring himself a glassful, sat down at the table to cut bread and butter. He ate huge slices ravenously, scattering crumbs.

"It doesn't mean anything, just being up on the term," Patrick persisted. "You might follow a tipster and do that."

"You know damn all about it, there's the hell of a science in betting. You have to work on a system——"

"Where's this lad been?" demanded Patrick, pointing at John. "Why isn't he dressed properly?"

John chewed for a few moments in silence, staring at Patrick. "I went to Huddlesford."

"Why?"

"I live there, that's why."

"Do people live there?" inquired Patrick, with an air of surprise. "I thought it was a music-hall fiction."

John was cutting himself more bread. "Yes," he said, "quite a lot of people live there."

"I'd forgotten," said Christopher. "Is there a lot of damage?"

"A fair amount, yes."

"The blitz is like a good show," Patrick remarked, putting his feet up against the fireplace. "After a long run in town, it's touring the provinces." Eddy coughed, and put his cigar back into his mouth. "See much of it?" he inquired, not without truculence. John thought he was being addressed, and said:

221

"The centre was all barricaded off."

"Is that so," said Christopher. "Of course, there's not much to hit in these provincial towns, they can hit it all at once. I must say, I found the blitz rather fun. One was nearly always tight, and it seemed quite natural. Did I ever tell you how when we were having that party of Julian's, how one came down and put all the lights out, and when he got candles we found all the corks had been pulled out of the bottles?"

"Oh, I don't believe that, Chris," said Eddy, grinning broadly. "Not unless you'd done it yourself."

"Well, near Shepherd's Bush, when I was doing special constable's duty," said Patrick, "we found a shelterful of corpses, not a mark on them. There hadn't been a bomb within twenty yards. We thought it was gas or something. But it was only blast, all their lungs had been burst with the blast——"

"Cheery," said Eddy. "Of course, I shouldn't be surprised at anything happening at a party of Julian's. If the Archangel ruddy Gabriel came in and blew the Last Trump, it would never surprise me. Lord, what you can do with money."

"Money!" exclaimed Christopher, theatrically clapping his pockets. "Have you got any?" he inquired of Patrick with interest. Patrick stared back at him and gave a sudden, barking belch.

John finished his bread and pushed his plate aside. "I could do with some," he said. "Just now I've got two and threepence in the wide world. Have you a cigarette, Chris?"

Christopher threw him the packet. "I think we should have a party before term ends," he said. "I think that would be a very useful contribution to the war effort. "

"Not in this college it wouldn't," said Patrick. "Not after all that damn row about Semple."

"That twerp," said Eddy. "Well, bring it round to my place. You can have women in there."

Patrick frowned. "I think women mess up a serious party."

"Well, you needn't have anything to do with them," said Christopher, throwing the end of his cigar into the fire. "You can leave them alone."

"*You* can't," chuckled Eddy. "We all know what you're after."

Christopher attempted to tip Eddy's chair over backwards and only succeeded in making him spill his beer. They scuffled for a few moments, knocking over a pile of books and papers.

"Don't fart about," said Patrick wearily.

"Well, when are we going to have it?" demanded Eddy, mopping himself. "I think it's hell's good idea, if we can get the stuff."

"Oh, we can get the stuff all right," said Patrick. "And you can pay for it out of your turf winnings."

"You're a mean sod," said Eddy, simply and sincerely.

"This is the last week, isn't it." Christopher lolled by the fireplace, twisting the signet ring on his finger. "It's happened fast, this term. No good starting work now."

"How about Thursday night?" suggested Eddy. "Thursday, at my place."

"I've got a tute on Friday." Patrick leant back deeper in his chair.

"Well, Friday night."

"I'm going to a dance."

"Well, damn it," Christopher was impatient. "You can work on Thursday."

"I've got Corps."

"Lord!" said Christopher sarcastically. "The man about town. You were a b.f. to join that racket."

"I don't think so. Wait till you're pitched into the ranks."

"Ranks my arse! They won't get me yet."

"I'll lay half a dollar," said Patrick judiciously, "that they register the nineteens in the next three months."

"Half a dollar it is."

"All right." Patrick drew out his tiny notebook.

"All right yourself. I'll join the Corps fast enough, when there's any monkey business."

"What closed down the nunnery?" chortled Eddy. "They'll catch up with you!"

"You've said it," said Patrick, stretching out his legs. "You can't fool all the Ministry of Labour all the time."

223

"Man alive!" Christopher exclaimed. "You don't think I care that much, do you? I'll be sick of this place by the summer, I'll be glad to leave. Your trouble is," he said, pointing to Patrick, "you're as windy as hell yourself."

"Urcher," said Patrick, in a bad-tempered voice.

"Well, we can't have it Saturday, we'll all be gone," said Eddy. "And I think Wednesday's a bit soon, don't you? Make it Thursday night."

"But——"

"Oh, sod your bloody essay!" shouted Christopher. "As if you don't know enough to walk through a tute blindfold! . . . Tell your tutor you've got pneumonia."

"Or pox," chuckled Eddy. "Ha, ha, ha!"

John left them at this point to have a bath. It was nice to be back. On Monday morning he had a letter from his parents at Preston describing the air-raid they had endured. It was not vivid enough to move him, but he was perturbed to hear that his mother was still suffering from nervous shock. He slipped the letter back into his pocket and forgot it in three minutes.

While he was having coffee that morning (a thing he did automatically now, without reference to its original cause) he saw Elizabeth at a different table with some girl friends, and he watched her with amusement, the way she talked and the way she listened, as if she were part of a comedy he was privileged to watch. Indirectly she reminded him of Jill, whom he did not expect to see again. When they all rose to go, she came swiftly across to his table. "*John!*" she exclaimed, "*do* tell me . . . I've been *so* worried. . . . Are your family safe? Were they in that dreadful raid?"

Her face hung before him, ludicrously, like an advertisement for cosmetics. There was a piece of fluff on her left shoulder.

"Yes," he said. "They were. But they were lucky." He sat back.

"Oh, good." She looked relieved. "I'm *so* glad. It must have been terrible."

"It was pretty bad, I think."

"And there's another thing. . . ." She looked at him acutely, then frowned slightly into the distance. "I hope you aren't too offended about . . . the other day, you know. I must have seemed a bit rude. Do tell me, was I?"

"Rude?" John laughed, frankly trying to remember. "Well, a bit, perhaps. But not very, considering."

"I'm sure I was. . . . Well, I do want to apologize. I didn't mean to be nasty. It's only that Gillian . . ." She paused, expecting him to cover up her uncompleted sentence, but he only smiled at her. "Well, it's only that she's so young. She's only fifteen, you know."

"Fifteen? Really!" John was bland. "Is that all?"

"Yes, only fifteen. . . . And she didn't really want to—you know—she asked me to—well, you see how it was," she concluded lamely.

"I see," said John. "That's quite all right."

"Are you sure? Well, so long as you aren't nursing a grievance or anything." She looked into his eyes with a brilliant smile.

"No, that's quite all right. I understand."

"Good. I must fly now. Good-bye!"

"Good-bye," he said, yawning. "Bitch," he added to himself, stirring his coffee, wondering what had prompted her to feint this submission, and tell all these lies. He wondered, too, if that had been the epitaph on Jill: in the circumstances, it seemed likely, and as he smoked and sipped his coffee he surveyed the experience with a surprising lack of shame.

It was December: the many trees were quite leafless: the views which in summer had been reproduced on postcards were now forsaken and austere. The boats had long been slung up in the boathouses: in the Common Rooms the Christmas numbers of magazines began to appear. And the term was coming to an end. He made an effort to clear up some of the work he had left undone.

Fortunately, he was working just before lunch on Thursday when there was a tap at the door and a yellow face under a soft brown hat peered in. "Hard at it?" inquired an ironical voice.

John jumped up. "Why, come in, sir. What are you—come in and sit down."

He took Mr. Crouch's outstretched hand. The master shut the door and put his hat on the table, coming round on to the hearthrug. He wore a thick brown overcoat with the collar turned up.

"This is a nice room you have. A pity you have to share it."

"Yes, it is a nice room." John looked round it vaguely.

"A great pity. I always found it essential to have a room to myself, however small. But perhaps you're different. Cigarette?"

He held out his case, amused when the boy unconsciously took one. As far as John was concerned, Mr. Crouch looked unexpectedly young and it seemed natural for him to be there.

"Surely you haven't broken up already?"

"Broken up? We've *been* broken up. I suppose you've been too secluded in your academic fastness to know that we had a little raid last week."

"Did they hit the school?" John exclaimed.

"Fair and square. Almost completely burnt out, except for the labs and the gym and one or two of the new classrooms. So we are prematurely disbanded." He blew out smoke. "I don't think there was much up your way."

"No, I was there on Friday—nothing, no damage."

"You were, were you? Pity I didn't know. You could have looked me up. Did you know I was married now?"

"Why, no—well, many congratulations," said John, with a return to his old shyness and a movement of his hand.

"Thank you," said Mr. Crouch lightly. "Thank you very much indeed." He looked at the boy a moment with a smile.

"Then where are you living now, sir?"

They discussed Huddlesford for a while, Mr. Crouch standing with his back to the fire and John straddling the arms of the sofa. "Still, for all that, I'm not as comfortable as you," he said, his eye travelling over the room. "You've done very nicely for yourself. Not that you haven't earned it. Why didn't you write to me?" He grinned in his old manner, seeing the boy confused.

"Well, I started to, several times. . . ."

Mr. Crouch lifted a yellow hand.

"I know how it is: you needn't bother to explain." He inspected the cigarette he held. "I know what one's first university

226

term is like. One feels one's never lived before." John looked at the carpet. "It's been worth it, hasn't it? Worth all that grind?"

"Oh, yes," said the boy shyly.

"Good. Now will you come and have lunch with me? I don't know where the best place is."

John put some coal on the fire, and they went out to a restaurant he had heard Christopher talk about. Mr. Crouch looked about him with interest as they walked through the streets. The chance sights he saw troubled him—an art student in a red skirt sketching some vaulting, a flower-seller and a white-coated kitchen boy carrying a tray of covered plates to a don's room. These things expressed a life he had not shared, and which he now never would share. He knew the boy at his side would not have noticed them.

"Tell me what you've been doing," he asked, when they were settled at their table, his nicotine-stained fingers locked before him.

John, recounting the work and lectures of the term, at first unconsciously and then consciously tried to make it sound more impressive than it was. "Have you read my tutor's last book?" he inquired. "It's very good. He's the authority on eleventh-century England. I've been reading a lot of his papers. I'm lucky to be under him.

"It's a pity he can't take you alone," said Mr. Crouch, breaking his roll. "Have you ever thought of asking him? Of course, the war's mucked everything up."

John did not reply, and presently Mr. Crouch asked what else he had done, apart from working. The answers he received were not definite. John did not seem to have joined any societies or made any friends, and to be turning the conversation different ways in order to avoid admitting this. Mr. Crouch studied his face across the artificial flowers. After a time he said:

"Of course, I expect you're only just beginning to find your feet here. It's a slow business." He lit a cigarette in a preoccupied manner. "But if I might be so bold as to give you a bit of advice—and it may be the last bit for some time, if not for

227

always—I would advise you to get out of the idea that the only thing that matters here is work."

John nodded vaguely.

"That isn't so at all. A very tiny percentage—very tiny—of the people up at the moment will become dons of one kind or another. But unless you're thinking of that—and if you are, remember the competition is very keen, because they're very, very plush-lined jobs—you must look at your time here from the point of view of what is going to happen to you when you leave." He settled himself more comfortably in his chair. "You can look at this place as a big railway terminus. Thousands of people. Trains starting in every direction. What you've got to decide is, where are *you* going? And having decided, get in with your fellow passengers. They'll be useful to you. I dare say it sounds a very well-worn piece of cynicism to you when I say you can get a better job for ten minutes' social climbing than from ten years' hard work."

John shrugged his shoulders.

"Unfortunately that is how things are. What you must remember is that in normal times you find here a couple of thousand of the people who are going to be at the top of things in twenty years' time—or perhaps less. You are privileged to knock about with them while you're up here on more or less the same social footing—make the most of it. The more contacts you can get, the better. That's why I should advise you to join plenty of clubs, societies and what-not, even if you despise them or feel out of it there. You can't afford to despise them—and you can't afford to go through life feeling out of it. For better or for worse, you're in the swim now, for three years. Whether or not you stay in the swim depends entirely on how far you take your chances up here."

John nodded again. "Yes," he said. "I see what you mean."

"So don't become too much of a cloistered monk," said Mr. Crouch, as they rose to go. "It doesn't pay. And talking of paying . . ." He leered round for the waiter.

He believed he had given the boy helpful advice.

When they were outside, John said:

"But what will happen to the school now?"

228

"The school?" Mr. Crouch held his gloves in his right hand and smacked them against his left. "That I can't say. In any case, I was leaving at Christmas."

"Were you really, sir? Why?"

"I am going to join the Royal Air Force in some capacity or other." Mr. Crouch's face split into a smile at John's incredulous look, and his utterance grew more precise and formal. "I had pretty well decided, and this business has made it certain."

"Will they take you?"

"Perhaps not in any very lethal arm of the service. I may be able to get into the educational side of things. Does it seem so very surprising to you?"

"Well, yes, sir, it does rather."

"I don't think it is." Mr. Crouch shuffled quickly along, glancing through the gates of the various colleges they passed, nearly treading on a cat. "A record of war service will be very useful in gaining employment when peace is declared, and it will look better to have volunteered than to have been called up."

John had grown depressed when they parted about the middle of the afternoon. He walked back to his rooms in a bitter mood. There was a cold humidity in the air: the streets were wet though no rain had fallen that day. He felt that he had failed to conceal the fact from Mr. Crouch that he was making a mess of things, that he had broken the bargain that they had tacitly contracted. The advice (which Mr. Crouch had stressed on parting) seemed reasonable and well meant, but by some strange impotence of his own it was rendered entirely irrelevant. Everything seemed wrong.

He boiled the kettle and made himself some tea. Any self-reproaching or self-promises were out of the question now: he had fought himself to a standstill.

After doing the black-out, he went on no particular impulse of friendliness up to Whitbread's room. It was empty and the fire had not been lit. John remembered seeing Whitbread at breakfast wearing the academic dress necessary for taking an examination. One of the question papers lay on the table: John glanced through it. It was meaningless to him. The realization

229

that Whitbread was taking an examination when his own tutor apparently thought so little of him that the matter had not even been mentioned made him peculiarly angry. He opened the cupboard door, and, taking out the jam pot, put a large spoonful of jam on each of the open books lying on the desk. Then he snapped them shut. The rest of the jam he ladled on to the back of the fire, scraping out the pot thoroughly and licking the spoon. There was a nearly new pat of butter in the cupboard, too, and this he unwrapped from its paper and cut in half, putting each half into the toes of Whitbread's slippers. Then he filled the pockets of the jackets hanging in the bedroom with sugar and tea. In one of them there was a pound note with a slip of paper bearing its number pinned to it, and he put that in his own pocket book. As an afterthought, he poured Whitbread's milk into the coal scuttle and lit the fire.

A great cheerfulness came over him now and he sauntered out through the cloisters into the dark. There was a letter from his parents in the Lodge, but he did not even trouble to pick it up. When six o'clock struck, he went to the nearest public house and sat alone in the bar, the first customer of the evening. The landlady polished a glass or two behind the counter, humming a tune, then went into the back room. John drank steadily. The beer tasted so unpleasant that he asked a little timidly for whisky, and sipped it undiluted. This made him thirsty and his next order was for beer to cool his throat: not till after several swallows did he notice that he could no longer taste it. On this condition it seemed quite nice, and he drank it swiftly. Then he bought a packet of cigarettes and smoked, lighting one from the other.

He wondered in what exact spot at that exact time Jill was. He had not seen her at all since returning from Huddlesford, though he gathered that she was back in Oxford. The thought was at first quite theoretical and evoked nothing. He lingered over her memory, remembering her as a false light he had stopped following through strength of will. How right he had been. Then he began to reconstruct her face, as one might re-string a set of beads together, until it rose in his mind like an apparition over a cauldron. He ordered more to drink. The clock ticked cheerfully, the bar filled up with men talking in low, serious voices, and all the struggle in him had sunk down out of sight. He stared at the fire and at the mirror and at his own glass.

But the time! He was horrified to see that it was half-past seven. He jumped up so suddenly he knocked his glass on to the floor, where it smashed. Everyone looked round as the landlady came out from behind the bar to sweep up the bits, and John tried to pay for the damage. He got her to accept the shilling he was holding. Crimson, he hurried out of the place, banging his shoulder on the doorpost, thinking furiously that they must think he was drunk, which he wasn't.

The darkness was appalling after the bright room. He bumped into three people and scratched his bare hand on some railings, so that he cursed out loud. This made him chuckle. In the cold air he became conscious of a slight dizziness.

Somewhere a clock chimed the half-hour and this recalled him to his fear that he would be too late to get into Hall for dinner. Nevertheless, he hurried back to the College and found his gown. From the kitchens came a warm breath of food and there was a subdued chattering from the Hall itself.

As he expected, the steward would not admit him.

"No, sir, you're too late, sir."

John was much too afraid of him to argue, and, blushing deeply, walked away again, muttering some excuse about having been delayed. Hurrying, the cold air and the cigarettes all made him cough, and he coughed till he thought he would be sick, slipping off his gown as he walked. When he got back to his room he found he had left the light on. There was an open note lying on the table addressed to Christopher, and he began to read it, squatting in front of the fire and shielding his face from the heat. It ran:

Dear Chris, I suppose it will be all right if I bring Gillian to-night? It's her last evening here and I've got saddled with her as usual—and Eddy said vaguely that he was amalgamating with someone who was holding a kind of social with sandwiches—I mean do you think I could leave her there, somewhere people won't be too drunk. I'm afraid we shall have to leave early, too, but I do want to come. Can you ring me up between four and five? . . .

There were a few lines more, but he did not bother to read them, scratching his head and reading the first part again. The page trembled as he held it. Then he got to his feet and leaned against the fireplace, his head against his wrists, then he lifted his head and stared at his own reflected eyes. His face had gone very pale. Folding the note up, he threw it back on to the table, and walked up to the door and back several times. He wiped his hands on his trousers. The clock on the mantelpiece had stopped at twenty to five.

Pushing back his hair, he made his way through the darkness back to the Buttery.

"I wanted two bottles of sherry," he said, looking confusedly at the wine list. "That kind," he pointed out, indicating the most expensive. The steward took a key from a nail and fetched them, wiping each bottle carefully with a duster when he brought them back. "Will you sign for them, please, sir," he said. John wrote his name awkwardly on a slip of paper printed for the purpose, then went back with the bottles towards his own room. Half-way there he dropped one and it smashed instantly on the flagstones: he hesitated a moment, then hurried on, carrying the remaining bottle with both hands.

When he set it down it glowed in the light like a column of amber: the label was spotted with age. He did his hair in the bedroom, then put on his overcoat again, turned up the collar, and, picking up the bottle, made for the door. There he paused. He put the bottle back on the table and going to a drawer pulled out the folder that held all he had written about Jill. He lit a cigarette, leant against the mantelpiece, and turned the pages over one by one, slowly, quickly.

Awful at breakfast this morning. We were just starting the porridge when I remarked that it was significant that both schools and prisons began their meals the same way—with skilly—when old B. was passing and heard. "I don't think that's a nice thing

232

to say," she said, so mild and pained that I really felt it wasn't, and was quite deflated. Odd. . . .

And:

I mean I know things will get worse, but I don't mind because they'll get better and better, too. I wouldn't go back, not for millions.

With a sudden shrugging movement he pitched the handful of written sheets into the fire, where they burst alight. He watched them a moment. Then he went out, slipping the sherry bottle into his pocket and leaving the light on and his cigarette burning on the mantelpiece where he had laid it.

As he walked through the archway he trod on broken glass and wondered what it was.

It was so cold outside that he went into a public house and asked for whisky. They only had gin, which he swallowed at a gulp. It had no perceptible effect on the coldness of his hands, so at the next bar he asked for whisky again and this time got it, though he thought as he drank it down that he would have done better to stick to gin. He then asked for a pint of beer to quench his thirst.

Eddy's college was at the other end of the town, some five minutes' walk, and the sag of the heavy bottle was making his left shoulder ache. There was a trampling of soldiers' boots in the darkness: then enormous, minatory, the bell from Eddy's college tolled the quarter-hour, filling every crevice of the night. A very fine rain had begun to fall. Alarmed by the huge noise of the bell, he stood irresolutely at the gates looking in, seeing a little light from the Lodge, and the porter in a bowler hat. Two young men came out, and he stepped aside to let them pass. Then he looked in again. There were bicycles leaning against the wall.

This was the very peak of indecision. Somewhere in that vast ramble of buildings was Jill, unattended, most likely bored, waiting to be rescued and taken away. He had his bottle as a passport, yet he dare not go in. Elizabeth's note had sent him staggering back into his old longings: the realization of another

233

last chance gripped him, making him long to act. He forced himself towards the event, towards the last chance he would ever have. Yet he dared not go in. He was afraid that he would be turned out, or that he would find her happy with someone else. He had no idea of what he would do, only that he wanted to be with her. Oh, Jill, he thought despairingly, shivering. He longed for her so intensely that surely she could feel his longing. He put his forehead against the wall: his misery was imprisoned in him and he was imprisoned in his misery.

There was an alehouse over the road. Perhaps it would be better to wait till they had got warmed up, so that they wouldn't be so likely to resent his presence. And he need not actually go in for another three-quarters of an hour, till nine, when the gates were shut. He would let them get started first.

The landlord looked at him suspiciously as he came up to the bar and asked for a pint.

"Are you eighteen?"

John blinked: he had to collect the words in his brain to answer.

"I am eighteen. I am a member of the University."

The man turned away, saying something that John could not catch, and drew the beer. To cover his embarrassment John lit a cigarette at the tiny gas jet that burnt in one corner of the room, looking round him. It was an old-fashioned place, with sawdust on the floor and ornamental casks labelled brandy rum and gin along the shelves. At a table a party of workmen were playing dominoes and the landlord leant over to watch them, drinking occasionally at a pint.

"'Arold, 'Arold," he interjected once, "is that the best you can do?"

But if he left it too late, Jill might go home. He remembered in the note that Elizabeth had said they were going to leave early, and in any case they had to be out of the College at some time, probably half-past nine or ten. He would have to act quickly if he was going to do any good. He took the burning cigarette from his mouth and dropped it by accident on to the floor, where he abandoned it after a slight preliminary groping. While he stood at the counter, a ragged man picked it up,

234

pinched it out, and put it behind his ear. He was sitting by John's seat when the latter returned with another pint to drink.

"Just finished my day's work, locking the gates of the cemetery," he said to John affably. "Stop 'em all gettin' out. Well, 'ere's more lead in yer pencil." He finished off his half-pint, wiping his mouth with relish. John looked nervously at him, noticing that he had a glass eye. The man lit John's discarded cigarette at the gas jet and broke into confidential speech.

"Ah, I got a marble at Dunkirk. Yer know what I mean, don't yer?" He tapped his eye. "I was there all right. Ah, I got it there. A wonder I'm 'ere to say so."

He began talking so quickly and so intimately that John could not understand all he said, except that he gathered that he was telling the story of his Army life. At one point he took out a great bundle of papers, tattered military forms and certificates pinned together, and spread them on the table. He gave John first one, then another. John realized he was begging.

" 'Ere, sir, perhaps you can give me an 'and. I ain't no beggar. I 'ad a trade, same as anyone, I 'ad a skilled trade. I'll tell you what it was, it was carpentry, that's what it was. Now won't you give me an 'and, sir, I ain't no blasted moocher, I was at Dunkirk. I'm a discharged ex-Serviceman, and they won't give me no work or pension. Don't you think I ain't tried for work, I ain't work-shy, mister. Ha, ha, ha! I tried. I've stood two, three—four hours I've stood outside that damn Labour Exchange. It ain't right, I tell yer. Won't you give me an 'and, sir. I was at Dunkirk, I ain't 'ad an easy time like you 'ave, sir. I ain't a young fellow like you any more. They gets yer in the Army, mucks yer up, and then says you ain't no good to them. God's truth you ain't: you ain't no damn good to nobody."

John wished he would go, wished so heartily that he gave him half a crown and looked away. The man jumped up and departed as if he had been sent on an errand. The door banged behind him and John covered his face with his hands. As he did so, the circular movement in his head, that was kept at bay as long as he held his eyes open, rushed in upon him. In the darkness he felt as if his chair were sinking slowly sideways to the

235

left. He uncovered his face and the room slowly pulled itself upright, then started to tug at his eyes, wanting to start moving round to the left. It was painful to struggle against this, and he closed his eyes again. Once more his chair began to sink sideways.

It seemed necessary that he should get some fresh air and find a lavatory, so he finished his beer and went out, the fine rain being instantly laid across his face like a piece of wet muslin. Not knowing where the lavatory was and being afraid of finding the man from Dunkirk there, he crossed the road and went into Eddy's college. He stumbled over the gate and the porter looked round, though without saying anything.

All at once it seemed very cold. The stars marched frostily across the sky. He buttoned up his overcoat and, feeling the bottle of sherry, recalled Eddy's party, where there would be a fire and a corkscrew and more to drink. He must go there. Eddy's indecent remark about Jill also re-entered his mind, and he went off into a cackle of laughter, stretching out his arms before him as if literally pushing the darkness back. It would be sensible, he thought, to ask the way. But just at the moment all the walls were blank and the doors were great locked ones leading into kitchens and storerooms. He stumbled and swore and ran into a tree. At this he paused and told the tree what he was looking for. While he was talking he noticed a staircase quite near, lit by a blue light, and he went in and knocked at the first door he found.

"Come in," cried a voice. John rattled stupidly at the door-handle and at last it was opened from inside by a young man with fair, greased-back hair and horn-rimmed spectacles.

"Yes?" he said. "What can I do for you?"

"I——" John experienced some difficulty in getting his tongue to work. "I'm trying to find a party—a party, it's given by—by——" He could not remember Eddy's surname. "You know, Eddy what's-his-name. Here, have a drink." He pulled the bottle from his pocket. "Oh, sorry. Haven't opened it." He fumbled at the neck. "It's corked."

"I've got a corkscrew—come inside." The young man took the bottle and stepped back. John came in, frowning at the light, seeing a desk under a lamp littered with sheets of paper covered with half-finished poems.

"One gets so worked up," said the young man. "As regards your party, there are dozens all over the place. There's certainly an unholy row in the next quad."

He produced a corkscrew from a drawer full of knives and set two glasses on the table. John sank into an armchair, and when the young man gave him a glassful, gulped it.

"I say, this is remarkably good sherry. Where is it from? I must say I should like a dozen or so of these for myself. Where does it come from?"

John told him and a period of utter forgetfulness intervened. The next thing he noticed was that the young man was reading him a poem, in a slow voice that rose and fell, all in one sentence that seemed to go on for ever. John did not understand it, and had more sherry.

"I say, is there a lavatory about here?" he inquired, when the young man paused for breath.

"Yes, on the next staircase. Turn right when you get outside. Do hurry back or we shall lose the mood."

John left him lighting a long clay churchwarden pipe with a glowing cinder held in a pair of tongs. It was not hard to find the lavatory, which was lit by a ghastly blue light and smelt of a peculiarly choking kind of disinfectant. He turned the wrong way on leaving it, and the room he entered was empty, with a glum fire smouldering in the grate. He switched on the light and lay on the hearthrug in an effort to get warm; he put lumps of coal on the fire with his bare fingers, but it still would not burn up. How cold it was. To help the flames he took a book from the table and stuffed it among the dim coals. Then he lay perfectly still, like an open-eyed figure on a tomb, staring at a photograph lodged on the desk. It showed a girl: Jill in fact. Slowly he dragged himself across on his knees to look at it, and when he took it in his hands the expression on the photographed face changed slowly until it was not her. He began trembling. He shielded his eyes from the light and the book in the fire burst into flames with a loud flap; simultaneously something seemed to run across the floor close by him. Holding

237

the photograph, he waddled frantically on his knees for the door, pulling himself upright by the doorpost, and got away out. His dirty hands had left marks on the photograph: since it was dirty, he tore it up and threw it away.

But this would never do: straightening his tie, wiping his fingers on his coat, he knocked peremptorily on the door and opened it. The room was lit by three candles arranged symmetrically on the table; a man was standing on the hearthrug staring at himself in the mirror, and did not look round as John entered.

"Do you know where the party is?" said John.

There was no answer and John slowly realized that the man was laughing very softly with hardly more noise than a driving-belt makes on a machine that is not running very fast. Wind from the door caused the candles to stream out in elongated shapes. John went out on to the steps and was quietly sick. Then he pushed on, listening to what now was quite plain— singing and shouting and cursing. It came from all sides at once, echoing and re-echoing from the many dark walls, mingled with croaking noises from some musical instrument, a trumpet or hunting horn. It seemed to rebound from the sky as if the sky were a low damp vault. A lighted aeroplane crawled across, leaving a soft trail of sound: looking steadily at its lights, John ran into a wall.

All at once the darkness was full of people running this way and that, gasping, bumping into each other, calling out: "This way! No, this way! Watch the garden gate!" John leant flat against the wall to avoid being knocked over, and after a few minutes became aware that someone else was leaning by his side. He turned to examine them more closely and as he did so they bent slowly forward like a drawn bow and vomited at length. John waited patiently for them to stop, and then asked:

"I say, where's the party here?"

A burst of cheering from the middle distance announced that someone had been captured and thrown into the fountain. John blew his nose and reeled off once more, singing tunelessly. He could hear the swift beating of dance music woven in among the tramping feet and shouting, and he directed his steps to-

238

wards the source of the music. Strung out behind him, unseen, was a clamour of cries converging: he was leading the way back to the party. He saw at the bottom of a staircase in the light an unbroken bottle and a lump of coal: the music was louder and louder. He stumbled up the steps and sat on the bottom stair, his head in his hands, his brain feeling like a horse that was rearing up and trying to fall backwards to crush him. Very soon he thought he would be ill again. But he was disturbed as the drunks came clattering up the steps, half a dozen of them, panting, noise steaming off them. One carried a trombone. Sitting alone in the pool of light John lifted his head and looked at them with mumbling lips, fumbling for his bottle. It was not there. He was terror-stricken at the sight of their dishevelled hair, loosened neckties and mouths shining with saliva, knowing that they were going to trample him down, but suddenly their noise was stilled as if by a spell; a door opened above and a river of sound came flooding down the stairs. They were clustering together with their pale faces tilted back, looking upwards over his head.

John pulled himself upright and looked round. Jill, Elizabeth and Christopher had begun to descend the staircase, the girls with their coats on, going, and Christopher in his shirt-sleeves, with his cuffs rolled back. The knees of his trousers were wet, as if he had been kneeling somewhere damp. John stood back. In the weak light his face was quite expressionless. Everything seemed at that moment clear and restful. As Jill came level, he took her quietly in his arms and kissed her.

Elizabeth gasped something.

Christopher ran lightly down a few steps, pulled John forcibly round, and hit him hard in the face.

John twisted away, falling crookedly among the drunks, whose cries met over his head. Fighting to get a grip on him, they carried him into the darkness. The trombone crowed triumphantly. Christopher had followed them, and for the moment the two girls were alone on the stairs.

"The nerve," said Elizabeth hotly.

Jill did not reply: she had gone very red and her eyes had filled with tears, and when she stooped to pick up the umbrella she had dropped she began crying in real earnest, so that her hand beat fruitlessly around the steps without finding it.

Another muffled explosion of cheering indicated that John had been thrown into the fountain.

Four days later John lay in bed with a fairly high temperature due to bronchial pneumonia, and as the fever grew, his mind lost the chronology of things, so that the days of his illness faded away to something no more vivid than a memory of childhood, and the events of the evening swelled to a monstrous size. In remembering them, his mind felt like a fly crawling over the great stone face of a statue able to comprehend only one feature at a time.

For instance, although he was safe in bed, he could not rid himself of the idea that he was still lying face downwards, wet through, on the wet grass. The stalks tickled his face: he could feel his hands, outstretched before him to the level of his ears, cold upon the grass, the nails digging lazily into the earth. Then he would gradually realize that he was in fact lying on his back with his arms by his side, and there would be a sickening struggle as each impression pulled this way and that. At length reality would submerge once more, and he would be lying face-downwards, the grass making a cold pattern on his cheek.

The kiss, too, grew realler every hour. He could feel the quiet pressure of her lips perpetually, and in response she would fill his arms again. The memory was keen. At intervals he would become aware that it was his bruised lips and jarred teeth that remained with him, and another struggle would ensue, filling him somehow with nausea. The sensations tugged this way and that.

Nor had he freed himself from the tempest of sickness that had ruled him that night. He had crawled along the back lawn on his hands and knees like a dog, every now and then stopping and hanging down his head to vomit. At the end of the lawn he

240

had collapsed again, which was the last thing he remembered: his mind then ran back to the beginning to start all over again.

As his temperature rose, untruths took their place quite naturally among these recollections. One of the earliest was that they were lying together on the floor of some room in each other's arms. He could feel her lips pressed against his, but he could not feel the rest of her. He could not feel her with his body at all. He hugged her harder, rolling desperately against her, but it was all nothing, he could not feel her at all. Everything was confined to the mouth and he would wake up with burning lips.

This became a root dream, into which numbers of others would change. Time and again different climaxes of different dreams would end in this. One of the most vivid was in a sort of cottage where they had been for some time: it was near the sea and had a long overgrown garden full of weeds and raspberry canes. They sprawled together on the couch and John was filled with a lassitude so great that it alarmed him, it seemed a kind of treachery. They had lived there so long together that their love had worn thin like a coat; it was shabby with wearing. He looked at the young girl he held, at her perfect, composed face so near to his, and was frightened at his own indifference. His mood was easily definable: it was simply the boredom of no longer loving. Yet he covered it up, frantically, with layer after layer of dishonest thoughts, and kissed her neck, just below the ear. She wrinkled her nose slightly, but made no comment. He got up and crossed to the window with his hands in his pockets, staring moodily up the garden that was hung with trees. And there he saw Christopher, moving about half-way up the garden, poking about the bushes for something. An unreasoning terror seized him: he knew that Christopher must not see Jill or he would come in and take her away, and though he did not care much for her now, he was determined to stop this at all costs. He began talking to her very fast and insincerely, trying to occupy her attention, but to his horror she got up, wanting to go to the window. He gripped her, to hold her back, and as a last resort turned his grip into an embrace, hoping to cloud her mind with sensuality, pressing his

Q   241

face against hers, though knowing all the time that she looked over his shoulder out through the window, that Christopher had seen her and was coming towards the house. On this vertiginous note of expectancy the dream began curdling and slurring into the first one, and they were lying on the floor again together.

He was not conscious of outside circumstances to any degree. Things whirled about him as the grey clouds whirled about the white sky. He noticed that his bed was under a window and that the room was a strange one, with a tiny electric radiator plugged into the wall. Through the window he could see treetops moving uneasily. The room looked like the College sickroom, which he knew existed, but had never been inside. The College nurse attended him, bringing him food and sponging his hands. All such things he noticed at different intervals, fitting them together with a distrust of the picture they formed. It had not really occurred to him that he was ill.

Instead, he fell to pondering within the framework of the dream how the love they had shared was dead. For the fact that in life he had been cheated of her was not the whole truth. Somewhere, in dreams, perhaps, on some other level, they had interlocked and he had had his own way as completely as in life he had been denied it. And this dream showed that love died, whether fulfilled or unfulfilled. He grew confused whether she had accepted him or not, since the result was the same: and as this confusion increased, it spread to fulfilment or unfulfilment, which merged and became inseparable. The difference between them vanished.

He was watching the trees, the tops of which he could just see through the window. They tossed and tossed, recklessly. He saw them fling their way and that, throwing up their heads like impatient horses, like sea waves, bending and recovering in the wind. They had no leaves. Endlessly, this way and that, they were buffeted and still bore up again to their full height. They seemed tireless. Sometimes they were bent so low that they passed out of sight, leaving the square of white sky free for a second, but then they would be back again, clashing their proud branches together like the antlers of furious stags.

Then if there was no difference between love fulfilled and love unfulfilled, how could there be any difference between any other pair of opposites? Was he not freed, for the rest of his life, from choice?

For what could it matter? Let him take this course, or this course, but still behind the mind, on some other level, the way he had rejected was being simultaneously worked out and the same conclusion was being reached. What did it matter which road he took if they both led to the same place? He looked at the tree-tops in the wind. What control could he hope to have over the maddened surface of things?

The College nurse closed the door quietly behind her, leaving him sleeping. In the distance the clock was chiming eleven o'clock: this was the end of her period of morning duty, and she walked along the carpeted corridor towards her dispensary. As she turned the corner she met Rivers, the Senior Tutor. He was smoking a pipe and held a letter in his hand.

"Oh, Mrs. Crawford, I was just looking for you. . . ." His voice trailed off and he examined the letter he held closely. "It appears that Kemp's parents are coming. . . . They're coming today, in fact they're on their way and will arrive, according to this, early this afternoon." He looked up vaguely. "I'm afraid it looks as if you will have to be here to see them. . . ."

"But why are they doing that?" said Mrs. Crawford, energetically surprised. Rivers turned and they moved slowly in the direction of the dispensary. "Why are they coming? There's no need. . . ."

"I don't know why they're coming," said Rivers, taking his pipe from his mouth. "I wrote to them, you know, saying that Kemp would not be home for perhaps a week, saying he was ill. . . . I think I said he had slight bronchial pneumonia, but I can't really remember. . . ."

"It rather looks as if they've taken fright," said Mrs. Crawford. "There's nothing like the word pneumonia for frightening people." She was washing her hands at a washbowl in the corner.

243

"Well, heaven knows, I didn't mean to." Rivers inspected the letter again, then replaced it in the envelope. "Do you think they're alarmed because he's had this sort of thing before? . . . Is——?"

"Well, naturally, I can't be sure, but Kemp doesn't look like a bronchial subject to me," said the nurse, drying her hands. "They sound to me like fussy people, and that will be a nuisance. They've absolutely no need to come bothering about here."

"No, that's what I said, or what I tried to say," said Rivers eagerly. "Though it doesn't look as if I succeeded. . . . I said there was no danger. That's true, isn't it?"

"Oh, perfectly. The boy's in no danger now; in fact, he's a bit better today. I've just left him asleep and his temperature was down this morning nearly a whole point. He's in no danger. Really, he's never been in the slightest danger at all."

"Well, that's what I said." Rivers put the letter back into his pocket and took out a box of matches. "You'll have to tell these people so when they arrive this afternoon, and try and pack them off as quickly as you can."

The Kemps arrived at the station just after half-past two that afternoon. As the nurse had suggested, they had been alarmed at the news that John was ill in bed with bronchial pneumonia, but it had been Joe's idea that they visited him. He had been very touched by John's immediate post-haste visit to Huddlesford after the air-raid, and secretly he was ashamed that he had not been there to meet him. Of course, he did not say anything of this to Mrs. Kemp. But when the Senior Tutor's letter came, Joe announced that he was going straight to Oxford, full of a muddled concern which he concealed by obstinately refusing to explain himself. He felt deeply and illogically that by doing so he would be somehow repaying the love his son had shown. At first he demanded that Mrs. Kemp should stay at home. But she would not be left, still nervous as she was from the shock of the raid; and she concealed this by saying over and over again that she did not trust those nurses. So in the end they had both set out together, without any thought of how long they would be away or where they would sleep that night.

Their arrival was a sad mockery of the sight-seeing visit they had planned, when John would show them round, and something of this entered into their silence as they walked slowly down the dull streets, not thinking it would be far from the station. Joe Kemp clutched his cap in his hand, then suddenly put it on, staring about him at the traffic lights and cinemas, as if surprised to find that Oxford was a city like any other. He took his wife's arm when they crossed the streets.

"Is this where he said turn right?" said Mrs. Kemp doubtfully. They asked again.

They could not help looking curiously at the venerable buildings and the shops with strange names, and the different-coloured omnibuses, though the anxiety that lay hidden in their silence prevented them commenting on what they saw. The only remark Joe made was when he paused in front of a large bookshop, seeing displayed a large volume with the University crest and motto stamped intricately in gold on the cover. His forehead wrinkled as he spelt it out. "*Domimina*," he said haltingly. "*Domimina . . . nustio . . . illumea*." He turned slowly away. "That's Latin," he said.

"This must be it," said Mrs. Kemp, as they approached the College, coming as nervously as their son had first done up to the gates that he had entered so many times now. They hesitated timidly, reading the rules concerning the entrance of visitors to the College which hung framed outside. As they stood there the Chaplain came out, stared at them and walked quickly away.

"Go on, Joe, you ask in there," urged Mrs. Kemp. Joe stepped deferentially into the Lodge, taking his cap off again, catching sight of the porter peering round the inner door.

"I want to see John Kemp—I'm his father," he said.

The porter used the telephone. Finally he told Joe that he could go straight across to the dispensary, where the nurse was waiting for them.

"And where would that be, could you——?"

The porter told him, Joe listening attentively and nodding his head. Mrs. Kemp waited outside, looking at the green baize notice-boards which now, at the beginning of the vacation, were nearly empty. She searched for a reference to her son, and did not find one. One notice, referring to the activities of a literary society, had been signed by Patrick Dowling as secretary.

Joe did not quite follow the porter's directions, but did not like to ask him to repeat them, so they set off across the quadrangle hoping that they would find another person later on who would help them. The wind blew. Most of the rooms were empty now and their shuttered windows looked blank: only the ground-floor rooms were still in use for people who for one reason or another had not immediately gone down when term ended. In the mid-afternoon the place was deserted.

"Old!" said Mrs. Kemp, pointing to one wall where "1610" was carved on a stone plaque.

Inside the Founder's quadrangle they paused, at a loss. "He said, to go through another arch," said Joe uncertainly. "Into t'Garden quad, or something."

"Here's a student—ask him," whispered Mrs. Kemp, clasping her handbag tightly.

It was Christopher, who came striding quickly along from his own room dressed in his overcoat and porkpie hat, carrying a suitcase and looking neither to right nor left. He had just taken a final look round his rooms before leaving them; John's few belongings, noticeable at last, were pathetically scattered about. Christopher's trunks had gone off in advance. He stopped impatiently as Mr. Kemp moved into his path.

"Excuse me, is the Garden quadrangle—how do I find it?"

"Through there." Christopher pointed with his free hand. "There, you see? That third archway."

"Thank you, and where would the dispensary lie then?"

"The dispensary? Oh——" Christopher frowned: "Second doorway on the right. At the end of the passage."

"Thank you—thank you, sir," said Joe Kemp, relieved. "I'm greatly obliged—greatly."

Christopher walked away without answering to the Lodge, not troubling to realize who had just spoken to him. At the Lodge he was met by Elizabeth, who had gone for a taxi while he cleared up his room. She had no hat, and, though the day was not unduly cold, wore a fur coat.

"At last."

"Did you get one? Good girl."

She took his free arm. Without once mentioning the matter she had managed to convey to him that when they once got to London she would be willing to become his mistress, and things were easy between them now.

He put his bag down at the Lodge to find two half-crowns for the porter, who emerged, knowing that Christopher was going to tip him.

"Well, so you're off, then, sir?" he said, looking round the empty quadrangle. "Going to leave us in peace?"

"That's right, Herbert. A release from my arduous studies. Drink my health while I'm away." He gave the man five shillings.

"Well, thank you, sir. Thank you very much. You going to keep 'im in order, miss? I don't know what 'e'll do without the Dean to look after 'im, I don't really. 'E'll be like a lost dog."

Elizabeth grinned. "And talking of lost dogs," said Christopher, "has the College started keeping pets?"

He indicated a small white dog that came wandering aimlessly round into the porch, going by the wall, sniffing with dropped head.

"It must 'a' got in from the street," said the porter, annoyed. "'Ere! This isn't the place for you."

The dog shrank from his formal threatening tone and sidled up to them. Christopher glanced at his wrist watch and picked up his bag. Outside, their taxi was swinging in a long arc into the kerb.

"Time we were going," he said. "Farewell, Herbert, a long farewell."

Elizabeth, her handbag tucked under her left arm, stooped, holding out one hand, making a coaxing noise. "Come on, then," she said wheedlingly.

The dog looked up at her and began to growl.